RISK OF RUIN

Paul —
You've long been
one of my heroes.

ARNOLD SNYDER

VEGAS LIT • LAS VEGAS, NEVADA

Risk of Ruin

Published by

Vegas Lit
3665 Procyon Street
Las Vegas, NV 89103
Phone (702) 252-0655
e-mail: books@huntingtonpress.com

ISBN: 978-1-935396-60-4
$11.95us

Cover art: Joseph Watson
Author Photo: Lisa Micklos
Design & production: Laurie Cabot

DEDICATION

In memory of Martin Rosenberg,
1943—1988
Alias "Paladin"
Berkeley poet and artist.
I miss you, bro.

ACKNOWLEDGMENTS

This novel has had a virtual army of editors. First and foremost, I'm indebted to my wife, Karen, who's been editing not only my verbiage, but just about everything else in my life for the past eleven years. You have no idea how awful this novel was when she read the first draft. Her initial comment: "Please, don't make me have to file for divorce." Then, there was Deke Castleman. Deke had me rewriting just about every chapter, but only after he had me cutting half of them and rearranging the rest. Basically, he pretty much agreed with Karen, and I have to admit, they were right. Then Deke quit his job with Huntington Press and moved to Ecuador. Thanks, Deke! (Is it possible I drove him over the edge?) So, Jessica Roe took the editorial helm. There was more blue ink than black on the pages when she got done with it. And I have to admit, for your sake, she did the right thing. But that still wasn't the end. Unsure if some of the esoteric topics I'd woven into the tale were accurate, I looked for experts. Was the tattoo stuff right? Heidi Barwell said: "No, you've gotta fix this, this, and that." How about the motorcycle stuff? Mark Cannata said, "Close, but no cigar. Fix this and this." What about the blackjack hole-carding stuff? Ben W. said: "Not bad, but why don't you explain a bit more about this?" How about the lock-picking stuff? Sam Case said: "By George, Arnold, you've got it!" (Hey, I did something right!) Others who read early versions of this novel and provided valuable feedback: Laurie Cabot, Avery Cardoza, Jennifer Starling, and Chelise Stroud Hery. I made changes based on all of their comments and criticisms, and without this team of eleven editors, this would be a much different book. In fact, I have no idea why my name is still being listed as the author of this pot-boiler. There isn't a single line left in it that was in the original manuscript! Wait a minute: The second line of Chapter Twenty-five was there, and that line is mine, *all mine*. And I'm damn proud of it!

PART ONE:

The Crime

ONE

SOMEHOW, HE HAD to get in touch with Stacy. He didn't know if she was in police custody, if she was hurt, or if she had any way to contact him. He had to find out what had happened to her and, in his current predicament, that wouldn't be easy.

He was in a hospital room. He'd figured out that much. From what he could gather listening to the conversations around him, he was fucked. Royally fucked. He was trying to remember the fight, but the only thing he was dead certain of was that he'd lost. Precisely what his injuries were he had no idea. His body was unresponsive to his weak attempts at movement, but he wasn't numb. He felt pain all over. His shallow breathing caused stabbing pains in his chest and his heartbeat was irregular. He couldn't see. Was he blind? He wondered if his eyes were bandaged and if so, why?

For a short time, one of the doctors had attempted to engage him in conversation, but that was before he knew where he was, while he was still in some semi-dream state. The same dream he always had. The worms. But they were talking, laughing, and big. When he realized he was awakening in a hospital bed and it was a human being who was trying to talk with him, he clammed up. For the next hour or so, he just listened to the activity around him.

He learned that they thought he was on the brink of death. It wasn't a question of if, so much as when, and when could be days to live, or even hours. A nurse was continually updating his heart rate.

Someone in the room used the term "cold storage." What was that about? Is this official hospital terminology? Was he nothing more than meat with a pulse?

But death was out of the question. No matter what his injuries, he wasn't going to die. Of that, he was certain. His heart was beating. His brain was working. The flesh and bones would heal. He'd die only when he was good and damn ready to die and that wasn't in days or hours. No matter what condition he was in, he had to get word to Stacy.

That was job number one.

He could almost hear her voice—*another load of cosmic shit*—and it brought a slight smile to his lips, one of the few areas of his body where his muscles still worked. With his swollen tongue, he could feel that many of his front teeth, upper and lower, were broken or missing. But despite the pain and those hideous worms that kept squirming into his consciousness, he felt his strength gathering.

A voice broke into his thoughts. "Mr. Black, can you hear me?" He pictured a worm, a huge worm, a worm bigger than himself, with a fleshy mouth and no eyes. Should he answer? Did he really want to talk with a worm?

"Mr. Black, can you hear me?"

It was a new voice, not the doctor who had been attempting to engage him earlier. Not one of the voices that had been discussing his dismal state in the past hour. Someone new had entered the room. The worm image faded. He was trying to picture the human that belonged to this voice. It was male, younger than him but an adult, not a kid.

"Mr. Black, can you hear me?"

"'Course I hear you—" his voice cracked. His slurred words sounded strange to him, slow and wet. He wanted to add, "you fucking moron," but it hurt his throat to vocalize. He tasted blood.

"Do you know where you are?"

"Lemme guess—" He wanted to make a joke, but ran out of breath before he could get it out.

"You're in the hospital, Mr. Black, in the intensive care unit."

He wanted to say, "That would have been my second guess," but the impulse died to a wave of pain in his lungs. Instead, he said, "Can you turn on the fucking lights?" The last words sounded like "fun lice."

"The lights are on," spoke the worm. "Your eyes are swollen shut. Do you know how long you've been here?"

"Too long … Coupla hours … "

"Four days, Mr. Black. You've been in a coma. Do you remember what happened?"

Four days? Jesus Christ …

"Got my ass kicked."

"Do you recall the circumstances?"

"The fuck are you?"

"I'm Sergeant Bruce Dorsett. Las Vegas Metropolitan Police. I just want to ask you some questions, Mr. Black. May I call you Bart?"

"'At's my name."

"I just have a few questions for you."

"Fuck off."

He had to get rid of the cop. Was it even worth mentioning Stacy? Would the cop at least tell him if she was in custody? He'd humor the cop for a while. See if he could get any information out of him.

"It would be in your best interest to cooperate, Bart. Some pretty serious charges are pending against you."

"What about Miranda?" Sounded like "veranda."

But the worm responded, "You have the right to remain silent. Anything you say can and will be used against you in a court of law. Would you like an attorney?"

"You arrestin' me?"

"No. But it might be helpful to you to be cooperative. I just want to ask you some questions."

The cop had nothing on him. His threats were bullshit. "What happened?" Bart said, then added, "to the girl … "

"I assume you're referring to Miss Thomas?"

"Referrin' to Stacy."

"Miss Julia Thomas."

"Name's Stacy."

"She's also been hospitalized as a result of the injuries she incurred at … Do you recall the circumstances? Do you remember what happened to you?"

Four days later and she's still in the hospital? Was the cop telling the truth?

"Like I said … Got my ass kicked. How long will I be here?" His words were slow and garbled, broken by his short, shallow inhales.

"The doctors didn't expect you to come out of your coma."

"Doesn't answer my question."

"You'll have to discuss that with your doctor, Bart. I'm just a cop, trying to get a handle on what went down. Your injuries are extensive."

"I was outnumbered."

"That's an understatement. We have two dozen suspects in custody right now for participating in the melee and more than a hundred were arrested. Your internal injuries are massive. Your skull is cracked and your brain is hemorrhaging. They were about to pull the plug on you this morning when you started talking. They couldn't understand what you were saying. The nurses had instructions to notify us immediately if you regained consciousness. It looks like you're going to make it. We have a lot of questions. Maybe you have some answers."

Was Dorsett lying? Did they really think he was going to make it now? Or was this alleged cop just the worm of his dreams and this would all go away when he woke up?

"Go ahead."

"Bart, I want you to be straight with me. I'm sure you're aware of the fact that you're wanted for serious crimes relating to Miss Thomas and you might ultimately be held accountable for her death if she doesn't survive her injuries. But from the witness reports, it appears you were defending her … I'm hoping you'll tell me what you know about the incident. I'm on your side. Believe me. Can you just tell me what happened?"

So suddenly, Dorsett's a good guy?

Bart was on the verge of saying, "You got nothing on me so fuck off," but changed his mind. "An' I should do this why?" he said.

"Look, we know you were living with Miss Thomas in Reno and

that you came here with her some three or four weeks ago. Why did you come to Las Vegas?"

"Long story, Dorsett ... Hope you got a lot of time." His saliva was thick, almost like mucous. When he tried to swallow he could feel a tube running down his throat.

"I have nothing but time. Do you mind if I tape this?"

"Why don't you video it? Stick it on YouTube? Dead man talking."

"All right, I'm taping this with your permission."

"Came here 'bout two weeks ago ... Stacy came here couple weeks before that."

"Didn't you come here together?"

"No."

"But you both left Reno almost four weeks ago. Together."

"No. I went to California ... Came to Vegas later."

"Where in California?"

"Bay Area."

"Where'd you stay?"

"Friends ... That's where I'm from ... Berkeley, San Fran, Oakland ... Crashed around ... Took care of some old business ... "

His words were coming slowly, with long pauses between breaths. "Business" sounded like "fizzes" to him, but Dorsett didn't seem to be having any trouble understanding him. Not that it made much difference, as all of it was a lie. He'd never gone back to California and he'd come to Vegas with Stacy, just as Dorsett thought; in fact, he'd brought her to Vegas on his bike, a chopped 1947 Harley Davidson. But even in his present condition, he knew better than to tell that story. Even if he believed he was dying—which he didn't—he still had to protect her.

Since meeting Stacy, he'd lost his job, his best friend, all of his money, his scooter, most of his teeth, his eyesight, his ability to get up and take a leak, and now, the cops were grilling him for an explanation. Right. Like that was about to happen. *Why did you come to Vegas?* Like he had any intention of ever telling anyone that story.

The night he brought Stacy to Vegas was in many ways similar to his current predicament. He'd found himself waking up in pain, confused and unable to move. He was just helping her move to Vegas, or get the hell out of Reno was more like it.

The story of that night was one he'd take to his grave, he hoped not in the too-near future.

TWO

HE WASN'T A flying saucer nut, nor was he investigating crackpot government-conspiracy theories. His concerns with politics had never stretched further than thinking the government ought to decriminalize pot and repeal the motorcycle-helmet laws. He had no business being anywhere near Area 51. He knew that.

But there he was, slowly awakening to the cool night air with an aching head, a stabbing pain in his back, and a confusing immobility. He remembered the sign he'd seen that made him turn away from the restricted area that would have gotten the feds on his tail:

Nellis Bombing and Gunnery Range
Restricted Area
No Trespassing Beyond this Point
WARNING
Photography is Prohibited

So he cut back east across the desert to get away from Area 51, and now he was somewhere between a major life catastrophe and deep shit. He didn't know exactly how much trouble he was in, but he knew it was more than he could afford. The state trooper's car was maybe twenty feet away, the headlights not quite pointing at him, but in his general direction, illuminating the dusty desert scrub. The engine was running, but where was the trooper? The driver's side door was wide open. With the headlights glaring in his direction, he couldn't see inside the vehicle, but he had a feeling the trooper wasn't in there. He could smell the exhaust fumes. That car had been sitting there idling for some time. He wondered how long he'd been unconscious. The last thing he needed was trouble with the police. Cops never took kindly to him. A throbbing pain was developing just to the right side of the crown of his head. He'd taken a really good whack. He saw the beam of a flashlight waving in the distance off to his right, maybe a hundred yards away, maybe more. When he attempted to turn his head to better see the light that was bobbing and weaving erratically, like an insect searching for a place to land, a different stabbing pain, deeper inside his head, stopped him. But even in his semi-conscious state, he knew what was happening.

The cop was looking for Stacy.

From the way the beam was moving, the trooper was obviously facing away from him and moving even farther away. That was good. That would buy him some time.

His inability to sit up straight and the pulsing knot on his head were just starting to make sense. Ah, yes ... he remembered now ... the cop had knocked him in the head with his baton and, he surmised, handcuffed him. The jabbing pain between his shoulder blades told him he was handcuffed to his own bike. He had a Swedish-style chopper frame with a long stretch, and the way the knuckle cover was jabbing his ribs, he figured he must be cuffed to the down tubes.

It slowly came back to him ...

They were tearing down Highway 375 with the trooper in pursuit. Speeding. That's all it was. Speeding. He remembered glancing at his speedometer, midway between 85 and 90 mph. Normally, he'd just pull over and take the goddamn ticket. But he didn't figure Stacy's phony ID would hold up, especially with the cops actively looking for her. He wouldn't even be in this godforsaken desert if it wasn't for Stacy's problems with the law.

"Cut her loose," Clance had advised him just a few hours earlier. "Otherwise, your ass is fried." Why didn't he listen to Clance? Why didn't he listen to himself?

It's not hard to lose a cop car if you're on a bike in the city. If the traffic's heavy, you can cruise between lanes, weave in and out between cars, turn around and drive the wrong way down the shoulder, even escape on the sidewalk if need be. If he doesn't have your plate number yet, fuck him. And Bart always kept his license plate smeared with grease and just enough dirt to ensure illegibility at anything less than about ten feet. But out on the open highway, it's just a speed test, and with Stacy riding bitch and all of their stuff crammed into the saddlebags, he couldn't chance trying to outrun the trooper. He had to outmaneuver him.

So he pulled off the highway onto the desert terrain. The trooper slowed to a crawl on the road, trying to decide if he should attempt to chase him through the thick brush and cactus. Bart cut his headlamp to make it more difficult for the cop to see him. A thin sliver of moon provided enough light for Bart to see a few yards ahead of him, but he also had to slow down. If he could just get far enough into the scrub, the cop wouldn't see him at all. Then the cop's spotlight hit him. Fuck!

As he put distance between them, he was praying the cop would give up, just call the feds and report a crazy biker getting close to Area 51. He was already planning an escape route once he got out of spotlight range, cutting south through the desert about 50 miles to come out on Highway 93 on the east side of the restricted area. There wasn't much out there but empty desert—other than the Nellis Air Force Base Bombing Range, which, he hoped, wasn't in active use at the time. Surely they'd assume he'd try to get back to Highway 375. Who'd expect a chopped Harley to try negotiating 50 miles of rough desert terrain in the darkness of night? With a helicopter, they'd have no trouble finding him. But they wouldn't send a helicopter if he avoided Area 51, not for some pissant biker who was just speeding.

Then he saw the trooper's headlights turn in his direction after he'd gotten a hundred-yard jump on him. Persistent sonofabitch.

Unfortunately, a Harley isn't a dirt bike, so this was slow going. It was also pretty dark, despite the waxing crescent moon hanging low in the eastern sky. He was doing his best to avoid ruts, cactus, tumbleweed, large rocks … He went on for quite a ways with the cop not quite keeping pace. He knew that without Stacy on the bike, he could definitely lose the cop. It was time to lose the baggage.

"Look, Stacy, you're going to have to make a run for it. I'll shake this jerk and come back for you."

"No way, Bart! You're losing him! Don't stop now!"

He pulled to a stop. "Get off the fucking bike! I'm going that way." He pointed. "I want you to run that way!" He pointed in the opposite direction. There was no time for an argument. "Now! He'll follow the bike. Trust me."

"That cop wants to kill you, Bart!"

He felt her arms tighten around his midsection. Jesus fucking Christ.

"He wants to write a speeding ticket. Now it's evading arrest. Much more serious. I can't let him catch me! Get off the bike!"

"But he turned his siren off. He turned his flashers off. He's crazy!"

"He doesn't need a siren off-road. Look, I'll come back for you after I ditch this asshole. Just stay low after you get out there a ways. He'll never find you."

"But he's going to kill you!"

"Well, if he catches me with you on the bike, you'll be kissing mommy and daddy hello tomorrow morning."

That was the threat that hit home. She slid off the bike. "You better not leave me out here," she said and took off running.

Wondering if that would be the last time he ever saw her, Bart turned his headlamp back on to make it easy for the cop to see him as he took off in the opposite direction. Just as he'd thought, the cop car turned to pursue him. The trooper was definitely picking up speed as he got the hang of negotiating the desert foliage, but Bart knew he could outrun him now. No contest. He couldn't go too fast right away or the cop might decide to give up on him and go after Stacy. He had to give her some slim chance of getting away. So, he led him on for a while, letting him keep up, giving him some hope while he was giving Stacy time to disappear. He figured she'd probably head for the highway and stick her thumb out. He was envisioning a half-dozen more troopers converging on the area. Surely the cop had radioed for assistance by now. Was there any chance they wouldn't find Stacy? The whole situation was fucked up. But even if they did catch her, if he could get away, he knew she wouldn't rat him out and she wasn't in nearly the trouble he'd be in if he were caught.

He hadn't traveled much more than a mile or so, slowly putting more distance between him and the cop, when he came to a dirt road and saw that Nellis warning sign. He sure didn't want to get the feds involved, so he headed east until smack! He dumped his bike. He didn't know what he'd hit. A rock? A ditch? A cactus root? He went flying off the seat and by the time he got up and managed to get the bike upright, the trooper was there, out of his car with his gun drawn, and all Bart could do was reach his hands up and pray the bastard didn't shoot.

What could he say to the cop? What the hell was he doing so close to a restricted area at three a.m.? The truth? That he was just trying to entertain Stacy?

They were making the trip from Reno to Vegas and she just had to see the flying saucer area. Had to see it! *Had to see it!* How could he have let her talk him into it?

"Please, Bart, we have to see the Extraterrestrial Highway!" She showed him the map in a guide book she'd picked up at a gas station convenience store in Sparks before they'd left. Damn if there wasn't a stretch of road out in the desert wilderness called the Extraterrestrial Highway. *Is that the official fucking name?* Now his ass was going to be dragged to jail, and who knew what would become of her? If they somehow managed to find her—and that was a pretty good bet since they got him—he was really up piss river. Harboring a runaway sixteen-year-old girl isn't just a speeding ticket. Was there any way he could talk his way out of this?

But the trooper didn't ask any questions. He simply said, very calmly, "Remove your helmet and drop it."

Bart did as told, then again raised his hands. But despite the fact that he was standing there with his hands in the air, the cop pulled out his night stick and whacked him on the head. Then, apparently, he'd handcuffed him to the frame of his bike so he could go after Stacy on foot. It occurred to Bart that this nitwit of a cop must have an IQ about half his age. You'd think he'd at least drive back toward the area where Bart had dropped her to cover a good portion of the territory a bit quicker than going it on foot. And why the hell wasn't he waiting for reinforcements?

As he was thinking about how he got into this jam, he remembered that he had about thirty-two thousand dollars in cash in one of his saddlebags and ten thousand or so in the other. How could he have been so stupid? If he was making a run from Vegas to Reno with an underage girl and a shitload of unexplained cash, why in God's fucking name was he speeding? He just hadn't figured on a cop patrolling such a godforsaken stretch of highway.

Three things were going against him. First, the girl. That wouldn't sit well with the authorities, no matter how he tried to explain it. Second, the money. There was just too much of it. He could probably kiss that goodbye. And third, those gorgeous tattoos of Satan on his right bicep, his chest, his back, even one of his calves. Of course, the first one they'd see would be the reversed pentagram on the back of his left hand with the name S-A-T-A-N spelled out in the five points of the star.

Although his ninth-grade IQ test gave him a score of 165, he was now trying to decide where he ranked among the severely retarded. In the 1940s, the American Psychiatric Association determined that the official classification of someone with an IQ below 30 was "idiot." An IQ of at least 30 but lower than 50 was officially an "imbecile." And with an IQ of at least 50 but less than 70, you were a "moron." A lot of people think that idiots, imbeciles, and morons are all equally stupid, when in fact, in a room full of idiots and imbeciles, the moron is a mental wizard.

He decided to stop thinking about Stacy, the money in the saddle bags, and his classification as a mental deficient, and buckle down to the business at hand. *Satan, help me. Into your hands I place my fate.* He had to free himself from the handcuffs before the cop returned, and only if he returned with Stacy would he have to come up with some kind of an explanation for what the fuck he was doing out in the middle of nowhere at three a.m. with a runaway teenage brat. He asked himself the question he always asked himself when faced with any dilemma:

What would Satan do?

Gee, your honor, I saw her hitchhiking and it looked awfully danger-ous for an innocent young girl to be out there alone in the desert with all the rattlers and rapists, so I was trying to do my duty as an upright citizen and give her a lift to the nearest phone booth where she could call mommy and daddy whom she misses so much.

THREE

THE WORM WAS barking, baring its fangs. He was up against a wall, couldn't back away any farther. Its breath reeked of ammonia and disinfectant and death …

"Bart? Bart?"

There had to be a way out, an escape …

"Can you hear me? Bart?"

The ICU.

The cop.

The fucking pain.

"Loud 'n' clear, Doormat."

"Are you still with me?"

"The hell do you want?"

"You're fading out on me, man."

"I'm right here … Don't get your panties in a bunch."

He couldn't shake his mental image of Dorsett as a talking worm, now with razor-sharp teeth, drooling, licking its fleshy pink lips.

"Yeah, well, all I asked was why you came to Vegas and you start asking me what Satan would do. What's that about? And what's with all the devil tattoos anyway? Are you really some kind of satanic priest? That's what they're saying about you, you know."

"Not a priest, Doormat … Just an apostle … Want to talk to a doctor … Find out about Stacy … "

"It's Dorsett, Bart. So, was this whole event, this riot downtown, some kind of satanic group or what? Tell me what happened."

"Not into Satanism, Doormat ... Tattoos? Just art ... I like art. No meaning. They're pretty. That's all ... I'm an atheist." More lies.

His tattoos had a lot more meaning to him than Dorsett would ever know.

FOUR

BART WAS IN the ninth grade when he first embraced Satanism, but he had no more use for the formal doctrines of Satanism than he had for any other organized religion. In his opinion, Madame Blavatsky was a phony and her Theosophical Society was a scam; Aleister Crowley was a blowhard snake-oil salesman who pretended to be connected to dark magical powers; Anton Szandor LaVey was a self-promoting opportunist, probably a run-of-the-mill atheist, who'd never even considered the true meaning of Satan worship.

But at the age of fifteen, Bart declared his undying love for the devil over breakfast with his parents. His father was leafing through the Berkeley Gazette while his mother was grading term papers.

"God's a prick," Bart announced casually.

His mother pursed her lips and looked at him disapprovingly over the tops of her wire-rimmed glasses.

His father said, "Don't use language like that, Bart," without looking up from the newspaper.

"I've been reading the Old Testament," Bart said. "Have you read it?"

"Yes, I've read it." His father was Jewish. He looked up from his paper, but not at Bart, to signal he didn't like being interrupted. "But I have an agreement with your mother not to discuss these things with you until you're older. I'm not practicing and you're being raised Catholic." His father went into one of the phlegmy coughing fits that had been plaguing him for months. Within the next year, his father would be dead from esophageal cancer.

"But is it true what the Old Testament says?" Bart asked when his father was through spitting into his napkin. "In Exodus, it says God slayed all the firstborn sons in Egypt. All of them, sparing only the Israelites. Is that true?"

"That's the story of the Passover. It's sacred to both Christians and Jews."

"That's sick. Did God really go and murder all these innocent babies just because they weren't Jewish?"

His father cleared his throat and again spit into his napkin.

"Do you have to do that at the table, Harv?" his mother said.

"How about when God orders the Jews to go around slaughtering anyone who isn't one of the 'chosen people'? No wonder the Arab world hates us. I'm ashamed of my name. You should legally get our family name changed from Rosenfeld to something else. Smith, or Brown, or Johnson, anything."

That got his father's attention. "The truth of the matter is I'm an atheist," he said. "Your mother didn't want me to tell you that, but it's a fact. But I'm very proud of my name and my ancestry. We're not just a religion; we're a race of people."

"Well, I just want you to know I'm not a Catholic anymore. I've decided to worship Lucifer."

This announcement got a genuine gasp out of his mother. His father just shook his head.

"Did you ever think of how much courage it must have taken for Lucifer to rebel against his own Creator?" Bart said.

"Bart," his mother said, "I think you should spend more time on the New Testament. That is sort of our Lord's revised edition."

"Have you read the Gospel according to John?" he asked her.

"What do you mean?" There was exasperation in her voice.

"Did you read the line where Jesus says, 'Verily I say unto you, whatsoever ye shall ask the Father in my name, he will give it to you'?"

"Yes."

"It's a bald-faced lie, Mom. Have you ever asked God for something in the name of Jesus? Might as well be asking Santa for a pony."

"Bart, you don't ask God for frivolous things—"

"Jesus didn't say, 'Whatsoever you ask, he'll give it to you, unless it's a frivolous thing.'" Bart looked up toward the ceiling. "Oh, God, in the name of your son, Jesus Christ, I'm asking you right now to turn my eggs and potatoes into chocolate-covered marshmallows."

"You know God isn't going to start delivering marshmallows to people."

"I asked God a hundred times to make me taller. That's not frivolous, not to me. I just want to be normal."

His mother sighed and gave his father a look. His father had the shrimp gene. Bart knew he was an accident, because no one would willingly pass such a trait to an offspring.

"God's had more than enough time to make me see results," Bart said. "Did you ever stop and think, Mom, that maybe the Bible is really just a test? That God purposely made himself look like a mean bastard, just to see if we'd fall down and worship an evil god just to save our souls? I think if we do worship him, it'll just show him what cowards we are. That's what I think. The only people he'll take to heaven'll be the ones who refuse to worship an evil god."

"I think you should talk with one of the priests," his mother suggested. "A priest could answer your questions. Right now, I have these papers to grade."

"Well, there's a lot of other stupid stuff in the New Testament," Bart said, once more raising his voice. "When Jesus begs his father to let him off the hook so he doesn't have to be crucified, God insists that the crucifixion go forward *to pay for mankind's sins*. But when Jesus dies on the cross, does God abolish Hell and allow all men into heaven because Jesus paid for our sins? No! Even today the church says we'll burn in Hell if we sin. Hey! I thought Jesus paid already! My sins are supposed to be fucking paid for!"

"That's it, Bart!" his father said, rising from his chair. "Away from the table! Now!"

Bart got up from the table and picked up his plate. "Lucifer saw

God for what he was and he stood up to him. If the Bible's right about God, then I'll stand proudly with Satan in Hell when I die!"

He headed off to his bedroom, but when he looked back down the hall into the kitchen, his parents had returned to their reading.

† † †

By the time he was twenty-one, Bart had the tattoos that attested to his religion. The ink on his left forearm was a beautiful piece of skinwork, the face of Satan crowned with thorns. Bart had designed it himself, a mockery of Rubens' famous oil painting of Christ being presented to Pontius Pilate after the scourging at the pillar. The face of Lucifer was modeled on Gustav Dore's "Fall of Satan," the only work of art Bart had ever seen that showed the suffering of Satan with empathy for the heroism of this angel who'd dared to challenge God himself.

His chest piece was a rendering of Dali's "Corpus Hypercubus," with the body of Christ replaced with the blood-red body of Satan, his barbed tail wound limply around one of his legs. The cubic cross itself was in flames.

Across his back, in Olde English lettering, were Satan's words from Milton's *Paradise Lost*: "I'd rather reign in Hell than serve in Heaven."

FIVE

"BART? BART? BART!"

Not the worm again.

The stabbing pains in his arms, legs, insides. The pressure in his eyeballs. The pressure in his brain. The worm …

"Bart!"

"Yeah, man … "

"Are you still with me?"

"Not goin' anywhere."

"You keep nodding out on me, Bart. If I stop talking for a minute, you disappear. Do you want me to turn the TV on? Get a little background noise in here?"

"No."

"Try and stay with me, man."

"Sorry, Doormat."

"The name's Dorsett, Bart. Are you trying to irritate me? Look, we found more than fifty-nine thousand in cash in your room. Where'd you get it?"

"Reno. Tell me where Stacy is."

"How'd you get it?"

"The hell you doin' in my apartment?"

"We got a warrant."

"Motherfucker."

What he wouldn't give for a couple hits of weed right now, just enough to put him into a nice stoned slumber. He wondered if his lungs could take it. He wanted to sleep.

"How about an explanation?"

"Huh?"

"The money, Bart. Where'd you get it?"

"It's mine … Earned it … Saved it … Motorcycle mechanic … Fix bikes … Mostly Harleys."

"I don't buy it."

"Tell me where Stacy is … Or fuck off."

"I'm supposed to believe the garage pays you in cash?"

"Garage? Work on the street … Cash only. Never take a check from a biker … Don't even have a bank account."

More lies. True, he didn't have a bank account. And he got a lot of the money in Reno. It was what was left of the forty-two thousand that was in his saddlebags when they left Reno a month earlier, plus a good chunk of dough he'd made in Vegas. But it didn't come from fixing bikes.

SIX

JUST TWENTY-FOUR HOURS before running into that cop near Area 51, Bart was sitting at third base on the best blackjack game of his life. In the parlance of professional gamblers, he was a hole-carder, what casino surveillance would call a "peek freak." The strategy is legal in the state of Nevada and the edge that hole-carders get on the house is so big they have to misplay a lot of hands so the eye in the sky doesn't start weeping blood.

He was working with Johnny who was assigned to the play by Clance, the team manager, specifically because Johnny was Asian. Asians have a reputation in casinos—well-deserved—for spreading big and playing crazy. Clance needed a player who could get away with a lot of unusual plays. This was a very special game.

Bart had found it the previous night when he was on a game with Jersey Jimmy. He was at third base catching the hole card and signaling the info to Jimmy. Stacy was standing behind Bart with her hand on his shoulder, just watching. Jimmy was betting the money. The dealer was an old-timer named Dewey who had badly-dyed thinning hair and a bristly gray mustache, one of those porcupine jobs with stubbly thick hair poking every which way. Bart wondered why anyone would dye the hair on his head Hershey-bar brown, but leave the mustache chimney-soot-gray? Kind of defeats the purpose of the dye job, doesn't it? Dewey was a man who probably hadn't been kissed in a very long time.

Bart had never seen Dewey before, but because of his age and the way he handled the cards and payouts, he knew Dewey had been around a long time, so he should have known better. But every time he loaded his hole card under his upcard, he gave up just enough of a flash of the face for Bart to read it. Not read all of it, not every detail. Just enough. Sometimes it was just the flash of yellow that told him he'd just seen a face card, the only cards with yellow on them. Stuff like that. On this night, every hand, Bart knew what Dewey had in the hole. A dealer who gives it up every hand is called a hundred-percenter. This gave Jimmy—who was betting four-hundred bucks a round and playing his hands according to Bart's signals—more than a bit of an edge on the house. Much more than a bit. More like eight percent— roughly, a brain surgeon's salary for playing a game of cards.

But that's not what made Dewey a special case. There were a lot of flashers in Reno just like Dewey. They're the bread and butter of any hole-card team. It was Bart's job to find these dealers and surreptitiously call plays for the guys on the team who bet the money. He was the guy with the scruffy beard at third base in the grubby biker duds, betting table minimum and keeping a low profile.

What made Dewey special was that not only was he flashing his hole card, he also had a habit of flashing the index of the next card to be dealt from the top of the deck. This guy was a hole-carder's gold mine! It was Stacy who noticed it. On a hand when Bart had a total of thirteen, she leaned over and whispered in his ear, "Hit. The next card's a seven." He didn't hit, but when the dealer hit his own hand with the seven, Bart was astonished. How the hell did Stacy know the next card to be dealt? She didn't leave him bewildered for long. "Watch the deck when he pulls it up to his chest," she whispered.

Shortly after he started catching the index, Bart called off the play, left the table and buzzed Clance.

"I nixed the play," he said.

"Too bad," Clance said. "I thought you said Dewey was a hundred-percenter."

"He is. But he's also flashing the top card."

"No shit? Plus the hole card?"

"A hundred percent on the hole card. Maybe seventy-five percent on the top card."

"Why didn't you stay on the game?"

"I've never played a dealer like this before. Have you?"

"Never found one," Clance said. "You should have crushed him."

"I started to play him," Bart said. "But we need some new signals, maybe some new procedures. If I know the next card to come off, I really need to know what Jimmy's hand is. Just telling him if the dealer's pat or stiff doesn't cut it. If I know the next card's an eight, there's no way I want Jimmy to hit if he's got a fifteen or sixteen. But if he's got a twelve or thirteen, then I want him to take that card. The way we play now, Jimmy doesn't show me his hand. We've got to think this thing through, Clance. We're going to need some new signals if we really want to milk old Dewey for what he's worth."

"I'll call Johnny," Clance said. "We'll meet at my place tomorrow afternoon and work it out."

"It was Stacy who started catching the indexes," Bart said. "I didn't even notice it till she clued me in."

"We'll cut her ten percent on the play. Two p.m. at my place to work it out with Johnny."

"Why Johnny?" Bart asked. "Jimmy's pretty hot to play this guy."

"Let's say the top card's an eight or nine," Clance said. "And your big player's got a twelve. If it's Jimmy, you'd have him hit. With Johnny, you can have him double down."

"Double down on a hard twelve?"

"Why not? Johnny's a crazy Asian. Anyway, it looks kind of funny if you're back on the same game tomorrow with Jimmy since you two aren't supposed to know each other. We don't want to raise suspicions."

Jersey Jimmy would be pissed. He wasn't especially fond of Johnny the Jap. Jimmy was a stocky guy in his early thirties. His head was shaved, the style for guys his age. He had massively muscled arms and broad shoulders from pumping iron. His bike was a late-model Harley Sportster, chopped, but with lots of chrome and a custom-painted gas tank. He had a very cocky air about him that bugged the shit out of Bart.

The day Bart first met Jimmy at Clance's place—which was the day after Bart got to Reno—Jimmy never sat down, just paced the floor in his leathers. He had a long stringy blond beard that would compete with the best of ZZ Top. Both of his arms were sleeved in ink. Some of the work was nice, but a lot of it was pretty crude.

"I want you to shave tonight," Clance said to him after making introductions. "Tomorrow we'll take you shopping for clothes. You're gonna have to wear long sleeves."

"Everybody's got tats now," Jimmy protested. "Tats don't mean nothin'. My banker's got more ink on him than me!"

Clance reached across the table and tapped Jimmy on the forearm just above the wrist. "Does he have one like that?" he asked, indicating one of the better designs—a baroque script lettering in royal red and gold with light blue highlight work. It said, "Eat Shit."

Jimmy just shrugged and didn't argue it further.

Johnny the Jap wasn't Japanese; he was Korean—a huge Korean, about six-foot-six and well over three hundred pounds. He rode a Japanese bike, a chopped Honda VTX 1800. There aren't many bikers who ride Hondas and hold their own with the outlaw factions of the biker community, most of whom tend to be rabid Harley-Davidson freaks. But Johnny was such a mountain of a man, he stood tall in tough crowds.

That didn't stop Jersey Jimmy from breaking his balls over beer at Clance's kitchen table shortly after Johnny arrived. It was the first time Bart had ever met either of them, as he and Stacy had just gotten to Reno the night before.

"Is that your rice burner out there?" Jimmy said.

"Point of fact," Johnny said, "the Honda VTX burns high-octane gasoline, not rice."

"You're livin' in the U.S. of A. now."

"I was born in Los Angeles. Never lived anywhere but the U.S.A."

"So why don't you get yourself an American bike?" Jimmy said. "Harleys are made in Milwaukee, not Tokyo."

"I've got nothing against Milwaukee," Johnny said. "They make great beer. But a Harley-Davidson is just a heavy slow-ass beast. I prefer to go fast. My bike was manufactured at the Honda factory in Marysville, Ohio."

"I'm talkin' about gettin' an all-American bike—not a bunch of Jap parts slapped together on some assembly line here to save on shipping costs."

"Next time you pull your fender off, I'll show you where it says 'Showa Japan' on your authentic all-American Harley front end."

"Horseshit."

"I've got a set of wrenches if you want to go outside right now. You want to put a couple hundred bucks on it?"

"You're full o' shit, man. Maybe my bike has some imported parts, but a Harley's an all-American bike. Hondas are strictly for tourists, man. Tourists and frat boys."

"Hey, any time you want to hit the highway and see who leaves who in the dust, let's do it. I'll be pulling a lot more weight, but I'm still willing to bet my bike's faster than yours. You know why Harleys go so slow, don't you?"

Jimmy narrowed his eyes.

Johnny said, "If you go any faster than sixty on a Harley, you can't see where all the parts fall off."

"Fuck you, man. That joke's older'n you are."

"There's a reason why it's an old joke. Just put your money where your mouth is."

That's when Bart decided to butt in. "You take that bet, Jimmy, and you lose your money."

"Shit, Bart, you're a Harley man. Ain't that your flathead out there? That greasy ol' rat bike?"

Bart turned to Johnny. "Your bike's faster, Johnny, but that's not the issue. It's a matter of aesthetics. I don't give a fuck how fast your bike is, how many trophies it's won, or whatever the fuck *Consumer Reports* has to say about it. Your bike doesn't look like a Harley. It looks like a bike that wishes it was a Harley." He turned to Jimmy. "And you're a fuckin' moron," he went on. "I shoulda let you take the bet. You don't even know your front-end's made in Japan? Maybe forgivable. You can't tell a flathead from a knucklehead? Unfuckingforgivable."

Jimmy listened to this with a sour expression on his face, then leaned back on his chair and clasped his hands behind his head. He narrowed his eyes at Bart and said, "I'd kick your fuckin' ass if you weren't one of the seven dwarfs."

Bart stood up so quickly his chair tipped over behind him with a loud bang. "You wanna run that by me again?" he said as he stepped in front of Jimmy.

Jimmy just sat there, the picture of sneering relaxation. He looked mildly amused, but he made no response.

"I asked you if you'd care to repeat your last remark," Bart said, moving as close to Jimmy as he could without touching him. "Didn't you say something about kickin' my ass?"

Jimmy snorted a nervous laugh. "Are you jokin'?" he said, flexing his enormous biceps without removing his hands from behind his head.

Stacy looked worried. Bart weighed in at somewhere around 130 pounds, while Jimmy was closer to 230, much of it muscle. But Bart saw her catch the calm smile on Clance's face as he shook his head. Clance had seen Bart do this a hundred times and didn't take it seriously.

"Let's get something straight," Bart said, his face not more than six inches in front of Jimmy's. "I'm not joking and I fight dirty, so watch your nuts. And don't ever let me get my face this close to yours again, because I bite. I'll take your fuckin' nose off. Unless you want to look like the ugliest motherfucker that ever kicked my ass, you better keep your fuckin' distance."

The look on Jimmy's face had gone from amused to alarmed. "Hey, Bart, we're just havin' a friendly discussion here about aesthetics. That's all. No need to get physical. We're on the same team, man."

Bart backed off a step, but continued to stare Jimmy down.

"Speakin' of aesthetics," Clance interrupted. "I got a hat for you, Bart."

Bart took another step back, then slowly turned to look at Clance. "I don't wear hats," he said. He turned to Debbie, Clance's wife, who was sitting at the far end of the kitchen table drinking a cup of coffee.

"You got another cup of that mud?" he asked her.

Bart had attended their wedding in Berkeley a year earlier, an outdoor affair. She was a big, buxom woman in her forties, with long, wild, curly blond hair that splayed over her shoulders. She wore tight clothes and looked like what she was, a tough biker chick.

"There's coffee in the pot," she said, without looking up from her smart phone. "You can rinse out that mug in the sink … And thanks for leaving Jimmy with his nose. I wasn't looking forward to cleaning up the blood."

"Here's the deal, man," Clance said to Bart. "We're not counting cards anymore. We're playin' the dealer's hole card. It's a lot stronger. How are your eyes?"

"They're not what they used to be," Bart said, rinsing the ceramic mug under the faucet.

"Are you wearing contacts?" Clance asked.

"I'm not required to wear corrective lenses. I read the DMV eye chart a month ago. That's all that matters to me. But I can tell you for a fact my eyes aren't what they used to be."

"Can you still read the shop manuals without a magnifying glass?" Clance had always kept a magnifying glass with his shop manuals and was always amazed that Bart never needed it.

"I haven't looked at a shop manual lately. I know my bike blindfolded and I haven't had much repair business lately." Bart sat down next to Debbie and spooned some sugar from a bowl on the table into his black coffee—two, three, four spoonfuls. Then he picked up Debbie's pack of cigarettes from the table in front of her, shook a few up from the pack and looked at her questioningly.

"Same old Bart," she said. "Go ahead."

He took a cigarette and tore the filter off, tossing it into the ashtray. "I owe you one," he said.

"You owe me a couple cartons," she said.

Clance dug a dog-eared Harley parts catalog out from under a tall stack of *Hustlers* on the floor behind him. He opened it and flipped a few pages, then held it out in front of Bart. "Read that," he said, pointing to some fine print.

Bart started to reach for it but Clance stopped him.

"Just read it from there," he said. He was holding it about five feet from Bart's eyes.

Bart started to read the text Clance was pointing to: " … metering device controls oil delivery to the top end, ensuring rapid lifter pump-up and reducing possibility of oil starvation to the bottom end—"

Clance yanked the manual away and looked at the page Bart had been reading from. He moved it closer to his eyes, then further away, then held it for a moment studying it at arm's length, squinting.

"It's right under 'Hydraulic Tappets' at the bottom," Bart said.

Clance fished a magnifying glass from a small drawer built into the underside of the table top. He examined the text. "Goddamn it, Bart," he said. "You've got the best fuckin' eyes on the planet! I've got a twenty-three-year-old kid working for me—twenty-twenty vision he says, never wore glasses in his life—and he can't read this damn thing at that distance."

"Actually," Bart said, "I'd've had more trouble reading it closer. I have to back up now when I'm slinging ink—for the detail work. I've lost a lot of my close-up focus."

Clance snorted a laugh. "Your focus is dead-on where we need it," he said. "The distance from your eyes to the dealer's hole card is about four to five feet, plus or minus."

Bart had known a few hole-card players he'd met at the tables. They called it "front-loading." The term comes from the type of blackjack dealer who loads his hole card beneath his upcard from the front—instead of the back or side—allowing an alert player to get a flash of the face of the card. "I've never been able to see a dealer's hole card," he said to Clance. "I've been counting cards for twenty years and I've never even spotted one accidentally. What makes you think I can do this?"

"You just have to know which dealers are flashers," Clance said. "We're scouting the joints on every shift. Usually it's the break-ins who haven't been properly trained. The ones that got juiced in, they're the ones that get shitty on-the-job training. We're pretty much only playing the hand-held games—one and two-deckers. Most dealers don't flash from a shoe. With your eyes, man, you're a natural. And you're short. You can get a good angle on the card without looking like you're restin' your head on the layout. All you need is a baseball cap to hide your eyes, man. You don't want the boss or dealer to see where you're lookin'."

"I don't wear baseball caps."

"Hey, man, it's just for the play. You don't have to change anything else about your appearance. You gotta hide your eyes."

"I'll wear shades."

"Shades won't work, man."

"Why not?" He pulled a pair of wraparound Oakleys from his jacket pocket and put them on. "Can you see my eyes?"

"Let's test 'em," Clance said. He opened the shop manual, then turned it toward Bart at the same distance as his initial eye test. "Read that line," he said, pointing to some fine print.

Even squinting, Bart couldn't make it out. "Mary had a little lamb," he said.

Clance put the manual down.

Bart took off his sunglasses.

"You see, man," Clance said, "I already anticipated this problem." He tossed Bart a small black plastic bag that had been sitting on the table.

Bart looked inside, then took the cap out. It was black with an orange and silver Harley-Davidson logo. "It's awfully damn new-looking." he said.

"Well, they weren't selling used ones at the bike shop. I'd be happy to fuck it up for you. I could take a shit on it or something."

Bart put the cap on and pulled the brim down to his eyebrows. "So why aren't you trying to clean up my biker act? Last time I was up here you kept trying to make me look like a socially respectable citizen. You think playing hole cards I'll be able to clean out the dealer's check rack regardless of what I look like?"

"You're not betting the money, man. You'll be signaling the hole card to a big player. You're just the grubby local biker dude who likes to play nickel blackjack. They won't even be lookin' at you, man. First off, you look like a biker—and by that I mean a biker of the road scum variety—which means you're probably a high school dropout, not exactly long on brains. And you're sitting at a six-five game—further evidence you're brain-dead. If you had any smarts you'd walk twenty feet and sit down at one of the shoe games where you get full pay on your blackjacks. Plus, you're bettin' a nickel a hand. You're a nobody, man. Totally invisible."

"What's a six-five game?" Stacy piped in.

"It's a crappy new blackjack game," Clance said.

"Are you going to be the BP?" Bart asked him. "BP" was card-counter slang for "big player," the guy at the table betting the money.

"No, man. I can't even be seen with you. I got a little too well-known in this town."

"Are you dead sure about the law on this."

"Damn straight. It's already been decided in the courts. State of Nevada versus Einbinder. Einbinder won. It's the dealer's job to conceal the hole card, not the player's job to avoid seeing it. So long as we're just finding sloppy dealers—exploiting their incompetence—we're clean in the eyes of the law."

"What if they figure out what you're doing?" Stacy asked.

"They kick us out," he said. "They might send a flyer out on us but they generally deal with it in-house because they're embarrassed to tell the other joints they've got poorly trained dealers. Usually all they do is eighty-six us and fix the dealer."

"How many dealers have you got right now?" Bart asked.

"About a dozen between Reno and Tahoe. Some of 'em aren't all that consistent. Maybe half a dozen really strong ones. Most are workin' grave. That's when they break in the rookies. But there's new ones showin' up all the time. It's these six-five games. They're spreadin' like a disease. All the card counters are pissed off, but we're getting' more hole-card opportunities than ever."

"What are six-five games?" Stacy asked again.

"Blackjacks pay six-to-five instead of three-to-two," he said. "That short-pay triples the house edge. The squares love 'em. What do they know about percentages? They just want to play single-deck."

"How do I keep under the radar so surveillance doesn't spot me?" Bart said.

"The main problem isn't surveillance. Those guys couldn't find shit in an outhouse. You gotta watch out for Barry's crew. He's our competition, a real fucking asshole. He's doing the same thing we're doing, but he keeps cutting in on our plays. When he spots us at a table, he sends in one of his players to pick off our signals. It blows the play. You can't have multiple players at the same table bettin' big money and all makin' the same types of weird decisions and all kickin' the dealer's ass when they should be losin'. With one guy doin' this, they can believe he's just a jerk on a lucky streak. What's worse, when you got that many chips movin' out of the dealer's check rack, it brings down the heat even if nobody was noticin' the weird plays. Worst of all, some of Barry's guys have been eighty-sixed so many times they bring down the heat just by showin' up. The dealer gets fixed and my players get branded in that joint. One of the reasons I wanted to get you up here is that Barry doesn't know you. It's a fuckin' war, man."

"Even if he doesn't recognize me," Bart said, "won't he recognize the BP at my table?"

"You're not going to be workin' with any of my old crew, man. That's why Jimmy and Johnny are here. There's a few more dudes comin' too. I recruited 'em at the Laughlin rally a couple months back."

"No shit?" Bart said. "A biker team? Are we gonna get jackets? I'll design the colors. The Socially Respectable Motorcycle Club of Reno."

"I want one of those!" Debbie said.

"Did you inform them they'd have to scrub the grease out from under their fingernails?" Bart asked, with a sidelong glance at Jimmy.

Jimmy gave him the finger.

"They're all good people, Bart. I hand-picked 'em. They know the score."

"Who hand-picked them?" Debbie asked.

"Debbie picked them," Clance quickly corrected himself. "The hard part is still going to be keeping Barry's crew from pickin' off our signals. Sooner or later, his scouts'll spot the play."

"Why don't you just change your signals?" Stacy asked him.

"Yeah, I've done that, but they still pick 'em off. There just aren't that many ways to signal that look natural."

"Have you ever studied semiotics?" she asked.

Clance grinned at her. "I think that was an elective course in my kindergarten class," he said. "But I signed up for Tinker Toys instead."

"It's the study of sign language," she said. "What you need is a pragmatic language system that's clear to the interpretant, but undetectable to any third party. You've created a sign language, but it's too transparent. Did you ever study cryptography?"

Clance was studying her intently. "I substituted Lincoln Logs for that," he said.

"It's the study of codes and ciphers," she said. "You need to encrypt your signals in such a way that your competition can't read them, even if they know you're signaling."

"Where'd you find this girl, Bart?" Clance said. "You know, Stacy, I could use a girl like you. I mean, aside from this signaling idea, you'd be a great distraction on the arm of one of my BPs. Then again, in the right outfit you could pass for a high class hooker with a gambling problem. You could get some real money on the table. You don't look twenty-one though ... "

"I'm nineteen," she said.

"Maybe I could get you some ID."

She chose to ignore the job offer. "Tell me about your signals," she said.

"You should bring her with you when you play, Bart. She'd be a great distraction. Those surveillance dudes will spend all their time focusing on her cleavage."

"I don't have a lot of cleavage," she said.

"Just wear something tight. Hot babes are the best distraction."

"What if they card me?"

"If you're not playing or drinking, nobody's gonna card you. And if they do, they just tell you to move along."

"I think you need decoy signals," Stacy said. "Keep using your current signals to confuse Barry's guys, but those won't be the signals your players will be reading. You can use different more subtle signals for your players."

"I can tell this is gonna be way too complicated," Clance said. "I've already got problems with missed signals when they're simple as shit."

Clance picked up the phone and ordered a couple pizzas.

Debbie started to question Stacy about semiotics.

"I think it'll lead to massive confusion," Clance interjected before Stacy could answer. "Our own guys'll be screwin' up."

"Then we'll have to get smarter players," said Debbie. "We can't afford to have our best dealers fixed and our players eighty-sixed."

Debbie asked Stacy a couple questions about how the decoy signals would differ from the real signals, but Stacy said she hadn't really thought it out. "I can try to come up with a set of signals if you show me how the game goes. I was never even in a casino until last night."

Debbie turned to Clance. "We've got to try this," she said to him. "This way if Barry's players sit down at our table, they'll think they can read the signals, but they'll think our guy is screwing up and they'll leave because the game looks too weak to invest in."

"Whatever," he said. "But I foresee massive confusion."

Listening to Stacy expounding on the merits of semiotics and cryptography, Bart was getting pissed off. He could see Clance was humoring her, while Jimmy and Johnny were engrossed in the merits of Clance's *Hustler* collection. For the moment, Bart held his tongue. But later that night, when he and Stacy were alone in their motel room, he lit into her.

"Semiotics," he said sarcastically. "Cryptography! You're gonna reinvent hole-card signals? Gimme a fucking break. Do you know how fast this game is? You think I wanna be giving two sets of signals, one decoy set and one real set? Jesus Christ, you gotta keep it simple. It has to be smooth and accurate. No mistakes. Clance thinks you're an idiot."

"I thought Clance liked me," she said.

"Yeah, he thought you'd make good eye candy."

† † †

The night after Stacy discovered Dewey was flashing the indexes, Bart found himself sitting on Dewey's game with Johnny the Jap. Dewey might as well have just cleared the chips out of his check-rack and pushed them across the table because they were all just going through the motions. Johnny was crushing the game, up more than eighteen large and he was betting only five hundred a hand. Stacy wasn't with Bart. Clance didn't want her presence in the casino that night—just his feeling for changing the look of the play.

There was a suit convention in the pit—the pit boss, two floormen, the shift manager, and some guy in a polo shirt Bart guessed to be from surveillance. All of them kept looking over at Johnny and mumbling and whispering to each other, generally appearing nervous and hot under the collar. One of the bosses was looming menacingly over the table, staring at Johnny like he hated his guts. But Johnny was perfect. He acted like he didn't even notice the boss's scowl and at one point put a wood-tipped Black & Mild in his mouth and asked the boss for a light.

Bart was thinking he had to call off this play soon, when a hand came up where Johnny held a pair of sevens and Dewey was showing a nine with an eight in the hole. The next card to come was an eight. Bart signaled Johnny to split the sevens and by the time the hand finished, Johnny had split and resplit sevens and doubled down on one of the hands, earning another two thousand when all of his hands beat the dealer's. This put him up over twenty thousand on the play—so Bart gave him the signal to walk.

Johnny stood up and started stuffing his massive stacks of black chips into all available pockets, waving off the dealer who wanted to color him up.

It was all Bart could do to keep from laughing. This big fat crazy Korean in a bad-fitting suit had just won more money in two hours than any of those bastards in the pit made in two months.

Bart stuck around, betting his quarter chip at third base for another twenty minutes or so. He wanted to hear what the suits had to say about Johnny's performance. Sitting there in his biker rags, he was, to all intents and purposes, invisible to the mucky-mucks. They made little attempt to keep their voices down.

Everything he heard was good. Johnny was a degenerate China-man, the worst player they ever saw, but the luckiest sonofabitch on the planet. They hoped he would come back. They planned to raise the table limits for him next time he played. His luck couldn't hold out forever. The surveillance dude assured one and all that Johnny wasn't counting cards and his weird plays couldn't have been based on hole-card information. One of the bosses pulled the deck off the table and instructed the surveillance guy to "check it out." But Bart knew the deck was clean. They wouldn't find any marks on the cards. They never stopped to consider that their veteran dealer might have a few weak spots in his technique. There would be a host meeting Johnny at the cage to try and give him a room for the night. Of course, they didn't know it, but Johnny wouldn't be stopping at the cage.

Bart left the casino feeling on top of the world. He'd been hole-carding for only three months, but he knew he'd found his calling in life. He'd discovered a skill that would earn him real money, maybe even make him rich, and he was better at what he did than anyone else he knew. He wasn't just a nobody scooter tramp anymore. He was someone the world had to deal with.

SEVEN

"DAMN IT. BART, don't fade on me!"

The dream again that he feared was not a dream.

"Not fading, Dorsett ... I'm right here."

"Thank you for getting my name right. Where'd you get the money? Five neat bundles of hundreds—ten thousand each—that's not the way your biker buddies pay you for adjusting their sissy bars. Where'd you get it?"

"Money's irrelevant ... Nothin' to do with what happened out there. In the desert."

"What desert?"

That's right ... Dorsett knew nothing about that night in the desert. That wasn't what he was asking about. That was a month ago, the night they came to Vegas. That was a different cop, a cop who asked no questions.

EIGHT

HE KNEW THAT the state trooper didn't find Stacy, his life would be a whole lot easier. Then all he'd have to explain would be the forty-two thou in his saddlebags, his refusal to stop for a cop in pursuit, and whatever the hell he was doing off-road only a couple of miles from Area 51.

He knew what the whole thing would look like to the cops, D.A., judge, jury … He was just some slimy biker tramp using and abusing some poor underage girl, a dumb mixed-up runaway who had problems at home and needed a friend and, like your friendly neighborhood Fagin, he'd pounced on her. And what was with all that unexplained cash in his saddlebags? He had no visible means of support. It had to be stolen, or drug money, or profits from pimping the girl, or ill-gotten loot of some kind. And it wouldn't take more than one look at his tattoos for them to deduce that he was some kind of Satanist to boot.

But being handcuffed wasn't as much of a problem for Bart as it would be for most people. He had two dozen lock picks of different types stuck into his belt. It was legal to carry lock-picking tools, but if you weren't a locksmith, getting caught with them could suddenly propel you into suspicion on lots of burglaries. So, he'd found a way to conceal a full set on him that wouldn't be found even if he was searched. The picks were evenly spaced about an inch apart all the way around his leather belt, each one having a steel ball tip he'd soldered on to act as a handle, disguising the set as decorative studs on the belt.

Just from the feel, he was pretty sure the cuffs were Smith and Wesson Maximum Securities. Either them or Peerless, but same difference: both popular police models, heavy-duty reinforced steel, with a similar tubular lock. He'd practiced on a set of S&W 94s at his Uncle Jake's lock shop for months on end when he was a teenager. His uncle would put the cuffs on him and he'd work on them with the picking tools until he got out. His uncle had a set of the S&W cuffs taken apart on his work bench so he could demonstrate how the locking mechanism worked and exactly what had to be done to unlock them with picks. It took him hours when he first started, but after a few weeks, he'd have them off in about fifteen minutes. Then his uncle showed him tricks that turned him into a Smith & Wesson master. By the end of that summer, he could get the cuffs off in thirty seconds flat if his hands were cuffed in front of him. Behind his back, it would take maybe ninety seconds.

The necessary tools were pretty simple, though not as simple as for some of the old-fashioned cuffs his uncle had that didn't have tubular locks and especially didn't have the double-lock feature of the maximum security cuffs. With no double lock, you could just slide a shim into the opening where the ratchet teeth of the shackle arm caught the locking dog. The shim smoothed out the surface and the shackle arm just slid right out. You didn't have to pick the lock itself, just foil the ratchet mechanism. Those old stories about Houdini being able to pick his way out of any pair of handcuffs with a hairpin weren't bullshit. He wasn't picking the locks on most of them; he was shimming the ratchet teeth. Hairpins made pretty decent shims for a lot of the old cuffs, though Houdini probably used piano wire with one end flattened, since hairpins weren't very heavy duty. His Uncle Jake all but worshipped Houdini, whom he always referred to as the "Maestro."

"Next week I'll show you some tricks for working behind your back," Jake said. "Maybe you're starting to understand why Houdini was the greatest escape artist of all time. He never knew how they were going to restrain him or even what kind of a lock they would use. He not only had to pick locks behind his back, sometimes he had to use multiple picks one-handed, or hold the picks in his toes, or in his teeth.

It's easy to pick a lock when it's sitting on a table in front of you. But can you pick it blindfolded? Or one-handed? Or behind your back? How many ways can you pick it?"

"What did he do if someone had a lock that he couldn't pick no matter what?" Bart asked. "I mean there must be some kinds of locks you can't get out of—combination locks or something?"

"The Maestro was always prepared," he said. "If worse came to worst, he would use his top-secret last-resort method. The method he never wanted anyone to know about, and nobody ever did know about … until after he died."

"What was that?"

"Well, he would sometimes get help from an accomplice," he said. "Not very often. Only when it was absolutely necessary."

"Isn't that cheating?" Bart said.

"Not when you're really in trouble. That's the cool thing about magic," Jake said. "There's no such thing as cheating. As long as you leave the audience baffled, you succeed."

Unfortunately, the double-lock feature of the modern cuffs made the shim useless. The double-lockers had a little toothed wheel in front of the locking dog, so you couldn't get your shim past it. You had to pick the lock; there was no way around it.

The S&W Maximum Security cuffs had four tumblers, each of which had to be picked to the shear line separately. For a tubular lock, in addition to a pick, you needed a tubular torsion wrench, and the one his Uncle Jake gave him with his first set of picks was fashioned out of the round sleeve of a ballpoint-pen clip.

The tricks his uncle taught him after he had the basic picking strategy down all had to do with the torsion wrench. You had to be very careful not to push it too far into the keyway, or you'd touch the tumbler you were working on, making your work more difficult. But with just the right pressure when it was perfectly placed, you could line those tumblers up, one, two, three, four, and you were home free.

The picking tools hidden in his belt were mostly made from various-sized bobby pins. He had only one tubular wrench and that would be a bitch to get to, as it was wrapped around one of the belt loops on his jeans, a loop on the right side, just over the front hip pocket. It was also squeezed tightly closed so it wouldn't come off the belt loop accidentally. Normally, with his hands cuffed behind him, he'd have no trouble reaching that little bastard. But with his hands cuffed behind him and around the frame of his bike, he couldn't maneuver his arms far enough to his side. It didn't help much that he felt dizzy from the whack on his head. If he kept his eyes open for any length of time, the sky—that deep black Nevada desert sky pin-pricked with a million stars—started spinning. He made a mental note to get another tubular wrench attached to a belt loop on the back of his jeans, but that wouldn't do him a lot of good right now. He was having what his Uncle Jake would call "a Houdini moment."

Bart knew what he had to do. First, he had to get his boots off, standard motorcycle boots, what some people called engineer boots. They were pretty easy to pry off over his heels just by using his feet. His jeans, on the other hand, were something else again. Without the use of his hands, he couldn't unfasten his belt, but by sucking in his gut and scraping his ass on the ground, he got the pants down to thigh level. Then it was just a matter of using his legs to get them past his feet and all the way off.

He had no underwear on—he always rode commando—so he was sitting there bare-assed in the dirt. With his feet, he was then able to move his jeans up to where he could reach them and he quickly had that precious little torsion wrench in his grip where he could unbend it from the belt loop.

He kept an eye on the cop's flashlight, now way the fuck out there, maybe a half mile away. Stacy had a big edge on the cop. She could see him, but he couldn't see her. And she was no dummy. Her brain worked faster than anyone Bart had ever known. Even if the cop managed to get his flashlight beam onto her, he'd never catch her. She was younger, healthier, and had a lot more reasons to not get caught than he had to catch her.

Still, there was something worrisome about the trooper's strategy. Why didn't he just stay with his car, radio for back-up, and get a few other cops out there to search for her? He'd also had no reason to knock Bart out. Why hadn't he just handcuffed him and stuck him in the back of his car? Bart had a sick feeling in his gut that this was some kind of rogue cop who didn't want assistance. He liked the idea of having a couple of captives out in the middle of the desert at three a.m. where he could do what he wanted with them, answering to no one. He remembered Stacy not wanting to get off the bike, insisting that the cop was crazy and wanted to kill him. Was she right? And why was the cop tearing after him alone so close to Area 51? Isn't this U.S. government property? Wouldn't he have to call the feds, the FBI, CIA, NSA, some government agency or other before he went racing around here?

Bart got the torsion wrench off his belt loop and unbent it to what felt like the proper diameter for use on an S & W tubular lock. He then went through a half-dozen pick choices on his belt searching for the best one. Doing this entirely by feel while he was shackled in a position that was becoming more uncomfortable by the minute—and with an unknown time constraint—was strangely exhilarating. This was the first authentic Houdini moment of his life. He wondered if Houdini had ever had to escape when he was dizzy, maybe from lack of oxygen or being bound upside down too long. The wooziness was causing mild nausea. He was breathing deeply to keep from vomiting.

Then he heard the cop shouting. Yes, he was shouting. In the city, at that distance, he never would have heard it. But out in the desert where the only sound is the wind and the bugs, the cop's voice rang through the night air. Did he actually say, "Stop or I'll shoot!"? He could see the flashlight beam bobbing frantically. The cop had spotted Stacy and now he was chasing her.

Run, baby, run. I just need a little more time.

NINE

"BART, CAN YOU hear me?"

Jesus fucking Christ, what the hell did Dorsett want from him? Wasn't it obvious he wasn't being cooperative?

"Bart? Bart? Can you hear me, Bart?"

"Goddamn you, Dorsett … Don't you have anything better to do? Trying to catch a little shuteye … "

"Don't let yourself fall asleep, Bart. Not yet."

"Afraid I won't wake up? Afraid you won't get your questions answered? The hell makes you think I'd tell you the truth anyway?"

"You haven't answered the first question yet, Bart. Why did you and Stacy come to Las Vegas?"

"Least you got her name right … Thank you … Why does anyone come to Vegas, man? Party center of the universe."

"So you came here to party? Were you aware she was being sought by the police? Did you know she was an underage runaway?"

"Just answer one question for me: How bad is she hurt? She in this hospital?"

"That's two questions. And I don't have any information about her. Maybe one of the doctors here can get some information on her. I'm just here to try and find out what happened from your perspective."

"Never heard anything about her bein' a runaway … Her ID said she was nineteen."

More lies. His troubles had really begun about twelve hours before that night-time flight from Reno. That was when he found out she was jailbait ...

TEN

IT WAS IN the parking lot of a Raley's supermarket in Reno. He was giving her a ride home from work and they'd stopped for a quart of milk and a chocolate bar. It was a sticky summer day. Leaning up against a side wall of the store, gulping down a few swallows of the icy milk, he saw her photo on the milk carton. He looked at the photo, looked at Stacy, looked hard at the photo again. It was definitely her. No doubt. He read the bad news …

> Have You Seen Me?
> Julia Gwendolyn Thomas
> Age: 15
> Height: 5'6"
> Weight: 112 lbs.
> Hair: Auburn
> Eyes: Green
> Last seen: Milpitas, California
> Call: 1-888-FINDERS

She was licking chocolate off her fingers.

"Julia?"

She looked up, responding to her name, then—in a split second—he saw a chill run through her. "Why did you call me that?"

"I've been reading about you."

Her eyes narrowed. "Cut the shit, Bart."

He turned the milk carton so that the side with her photo was facing her. "Thirsty?" he said, offering the carton to her.

She didn't even look at it. "Why did you call me Julia?"

He jiggled the carton at her.

She grabbed it from him, stared intently at the photo for a moment, then slowly sank to her haunches, holding it tightly in both hands, never taking her eyes off of it. Finally, with a sick look on her face, she said, "Shit, Bart! What am I going to do?"

"I'm asking myself the same question."

"What if somebody sees this?" she said. "I'll lose my job." She was working at a used bookstore in downtown Reno. Stacy was a book freak. They'd only been in Reno a few months and their apartment was nothing but books floor to ceiling. She devoured books. She could talk about any subject. Anything. Aeroballistics. Zymology. Anything. He suspected her IQ was higher than his and she was the first person he'd ever met about whom he'd had such a suspicion.

"Lose your job? That's the least of your worries. More likely they'll call the cops."

"Dottie wouldn't turn me in to the cops." Dottie was the bookstore manager, maybe the owner. He didn't know.

"Hey, any customer could recognize you and rat you out. You're fucked, Stacy. You can't go back to work. How in God's name did you get that job in Sunnyvale?" When he'd met her three months earlier, she was working as a stripper in California. At a nude club. No alcohol. The state law said the dancers had to be eighteen.

"I've got fake ID," she said. "And I have to go back to the store on Friday. They owe me a paycheck."

"Kiss it goodbye. Should I call you Julia?"

She shot him a look that said don't you dare, then said, "You're serious? I can't even pick up my paycheck?"

"Damn straight, baby. You have to leave town. Get on a bus to Vegas or something."

"They have milk in Vegas," she said. "This picture's probably all over the country."

"Yes, but they don't know you in Vegas. People here see that photo … 'Hey, that's Stacy!' In Vegas, nobody recognizes that girl. A week from now, a new photo comes out and nobody remembers last week's milk-carton kid. Besides, now you know which photo they're passing around. You can change your hairstyle, put on some glasses. You've got to get out of town. You've got no other options."

"You have to come with me, Bart. We'll go to Vegas together. You have milk in your beard. You look like a derelict."

He wiped his palm down his chin, smearing the white drops of milk into invisibility. "Stacy, you're fifteen years old. If you get caught, they send your ass home. If I get caught with you, they send my ass to prison."

"You can't just abandon me, Bart! You said you loved me!"

"I never said I loved you. I said I don't believe in love."

"You lied to me," she said.

"I lied to you? You told me you were nineteen! All those times you came into the casinos with me … Jesus Christ! It was bad enough I thought you were nineteen and they'd just kick you out. But fifteen? They could haul my ass to jail."

"I told you a white lie. Age is an arbitrary distinction. When I told you I loved you, I meant it."

"As I recall our exact conversation, Stacy, you said you loved me and I said that's because you're a girl. What I said and I repeat: 'Guys don't believe in love. Guys believe in gettin' laid.' Do you recall this conversation?"

She just looked at him. Hurt. Too proud to pout.

"Are you saying you don't recall this conversation?"

"I know what you said, Bart, but you said it in a way that meant you loved me."

"So it was all bullshit you gave me about majoring in chemistry at Stanford? You're not even out of junior high! Have you told me a single word of truth the whole time we've been together?"

"I graduated from high school when I was fourteen," she said. "And I was going to Stanford, majoring in chemistry. That's the truth, Bart. Honest. I only lied about my age."

Now he didn't know what to believe. "Baby, you're fifteen years old and you've been living with me for the past three months, with me thinking you were nineteen. I'm a middle-aged anti-social biker with no visible means of support and a list of prior busts for possession of controlled substances, shoplifting, and various minor infractions that may soon include the statutory rape of a fifteen-year-old girl. That's not minor. I could do hard time for this."

"You never raped me!"

"Believe me, if I'm living with you, the court is not going to be kind to me. In the eyes of the law, I'm an adult. You're a child."

"But we never even had sex!"

He stared hard at her for a few moments, then said, "Not because you weren't trying."

"I'm not fifteen anyway," she said. "I turned sixteen two weeks ago."

At this point, he had no idea if anything coming out of her mouth was true. "Well, a belated happy birthday, baby. Sorry I didn't get you a cake. But believe me, it won't make any damn difference to the judge. And you can't use that ID anymore. Even in Vegas, you can't use it. As soon as someone here recognizes that photo, they'll be looking for you and they'll know the phony name you've been going by. You've got to get a new ID with a different name."

"That's no big deal. I can get another ID."

"Where'd you get it?" he asked.

"Zoey makes them. She's got the whole works, hologram and everything. It's a real one. I mean, it's made from real equipment. That's how I got the job at Angel's."

He had initially met Stacy at Zoey's apartment in Sunnyvale about three months earlier.

"So you were fifteen when I met you?" he said. "You were fifteen and working as a stripper? Where'd Zoey get the equipment to make fake IDs as good as that?"

"She paid a lot for it. It used to be in the DMV, I think in Sacramento. It broke down or something. The guy who was supposed to be scrapping it took it home and fixed it."

"But why'd she buy it? She's not on the lam, is she?"

"Zoey has a lot of friends who are card counters. What kind of business did you think she was doing with Clance? She's living in Las Vegas now and has a pretty good fake ID business going, making IDs for professional players. That's where all the pros are. She says Reno's small time compared to Vegas."

All news to him. Zoey had never told him she could make fake IDs. Clance never told him Zoey was making them. Zoey had mentioned to him that she was planning a move to Vegas. "Then, what do you need me for, Stacy? You've got Zoey to take care of you. She knows your secret and she can whip you up a new ID. You can stay with her in Vegas and hide out till you get a different look together."

"You can't abandon me just because of my age, Bart. Age is an involuntary thing, like race or height. It's not my fault how old I am. You can't just hear a number and say 'I don't love you anymore.'"

"First off, I never said I loved you. Second, I never said I was going to Vegas with you. Third, you should have told me how old you were."

It pissed him off that she'd lied to him about something so important. If she'd told him the truth, he never would have brought her to Reno. What was most upsetting to him was that he did love her, but her age wasn't really why he'd never had sex with her. That was just what he'd told her. The fact was he couldn't fuck. Anybody. Broke dick. None of her business.

"Look at me, Bart," she said. "I'm sixteen years old. I'm just an innocent young girl with a hot body. Do you really want me to go to Vegas all alone and do whatever I have to to survive?"

"Don't give me that innocent crap," he said. "Are you going to drink that milk? You've been bogarting that carton for ten minutes."

She took a swig then passed it to him. "I guess I'll just hit the highway with my thumb out and trust my fate to the kindness of strangers," she said. She looked comical with her milk mustache.

"C'mon, Stacy … Won't Zoey help you get settled somewhere?"

She wiped her mouth with the side of her hand. "Oh yeah, we've talked about it before. Do you know why her husband is divorcing her? Because he found out she used to work at a whorehouse down in Pahrump. She made a lot of money and it's legal. One of her old customers saw her in the casino and he talked with Jeffrey about her. She's probably going back to work there again. She already told me she could get me a job in the brothel. Her IDs are perfect. I don't look sixteen." She said this as if she were bragging.

His stomach was churning. "You wouldn't do that, Stacy," he said. "Why don't you just go home till you're eighteen? The time will pass fast. It can't be that bad at home, can it?"

"Do I have to talk about all this shit right now? Do you need to know the creepy details of my home life or can you just accept the fact that I would prefer blowing strangers to living with my parents? I'm a survivor, Bart. I'll do whatever it takes to be in control of my own life."

He made a move to take her hand, but she twisted away from him with a look of defiance. "Don't put a guilt trip on me, Stacy." He paused, trying to soften the tone of the conversation. "I could be charged with kidnapping, rape, child molestation, corrupting a minor, god knows what else."

"I'm not trying to guilt trip you. I'm just telling you the facts. If I find myself working in a whorehouse next week, I'm not going to be fooling myself that it wouldn't have happened if Bart really knew my situation. Bart loved me. Bart wouldn't let this happen if he knew. He cared about me. He just didn't know."

"You're not trying to guilt trip me?"

"Yeah, and then two years from now, I'll be eighteen and I'll call Bart and say, 'Guess what, sweetie, I'm legal. I'm finally old enough for you to be in love with me. The magic legal number. Eighteen. Here's another magic number: *one thousand*. That's how many dicks I've sucked in the past year!'" There were tears in her eyes.

He started to respond several times, opened his mouth, but stopped. She was looking intently at him, waiting, as if daring him to put up his fists and have it out with her. The feeling in his gut was on the verge of panic. Finally, he said as calmly as he could, "I have never once come on to you. I never told you I loved you. You're not my girlfriend."

"Fuck you," she said through her clenched teeth.

He waited a moment, then continued at a slightly higher pitch. "Every time you came on to me, I told you you were too goddamn young for me and that was when I thought you were nineteen. Now I find out it's fifteen, not nineteen. Fifteen! *Fifteen!*"

"Sixteen!" she spat at him. "You're such a fucking hypocrite! You walk around in those biker duds, mister rebellion, riding your badass Harley, bragging about your disregard for authority, telling stories about all your wild rides and dangerous adventures, mister professional gambler, mister social renegade, the big casino scammer who's never been caught. But I guess I'm an adventure that's just a little too dangerous for you." She looked angry. She looked scared.

Once more, he tried reaching for her hand.

This time she slapped his arm away. "You can't even keep up with a sixteen-year-old girl, you wimpy sonofabitch! You call yourself a man? You and your fucking Satan tattoos? Big devil worshipper! You wimpy little phony. I'll go be a whore and you can ride your big bad Harley off into the sunset!" The look on her face was almost vicious.

"C'mon, Stacy," he said softly.

"Oh, fuck you! I've got more guts than you ever had! You're just like my father! You call yourself a man and you're just the same as every other ass-licking little turd who acts tough but does what he's told! Maybe I'll just kill myself! Like you even give a damn what happens to me! Fuck you!"

† † †

Clance was upset when Bart told him over the phone that he was leaving town.

"No fuckin' way, man! We're just startin' to get a decent bankroll together. I've never met anyone that can read hole cards like you. What the fuck am I going to do without you?"

"It's an emergency situation, Clance. I can't even talk about it right now. I'm going to Vegas. I'll call you when I get settled there. We can move the whole operation to Vegas. Reno's too small anyway. This move will pay off. I just need to pick up my cut of this week's win."

"Jesus Christ, man, are you shittin' me?"

"It's no big deal, Clance. It's time to move on. Barry's team knows who I am now anyway and they're going nuts trying to pick off my signals. Every time I scout, one of his guys sees me and starts following me. This town is too small."

"This is going to fuck up everything, Bart. We've got thirteen flashers now and you're the only one who can read half of 'em. And Barry left town last weekend. Didn't I tell you? He's gone. His team's gone. What do you want to bet he's in Vegas? Your eyes are worth a million bucks, man. Do you want a bigger cut?"

"Look, I'm sorry, Clance. It really is a goddamn emergency."

"What about tonight's play? You can't cut out on tonight's play, man. We've got to go after Dewey again before they fix him. I already got Sam and Lisa working on the new signals. Can't you just stay around for another couple weeks? If we pack up and blow Reno now we're leaving a shitload of money on the tables. I told you we'll be going to Vegas soon, like in a month or two. But we've got some great games here, man."

"Look, I'm going to tell you something but I don't want you spreading it around, not the guys on the team or anyone. Stacy's only sixteen."

There was a long silence before Clance said, "So what?"

"So her picture's on a milk carton right now."

"So cut her loose."

"I can't. I've got to get her out of town."

"You can't live with her. Why the fuck are you living with her anyway? You said you weren't bangin' her. Tell her to hit the road. She's got money."

"She's in trouble, Clance."

"Shit, man, you're gonna be in a lot more trouble than she is if you don't cut her loose. Are you pussy-whipped?"

"I'm not fucking her, Clance; she's not my type. She's just a kid, but I like her. I care about her. I've got to get her out of town and get her set up doing something in Vegas."

"They're going to fry your ass, Bart."

"So I should just tell her to beat it? I can't abandon her, man. She's not my girlfriend or anything, but … she's special."

Clance let out a mocking laugh. "You're PWed, Bart. You're not fuckin' her and you want her to live with you? Explain that to me, man. She's the hottest piece of tail in Reno and you're telling me you want to be her big brother? I don't buy it. As I recall, you've got one bedroom in that pad where you two live, and one fuckin' bed. I don't really give a shit if you're lying to me. If I was bonkin' San Quentin quail I wouldn't admit it to anyone either. But when you get to Vegas, at least rent a two-bedroom crib, because I don't think the jury's gonna buy it that you're sleepin' on the couch. And I repeat, your ass is gonna be fried."

Bart caught himself feeling pleased that Clance thought he was having sex with Stacy. She was so smart and gorgeous and totally out of his league that he couldn't bring himself to argue the point. "So I should just kiss her off and wait for the next girl genius to blow into town?" he said.

"That would be the smarter move."

"I'll stop by in an hour to get my money."

ELEVEN

"WHAT MONEY?"

"My cut, man! You owe me my cut. For this week."

"What cut? What money?"

"Jesus Christ, Clance. You owe me more than twenty large!"

"Who's Clance?"

"Huh?"

"Who's this Clance and what's the money for?"

"Goddamn it, Dorsett … Stay outta my fuckin' life!"

"What's the money for, Bart? And who's Clance?"

"None of your fuckin' business!"

"We will find out who he is, Bart. Can't you make it easy on yourself and just answer a few simple questions?"

"Can't you just let me fuckin' recuperate in fuckin' peace?"

"Is he part of this satanic ring you're in? Was he there at the rally?"

"Jesus, Door-prize … "

TWELVE

IT WAS DURING his early teenage druggie period when he met Clance and became fascinated with motorcycles—or, more specifically, with chopped Harley Davidsons and the outlaw-biker culture. Clance worked behind the counter at a comic-book store on Telegraph Avenue in Berkeley, just a half-mile or so from where Bart lived. The store sold used paperback sci-fi novels for fifty cents each and Bart was building a collection from the money he made working at his Uncle Jake's lock shop every Saturday. He'd seen Clance a hundred times before at the comic store but had never talked to him except to make a purchase. Clance wasn't the sociable type. Bart knew Clance was a biker; he'd seen him on his Harley many times and the bike was always parked in a back corner of the store when Clance was working. Clance also dressed the part—open, sleeveless, faded-denim jacket, no shirt, lots of silver rings on his fingers, tattoos on both arms as well as his chest, long unkempt hair, missing a bottom front tooth.

Bart chose a novel by Roger Zelazny, an author he'd never read, and tossed it onto the counter with a buck. Clance just sat there reading a comic.

"I need change," Bart said.

Clance stood up with a look that said Bart was pestering him, then picked up the book from the counter and said, "You like Zelazny?" He said it like Bart was an idiot to have chosen this book.

"Never read him," Bart said.

"Bad choice." Clance dropped the book back onto the counter top.

Bart looked at the cover. "It says here he won a Hugo Award and a Nebula."

"Not for that book," he said. "The one you want to get is *Damnation Alley*. It's down there on the bottom shelf with the other Zelaznys. Put this one back."

Bart looked through the half-dozen Zelazny titles on the bottom shelf, but couldn't find *Damnation Alley*. "It's not here," he said. He returned to the counter with his original choice. "I'll just take this one."

"I know we have it," Clance said. "It was right on top of a box of books I bought myself off some punk who came in two days ago. I guess Darrell didn't get them out on the shelves yet. It's in the back room. He'll be here at noon. Don't get that shit book. I've read every Zelazny novel and you just picked the worst fucking book he ever wrote."

Bart knew Darrell. He'd talked with him about sci-fi many times. Darrell was the one who'd turned him on to Philip K. Dick. "Why don't you just go to the back room and get it for me?" Bart said.

"Can't. I don't have the key."

A cheap hollow-core door behind the counter led to the back room.

"Can't you pick the lock?" Bart said, eyeing the standard Schlage doorknob.

Clance grinned an exaggerated gap-toothed grin. "No, I can't pick the fucking lock," he said. "It's eleven-thirty. Darrell will be here in half an hour."

"I could pick that lock in fifteen seconds."

Clance looked at him as if he'd just told him he could levitate. Then his eyes narrowed and he said, "Seriously?"

Bart pulled a small leather pouch from his hip pocket where he kept a set of picks. He opened the pouch, fished out a diamond pick and a tension wrench and held them up for Clance's inspection. "Fifteen seconds."

"All right, hotshot, show me," Clance said, motioning for him to come around behind the counter.

Bart went straight to the back-room door, inserted the pick, then the wrench, into the keyway and said, "Start counting."

Bart raked the pick in and out gently, applying delicate pressure on the wrench. The cylinder turned and Bart opened the door when Clance got to nine.

"No fuckin' shit," Clance said, seriously impressed. He pushed the door all the way open and turned on the light in the room.

Bart followed him in.

Clance took a paperback from a large corrugated cardboard box on the desk and tossed it to him.

Bart looked at the book. *Damnation Alley*. He liked the cover art, a head inside a transparent round helmet. You couldn't tell if the head was human or alien. "Thanks," he said.

"On the house," Clance said. "Can you teach me to pick locks?"

"Sure. But it's not easy. It takes a lot of practice, even when you know what to do."

"Some things are worth workin' for. Where'd you get the picks?"

Bart thought better of telling him about Uncle Jake. It was good to keep some secrets. "I've got connections," was all he said.

"Can you get me a set?"

Uncle Jake would have a fit if he heard this conversation, but this was business. What would Satan do? "It'll cost you," he said.

"How much?"

"Five bucks."

"Fuckin' deal, man! Where'd you get 'em?"

"Connections … They're illegal, you know, if you're not authorized."

"Bullshit."

"Try and buy a set sometime. Anywhere. Go to a locksmith and tell him you want to buy some picks for personal use. He'll tell you to take a hike. He could be busted for selling these to someone who's not in the business. The cops will bust you if they catch you with them." At least, that's what Uncle Jake had told him.

Clance took his wallet from the back pocket of his jeans and peeled out a five-dollar bill. His wallet was a big, fat, dirty black-leather one attached to a chain that hooked to his belt. Bart already regretted telling him the picks were five bucks. He probably could've gotten twenty from him. But he wouldn't actually have to pay anything for them and Uncle Jake would never notice he'd taken them. Uncle Jake had hundreds of picks that he'd made himself, mostly from hairpins and pieces of wire. Bart could easily make them himself. It was pure profit. Clance handed him the five-dollar bill. "You gotta teach me how to use 'em," he said. "How soon can you get me a set?"

He tossed him the pouch. "You can have these. I got more. But lessons are extra."

"How much do you want?"

"I don't know. I have to think about it. I never taught anybody before. It might take a long time. You don't even know how locks work, how the mechanism looks inside. You'll learn faster if you can see a lock taken apart."

"I can trade you books. Anything in the store."

Bart had a feeling that if Darrell heard this conversation, he'd be as pissed off as Uncle Jake. But this was getting better all the time. "That would be cool," he said. "But there's something you could teach me too."

"What do you wanna know?"

"How to ride a motorcycle."

Clance looked dead on into Bart's eyes like he'd said he wanted him to teach him some arcane form of magic. Then he said, "You're too small for my bike. Can you get a bike, somethin' more your size?"

"I can learn on your bike," he said with as much confidence as he could muster.

"Like hell. It's a fuckin' Harley. You have no idea how heavy that motherfucker is. What do you weigh, like eighty pounds?"

"No way! I'm about a hundred!" Actually, about eighty-eight.

"Your feet won't even reach the pegs, man. You can't ride a Harley. It would be a mistake to even try. If you dumped it, you couldn't even get it upright. Shit, it strains my fuckin' muscles. What's your name, man?"

"Bart."

Clance extended his hand. "I'm Clance. How old are you, Bart?"

Bart shook his hand, noting the crude black tattoo on web of his thumb. "Thirteen," he said.

"You're awfully damn small for thirteen."

"That's my problem."

"You know you can't get a motorcycle license 'til you're sixteen."

He shrugged. "So? I'll be fourteen pretty soon."

"C'mon out and sit on my bike, man. I want you to feel how heavy it is."

They exited the back room and Clance led him to his bike. Just looking at it, Bart knew Clance was right. It was too big, too heavy. But it looked so mean, so bad, so powerful. Why couldn't he be just like a normal-sized thirteen-year-old?

Clance mounted the bike and took the kickstand off, then dismounted, holding it upright by one of the handlebars. "Get on," he said.

Bart just looked at it. It was so damn big.

"Just swing your fuckin' leg over the seat and get on it."

Bart put his hands on the handlebars, which were a real reach for him, and swung his leg over the seat and sat down.

"Now put your feet on the ground," Clance said. "Get your ass off the seat and stand up. I'm going to let go."

Bart stood up, straddling the gas tank, and held onto the handlebars for dear life. Clance let go of the bike and backed off a short step when he saw Bart was holding it steady. Bart didn't feel any weight at all. It was perfectly balanced.

"It's a good thing it's chopped," Clance said, "or your feet wouldn't even touch the ground. Now lean it toward me just a bit so you can get a feel for the weight of it."

Bart angled the bike ever-so-slightly toward Clance and the balance was gone. He didn't have the strength to hold it up. Clance caught the bike before it crashed to the floor. He was laughing. Bart was petrified.

"All right. Get off," he said.

Bart took a deep breath and dismounted.

"Like I say, man, I can't teach you on my bike."

"Maybe I can get a Kawasaki."

"Get real. You're not going to be riding that Jap crap. I thought you said you wanted to learn to ride a motorcycle. I'll teach you to ride a motorcycle, but I won't teach you to ride one of those eggbeaters. We're gonna have to build you a bike. You know what a Triton is?"

"No."

"You take a Norton frame and you slap a Triumph engine on it, you got yourself a Triton. Not a V-twin, a little six-fifty Bonneville engine. It's a fast little motherfucker and we can chop it down to your size. You gotta put some muscle on though. If it tips over, you gotta be able to upright it. I'm not sayin' it's light—just a fuck of a lot lighter than a Harley. I'll supervise the building, but you gotta do the work yourself."

"Really?" Was he seriously offering to help him build a motorcycle? "Where do I get all the parts?"

"I've got a couple of frames and three or four old Triumph engines. They need some work but nothin' serious. I used to ride a Triumph Bonneville. Best limey bike ever built. My yard's a fuckin' motorcycle graveyard. Anything I don't got, we can get. You get me whatever the fuck I need to learn lock pickin', and while I practice with the picks, you'll be workin' on your bike. I got all the tools you'll need."

Just then, Darrell walked in.

"What the hell's going on, Clance?"

Clance looked at him for a second, decided to ignore the question, and just said, "What's up, man?"

"Why the hell is the back room door open?" He sounded more curious than angry.

"You left it unlocked, man," Clance said. "I didn't touch nothin' back there except that Zelazny book on the counter. *Damnation Alley.* Bart here just bought it. It was in the box I put back there a couple days ago."

Bart went over to the counter and picked up the book. His dollar bill was still on the countertop beside it. He figured this wouldn't be a good time to inform Darrell that Clance said he could have the book free of charge. He pushed the dollar toward Darrell. "I need change," he said.

Darrell took the buck and opened the cash register. He handed Bart two quarters. He never charged tax, but then he probably didn't record a lot of transactions.

Meanwhile, Clance had wheeled his bike out the door and onto the sidewalk. He kicked the engine to life, then revved it up. There's nothing quite like the sound of a Harley engine, the tremendous noise of it, the raw power. He stopped revving the engine and looked over his shoulder at Bart.

"C'mon, Bart!" he yelled. "Let's go!"

Bart was dumbfounded. Clance was actually inviting him to take a ride on his bike! After a stunned moment of staring blankly at him, he ran to the bike for fear Clance would change his mind and go racing down Telegraph Avenue without him. Tucking *Damnation Alley* into the front of his pants, Bart climbed up onto the raised leather pad behind Clance's seat.

"Put your arms around me!" he yelled back at Bart. "Tight! Hold on tight! Don't let go!"

Bart wrapped his arms around Clance's midsection and clenched his fingers onto his denim jacket. His scraggly hair was in Bart's face and he smelled like grease and sweat. The bike was vibrating violently.

Then it took off like a shot, literally bouncing down the curb from the sidewalk to the street, thundering down the avenue with that evil loud noise that only a Harley makes as it accelerates. In that moment, Bart understood everything there was to know about the attraction of man to motorcycle. The bike was just crude power harnessed between your legs. The bike told the world to get out of your way, to wake up, to go fuck itself. The bike was God on a leash, an insult to fear.

They roared down Telegraph Avenue for a couple miles into Oakland, then Clance turned onto Highway 580 heading east toward Hayward. As soon as they hit the highway, he really opened her up. The wind pummeled Bart's face and arms and legs. The exhilaration was so great he could feel himself laughing out loud, though he couldn't hear his own voice.

He knew right then that this would be his life.

THIRTEEN

"WHAT ARE YOU laughing at?'

"What?"

"What's so funny?"

"Nothin'."

"You're laughing at something, Bart."

"Laughing at you, Doorknob ... You're cracking me up."

"Well' you're pissing me off, Bart, if that's your intent. Who's Zelazny?"

"Roger Zelazny?"

"Who is he?"

"Ol' buddy o' mine."

"What can you tell me about Miss Thomas?"

"Who?"

"The girl you call 'Stacy.' Where'd you meet her?"

"Reno."

"Where in Reno?"

"Bookstore ... You read books, Dorsett?"

"Were you part of that satanic cult there?"

"Where?"

"In Reno. Isn't that cult where you met her?"

"No satanic cult in Reno ... Not that I know of."

"Don't play dumb with me, Bart."

"Met her at a bookstore ... Buying a Zelazny novel ... Roger

Zelazny ... Stacy was sales clerk ... Sold it to me ... Said Zelazny sucked ... Should buy somethin' else ... That's where I met her ... Stacy."

Another big fat lie ...

FOURTEEN

GODDAMN IT!

He'd dropped the torsion wrench in the dirt. Now he had to maneuver his body into a position where he could see the damn thing. Seeing it, however, despite the pain of his bike's valve cover gouging into his ribs, turned out to be helpful. He was able to ascertain that the diameter he'd opened the wrench to when removing it from his belt loop was slightly too wide for the tubular keyway. That, in fact, was probably why he'd dropped the damn thing trying to jam it in. He made another mental note to come up with a way to hook a tubular torsion wrench to the back of his belt that didn't involve squeezing the wrench end closed over a belt loop or anything else. He thought of what his Uncle Jake had told him a hundred times about Houdini: "The Maestro always found a way."

He got the torsion wrench back into his hand, squeezed it to what he thought was the proper diameter for the lock, and voila! He was finally able to slide it cleanly into the keyway.

But a new problem had developed. The cop was on his way back. All Bart could see of him was the beam from his flashlight, but it was definitely heading in his direction. He had, at most, maybe three to four minutes to escape from the cuffs. Technically, he only had to get one of them off to free himself. At the same time that he was working his tools on the tumblers, he was trying to figure out what the fuck to do once he was free.

If he was really crunched for time—meaning when the cop was like ten seconds away—he'd have to just upright his bike and get the hell out of there. Time permitting, however, it would be a nice touch if he could get his pants on. Riding a Harley bare-assed over rough terrain was not his idea of a pleasant evening. And pants or no pants, he would absolutely, positively, have to get his boots on to have any chance of escaping. There was no way he could ride his bike, or even kick-start it, barefoot. He was only five-foot-three and it was a miracle he could ride a Harley at all. It had taken him years of pumping iron as a teenager to get the muscles to handle that bike, but without those boots, that upper-body muscles wasn't going to cut it.

Disabling the cop's car was also on his mind. Technically, it would be a piece of cake. He wouldn't even have to get under the hood. He had a good selection of rocks at hand to bust the headlamps and spotlight. Sure, the cop could still drive the car, but with only his flashlight to guide him in this blackness, he wouldn't attempt to do much more than get back to the main road, and he wouldn't get there any too quickly.

Bart was pretty sure that the cop didn't have Stacy. That wasn't even a worry. He knew if he could just bust the car's lights, he'd have no problem finding her himself. She'd be out there waiting for him, looking for him, calling to him once he got anywhere near her. He just had to get to her before reinforcements showed up. Maybe he'd be able to save her.

He considered the possibility of disabling the car's two-way radio, but that would probably be an exercise in futility, a waste of precious time. The trooper probably had a cell phone on him. The important thing was that he had to get out of there before he had half the cops in Nevada on his trail.

Bart started to feel an anger rising in him, a familiar blind fury at whatever god had cursed him with his diminutive stature. It always started with a tightening of his neck muscles, then a clenching of his jaw and a shortness of breath. The cop had looked big—maybe six-two, broad shoulders. *Why does every other fucking asshole on the planet get to be six feet tall? What did any of them do to deserve physical superior-*

ity over me? Bart rarely got into fights, but when he did, he always won and he made sure everyone knew it. He was very good at picking his fights, just like he was good at picking locks. But this was not a fight he would have picked. You can't beat a cop with sheer viciousness and balls. Cops have guns.

He had to calm down. He had work to do and not much time to do it. He had to clear his head. He'd spent too many years of his life pissed off about this same unalterable factor of his existence. All of his concentration had to be channeled to the Smith & Wessons, the only obstacle that mattered in this Houdini moment. The Maestro himself was only five-foot-five.

He got the first tumbler lined up. He was just three tumblers from freedom. The cop was way out there, but he could tell from his bouncing flashlight he was still coming back. Bart couldn't see him at all, just the beam of the flashlight, but he knew he didn't have Stacy. He just knew it.

He got the second tumbler lined up. *Two down, two to go.* He estimated the cop was still a couple minutes away. Every once in a while, the cop would stop and scan his flashlight beam around himself, like he'd heard something, like Stacy might be following him. This was good for Bart, since he needed all the time he could get. It was going to be close.

It crossed his mind that if he didn't get the cuffs off and he was still shackled to his bike when the cop returned, he'd probably be less than amused to find that Bart was now sitting there bare-assed and barefoot. What would he think? He leaves a prisoner unconscious and shackled to a five-hundred-pound motorcycle, only to return a few minutes later to find the guy still helplessly cuffed to the bike, but bare-ass naked from the waist down? He actually got a chuckle out of it when he thought of how funny it would be if, when the cop returned, Bart acted as if he was still dead unconscious. Figure that one out, Einstein! The thought of the look on the cop's face almost made him laugh out loud, except he was pretty sure that however the cop reacted, it wouldn't be all that pleasant for him. By this point, he figured the odds were pretty good that this cop was a power-tripping sociopath. There was something seriously wrong with a cop who knocks an unarmed and cooperative suspect unconscious then shackles him in the dirt while he goes chasing a girl through the desert and never radios for backup. Pants or no pants, Bart was pretty sure he was in for a taste of hell. Stacy had this guy nailed from the moment he entered the desert in his patrol car. How did she know he was such a loose cannon? Was this more of her psychic shit?

Jesus, he was getting close ...

FIFTEEN

"WHY'D YOU CHANGE your name?"

"Where's Stacy?"

"I'm asking why you changed your name, Bart."

"She in this hospital?"

"Your name used to be Rosenfeld."

How the hell would Dorsett know that? Maybe this wasn't a cop. Maybe this was a dream after all.

"Does the name Lloyd Rosenfeld ring a bell?"

"Jesus fuck, Doormat ... That was a century ago ... Fuck does that have to do with anything? Was a legal name change."

"What was wrong with Lloyd Rosenfeld?"

"Gimme a break ... Are you on the clock? You bein' paid by my tax dollars? Must be no fuckin' crime in this town."

"Look, Bart, there was a riot. It appears that you were at the center of it. Six people shot. More than thirty injured, many in serious condition, some of them are still in the hospital. It's my job to try and glean whatever information I can from the only person who might know exactly what happened and why. You're the mystery man of the hour, Bart. Or should I call you Lloyd?"

"Call me Mister Black."

"Did you change your surname to Black because of this obsession with Satan? Something to do with the Black Arts?"

Bart laughed. It hurt his chest like hell and he stopped at once, but it made him smile that Dorsett was so far off base.

"Damn, you're good, Doormat ... Got me all fingered out ... Changed my name for the devil."

Another lie.

SIXTEEN

BART HATED ELEMENTARY school. He was always the smartest and smallest kid in his class, a good three inches shorter than any of the first-grade boys, and even the shortest girl had an inch or so on him. Academically, he was way ahead of all of them. When he entered first grade, he was already reading, writing, and doing simple math. His parents had encouraged him to read from the time he was about three, and since they spent most of their time buried in books, he became fascinated with books himself. He was also a comic-book addict.

He wasn't in the first grade more than two weeks when he was skipped ahead to second grade. Unfortunately, this made his classmates even bigger and his life that much more difficult. He was learning nothing and he was being teased mercilessly by the other kids. For the first few months, he was called runt, shrimp, midget, dwarf, tiny, pygmy, peewee ... The name that finally stuck was "Midge"—the one he despised more than any other because it was a girl's name. In the Archie comics, Midge was Moose's girlfriend.

The boys found it hilarious to hold his books or his lunch bag above his head, out of his reach. Did they actually think he'd make a fool of himself jumping to get his stuff? After a few A-pluses on homework, he learned that praise from the teacher had unpleasant repercussions outside of class. He purposely underperformed academically. He made no friends at school. He felt like a freak.

He could see no logical reason for going to school. They make you sit for hours every day watching stupid kids struggle. The teacher spends months reading a history book you could read at home in a couple nights, then they want to test you on the stupidest shit, like what date the Huns wiped out the Visigoths. Who cares? In his opinion, first grade would be more effective if they shit-canned the teachers and just locked all the kids in the classroom with about five hundred comic books for six hours a day. They'd all be reading in a week. The dumb kids would be begging the smart kids to teach them. Fuck see-Spot-run. See-Hulk-grunt would generate a lot more interest.

In the sixth grade he changed his name from Lloyd Rosenfeld to Bart Black. He'd become fascinated with American outlaws and he spent a lot of time at the downtown Berkeley Library, reading the histories of outlaws—anything and everything he could find, from mobsters like Al Capone to hit men like Baby Face Nelson, from loners like John Dillinger to the famous old-west gunslingers like Jesse James. He especially liked the lesser-known legends, men like Shotgun John Collins, Cock-Eyed Frank Loving, Thomas "Black Jack" Ketchum, Big Nose George Parrot, and the Native American renegade known as the Apache Kid.

The man who intrigued him the most, however, was Charles Boles, a stagecoach robber who called himself "Black Bart." Boles was so infamous in his time that, even today, some people could tell you that Black Bart was an old-Western bad guy, but few have read anything about him or have any idea of who he actually was. Only his name survived.

Boles' modus operandi was to stand in the path of a stagecoach with a flour sack over his head, two eye-holes cut out, a double-barreled 12-gauge shotgun pointed at the driver. Using this method of getting the drivers to stop, he successfully robbed 28 stagecoaches between 1875 and 1883. Every one of them was a Wells Fargo wagon and, in every instance he took only the bank's strongbox, never robbing the passengers and never once firing his gun.

What had most intrigued Bart about Black Bart, however, was that he sometimes left handwritten poems with the stagecoach drivers after robbing them. One poem he liked so much he memorized it:

I've labored long and hard for bread,
For honor and for riches,
But on my corns too long you've tread,
You fine-haired sons-of-bitches.

Black Bart was an outlaw with not only a sense of ethics, but a sense of humor, and for some reason he really had it out for Wells Fargo. Though Wells Fargo might disagree, Lloyd Rosenfeld thought the country could use more men like Charles Boles. So, in his honor, Lloyd Rosenfeld had become Bart Black and since then had refused to answer to any other name.

He didn't make the name change legal until he turned twenty-one, but from the sixth grade on, he refused to respond to Lloyd anymore. Even his parents stopped calling him Lloyd when they saw he refused to answer to anything but Bart. His father took a while to come around, but even he did, eventually.

In his own way, Bart was honoring the legend of Charles "Black Bart" Boles. It was probably lucky for Wells Fargo that they weren't transporting cash in stagecoaches anymore.

SEVENTEEN

"WHO'S CHARLES BOLES?"

"Huh?"

"You said 'Charles Boles.' Who is he?"

"Jesus Christ ... Am I talkin' in my sleep?"

"Can you answer my question, please, Bart? Charles Boles?"

"Outlaw."

"A biker? A friend of yours? Was he involved in this?"

"Outlaw in the old West ... Stagecoach robber."

"Yeah, right."

"Fuck ... Not authorizing the use of the tape recorder anymore ... What else d'I say?"

A small amount of light was starting to enter Bart's right eye. Was the swelling going down? He could move the eyeball and change the intensity of the light. He wanted to see, if for no reason other than to assure himself that this wasn't a dream and that Dorsett wasn't a worm. But he could see nothing recognizable, no shapes or forms, not even the source of the light. But it was another good sign. He was coming back, was on the road to recovery.

"Well, you're saying a lot more when you nod off than when you're awake. Unfortunately, Mr. Black, you're not making a whole lot of sense. According to my notes here, so far, at various points you've mentioned Area Fifty-One, Uncle Jake, the Theosophical Society, re-splitting sevens, Wells Fargo, and 'two down, two to go.' Does any of that refresh your memory about what happened last Friday?"

"Two down, two to go. Where's Stacy?"

"What's two down, two to go? Bart?"

"Fuck off."

EIGHTEEN

TWO DOWN, TWO *to go.*

The third tumbler was giving him trouble, primarily because the hand that was holding the torsion wrench was starting to go numb in the wrist, while the thumb muscles in his working hand were starting to cramp. But his vertigo was subsiding. That was good.

The cop was maybe a couple hundred yards away and it was starting to sink in that maybe he wouldn't make it. He truly might fail at his first real Houdini moment. To calm himself, he kept repeating his Uncle Jake's favorite dictum, like a mantra, "The Maestro always found a way. The Maestro always found a way—"

That's when the shot rang out.

Bart froze. Was the sonofabitch actually shooting at Stacy? For god's sake, she was just the fucking passenger on the bike!

A coyote howled in the distance.

The cop walked over to something on the ground and was kicking at it. Bart couldn't allow himself to think it was Stacy. Whatever it was, he shot it again, and the moment that shot fired, Bart's pick hit pay dirt and the third tumbler lined up.

One to go.

The sound of the second shot shook Bart into a state of heightened mental clarity. But the cop was so damn close. Even if the fourth tumbler just fell into place on its own, would he have enough time to get his bike uprighted? Now the fucker had his gun in his hand! Suddenly, the cop turned and started waving his flashlight around in the other direction, as if he'd heard something. He was slowly scanning the flashlight beam from side to side and, once more, started walking away.

It couldn't possibly have been Stacy he shot. Why would the cop be searching the area again? Was Stacy actually following him back? If so, she was buying him time, but why? She didn't know he could pick locks. He'd never mentioned it to her. So, even if she knew he was handcuffed to his bike, she wouldn't expect that he'd have any way to free himself.

NINETEEN

"DAMN IT, BART! Stay with me!"

"Look, Dorsett … Here's what's happenin' … My life's passin' before my eyes."

"Cut the drama, Bart. Just try to stay awake."

"Not that long of a life … but it's mine and I'd prefer not to miss any of it … "

"Who's Zoey Berrington?"

"Zoey?"

"We know Stacy was living with her."

"Where's Stacy? Damn you."

"Does Zoey have anything to do with this cult?"

"Fuck off … Tryin' to watch my life story … Appreciate it if you'd stop interrupting … "

TWENTY

HE WAS LIVING in Sunnyvale, a Silicon Valley suburb of San Jose, when he met Stacy about three weeks prior to their going to Reno. He'd gotten a call on his cell phone from a woman who introduced herself as Zoey, who said she'd gotten his number from Clance. She was interested in getting a tattoo. Zoey's apartment was in the better part of Sunnyvale.

She was maybe thirty years old and pretty, but also had a hard look about her. Her hair was in a punkish buzz-cut, dyed white with pink streaks. She had an eyebrow stud and a pierced tongue, but no visible tattoos.

"I'm Zoey," she said, taking his hand.

"My pleasure," he said.

She didn't let go of his hand even though he'd already stepped through her doorway. She wasn't really his type; she probably had about forty, maybe fifty pounds on him—very buxom, big ass, a lot of guys would say voluptuous. Not his type. He tended to go for skinny waifs. He guessed Zoey to be five-foot-four, which meant that he appeared to be taller than her, since he was wearing boots and she was in sandals. When she finally let go of his hand and turned to lead him into her living room, she seemed to walk like she wanted him to drink her in, check out that big bubble butt squeezed into her tight white denim shorts.

Her living room walls were adorned with large framed posters of rock groups, some concert posters, some album covers. Not his taste in music—Nine-Inch Nails, the Deftones, the Arctic Monkeys.

"My roommate's out walking my dogs," she said when they were sitting on her living room couch. "She should be back soon, but I just want to give you a heads-up: She's kind of weird."

"Aren't we all?"

"Yeah, but Stacy's one-of-a-kind. Anyway, I want a tattoo just like the one you put on Clance's back."

"I put three tattoos on Clance's back. Which piece did you like?" Clance was his showcase. Bart had at least ten of his best tattoos on Clance.

"I like the peacock."

He flipped through his portfolio to the design she was referring to.

"Yes," she said. "That is so beautiful. It doesn't look like a tattoo design."

"It's art deco," he said. "I got the basic design from an old sheet of wallpaper. The detailing and coloring are my own."

"How long would it take?"

"To pound the ink? It's not that big, but it's a lot of detail work. Two sittings. A few hours total."

"Can I just do one sitting?"

"With detail work like this, I'd prefer to get the basic outline done, then fill in the colors later. This is original artwork and I do the outline by hand." He knew he could do the whole thing in two hours, one sitting, no sweat. But if he made the job seem more complicated than it was, he could jack up the price a bit. She looked like someone with money.

"How much will it cost?"

"Three hundred bucks," he said. He was quoting what he thought she could pay, not what he'd expect to get from most of the bikers he did tattoos for.

"And you can do all of those same colors?"

"Not the white. I mean, I can do it, but it'll fade too fast. You don't want white, trust me."

"I love those colors," she said. "What can you substitute for white?"

"You're pretty fair. Turn around."

She swiveled sideways in her seat.

She was wearing a halter top. He pressed his index finger into the skin on her back just below her shoulder. "You either stay indoors a lot or you use a lot of sunscreen," he said. "Were you thinking of getting it in this area here?"

"I was thinking … on my cheek."

"Can I assume you're not talking about your face?" he said.

She pursed her lips. "My ass," she said.

"Maybe a light blue," he said.

She stood up and unfastened the button on the waistband of her shorts, then the zipper, then she turned her back to him and pushed the shorts down over her hips and let them drop to her feet. She was wearing a pink satin thong.

He'd done very few tattoos for women—a couple of small shoulder designs, one medium tramp stamp. Most of his work was for bikers.

"Which cheek?" he said.

She patted her left buttock softly.

He touched the skin. Tight.

"What do you think?" she said, looking over her shoulder at him.

As he was attempting to come up with some way of saying, "What a gorgeous fucking ass you have," just to be polite, without actually using those words, the front door handle clacked and the door pushed open.

In walked a tall blond in wraparound shades and a bright yellow sun dress with two leashed dachshunds yapping at her heels.

The girl looked momentarily puzzled at the scene before her and quickly turned away, embarrassed. "I'm sorry, Zoey," she blurted, starting toward the door.

"Stacy, it's okay," Zoey said calmly. "Come in and close the door. You're letting the air out."

"But—"

"It's okay, honey. This is Bart. He's the tattoo artist I told you about."

Stacy turned and looked at him, pushing her shades up onto her forehead. "Oh," she said. "You work for Clance?"

Weird question. She sounded like she'd known Clance all her life. She was looking at Bart like he was some dispensable blue-collar employee.

"I work for myself," he said. "You know Clance?"

"No," she said. "Zoey told me about him."

There was something about the way she talked that puzzled him, the tone of her voice, the careful way she intoned her words.

"How do you know Clance?" he asked Zoey.

"I did some business with him up in Reno," she said.

He figured Zoey was a card counter.

"Can I pull my shorts back up?"

"I'll think about it," he said.

She got her shorts on and sat back down beside him on the couch. Stacy unleashed the dogs and settled into an armchair across the room. She pulled out her cell phone and started texting. The dogs lay down at her feet.

"What's in the bag, Stace?" Zoey asked.

"I bought a CD."

"Stacy's a dancer," Zoey said.

"That's stretching it," Stacy said. "I'm not a dancer. I'm an ecdysiast."

"A what?" Zoey said.

"An ecdysiast is a stripper who's read H.L. Mencken," Bart said.

Stacy smiled. "Gee, what do you call a tattoo artist who's read Mencken?" she said. Now she was looking at him like he might be someone worth paying attention to.

"A showoff," he said.

"What are you guys talking about?" Zoey asked.

"Mencken was a writer," Bart said. "He coined the term 'ecdysiast' as a euphemism for stripper after he saw Gypsy Rose Lee. This was like fifty years ago. He didn't think the term 'stripper' did her justice. It's actually a bastardization of a biological term. When a reptile sheds its outer skin, it's called ecdysis. It's a Greek word."

"Oh my god," Stacy said, still texting. Bart couldn't tell if she was responding to what he'd said or to what she was looking at on her cell screen. Then she said, "Will wonders never cease? A tattoo artist who went to college!"

"Wrong. I'm a high school dropout. In fact, I'm a grammar school dropout if you want to get technical. So exactly where do you practice the fine art of ecdysiasm?"

"Angel's Showgirls," she said, putting her cell phone down.

He kept looking back and forth between Stacy and Zoey. Stacy had some kind of eye thing going with him. Was she flirting with him?

"Angel's," he said. "Never heard of it. Is it in San Jose?"

"No, it's right here in Sunnyvale," Stacy said. "It just opened a couple weeks ago. Can I see the peacock design?"

Zoey picked up Bart's binder and turned to the page with the peacock. She held it up for Stacy to see.

"It's art deco," Bart said.

Stacy got off her chair and came over to the couch. She took the book from Zoey and studied the picture for a moment.

Bart was studying her. She looked awfully young to be working as a stripper. Her hair was long and thick and blonde, but not naturally blonde. Hollywood blonde. Marilyn Monroe blonde. There were movie stars who would kill for her face, her high cheek bones, her full perfect lips. She had luminous green-blue eyes. She was wearing lipstick that was ghoulishly white and heavy black eye-liner that looked so out of place with her soft pale complexion and her pixie nose. But she could have shaved her head and smeared green paint across her mouth and anyone could still see she was stunningly beautiful.

Technically, Stacy wasn't his type either. She was too tall, for one thing. He tended to immediately disregard as objects of lust women who were much taller than him. They just didn't fit his fantasies. And Stacy had a good three inches on him. But something about her style instantly attracted him to her, though it wasn't until later that he realized it was precisely what she'd done to her hair and her lips and her eyes that drew him to her. It was like she'd made up a Barbie doll like a harlot. There was something so wrong about it, so rebellious. She was refusing to be defined by her physical attributes. She was going to make you think twice when you looked at her. He was trying to figure out her accent. Her English was too perfect, like she'd come from some other country and had taken lessons in how to get rid of an accent.

"That's not art deco," Stacy said. "That's art nouveau." She said this with authority, like there was no argument.

"I stand corrected," he said. "I take it you've studied art in addition to literature."

"Design," she said. "Not in school. My parents collect antiques."

"How do you distinguish art deco from nouveau?" he asked.

"Nouveau is more ornate," she said. "Deco has cleaner lines. It's more modern looking. This peacock is almost like an Aubrey Beardsley painting. Clearly art nouveau. It's beautiful, Zoey." She closed the portfolio and handed it to Zoey.

"Where are you from?" he asked Stacy.

She looked at him for a moment before answering, "Not from this planet."

"I assumed that much. Are you in the market for a tattoo yourself?"

"I have all the ink I need," she said. She extended her arms, palms up, to display two tiny, red, heart-shaped tattoos, one on each wrist. Neither one was much bigger in circumference than the head of a nail.

"They're awfully small," he said. "Can I assume it says 'Mom' inside the heart?"

She smiled. "Read them," she said, pushing her wrists toward him. "They're four-letter words, not three."

He had been joking. It was impossible that anything could be written inside tattoos so small. But he took hold of her wrists and positioned them to get a good look at them. It did appear there was some kind of scrollwork inside them, which made no sense. He couldn't imagine a tattoo needle capable of making such fine lines. Then he clearly saw that the tattoo on her right wrist had the word "ECCE" inscribed in it. The tattoo on her left wrist said "HOMO."

"I assume you were raised Catholic," he said, still holding her wrists.

"No."

"Well, I was. *Ecce homo* ... those were the words Pontius Pilate spoke when he presented Christ to the Romans after the scourging at the pillar. It means 'Behold the man.'"

"Very good," she said, as if he'd passed some secret test she was administering. "It was also the title of Nietzsche's last book."

He let go of her wrists reluctantly. "You sure know a lot of weird shit," he said. "I assume those are some kind of decals? I've never seen a needle that could draw lines like those."

"You make a lot of wrong assumptions," she said. "They're birthmarks."

Okay, so they're decals. But where would she get such tiny decals and why would she wear them? "Why ... " he said, but never finished. *Ecce homo.* The last words Pilate spoke before washing his hands of the crucifixion.

She smiled at him. "Actually, they mark my radial arteries in case I ever need to find them in a hurry."

That froze the room into an uncomfortable silence.

"Come on, Stacy," Zoey said. "Don't even talk that way." She looked at Bart. "Can you get started on it next week?" She handed the binder to him.

"I can get started on it tomorrow," he said. "Do you want to come to my place or do you want me to do it here?"

"Tomorrow doesn't work for me," she said. "I have to go to Vegas for a few days to finish up some business. Can you come over tonight? Say around nine?"

"I'll be here. It'll take me about an hour to draw the outline and ink it ... Nice meeting you, Stacy. Maybe I'll catch you molting sometime."

But she didn't look up or acknowledge his goodbye. She was texting again.

† † †

The moment he touched the needle to Zoey's flesh, he could see her body stiffen.

"How's the pain?" he asked.

She picked up her head to look at him. "It's tolerable," she said.

"It hurts more at the beginning," he said. "Your body gets used to it. Just think about something else."

"I am thinking about something else." She reburied her face and he went back to work.

The dachshunds outside her bedroom door started moaning along with the buzz of the needle. He was glad she'd thought to lock them out. She started tightening the muscles of her buttocks.

He lifted the needle. "You can't keep clenching your cheeks like that."

"It's involuntary."

"Well, you're going to have an involuntary mess on your ass if you can't stop." He looked at her nightstand where his power box was surrounded by the equipment he'd brought with him—disposable tubes, a couple bottles of ink, ink caps, A & D ointment, paper towels ... "Sorry I don't have a pussyball for you," he said. "Do you have anything you can squeeze?"

"What's a pussyball?"

"Just a rubber ball. A tennis ball. Anything."

"There are some dog toys in that box in the corner."

He lifted his latex-gloved hands, one of which was holding the machine, the other the paper towel he was using to wipe the ink after laying each line. "I'm sterile," he said. "I can't touch dog toys right now. Go pick out a ball or something, one for each hand. Just something you can squeeze instead of your ass cheeks. And be careful not to bump my work area when you're getting up."

She climbed off the bed and went over to the toy box, returning with a small pink rubber dumbbell in one hand and a green rubber frog in the other.

"Perfect," he said. "Now be careful getting back on the bed."

She stepped in front of him, facing him, and put her arms up over his shoulders. She closed her eyes expectantly, inviting a kiss.

"Can I take a rain check on that?" he said. "I'm kind of busy at the moment."

She opened her eyes. "I like bad boys," she said, and without waiting for him to make a move, she went in for the kiss, mouth open, tongue on active duty. She pressed her body up against him, those huge tits squishing into his chest.

He couldn't put his arms around her with his tattoo works in his hands, but he felt his dick spring to life inside his jeans. His brain was protesting. *She's not even my type!*

She pulled back from the kiss suddenly, looking him in the eyes from a distance of about eight inches, and said, "I want you to fuck me when the outline's done."

He snorted a mild laugh. "I don't know what position you have in mind, but I can guarantee you that an hour from now your ass will be in no mood for fucking."

She looked dead serious. "I am so turned on," she said.

"You like pain?"

"I hate pain. I like you."

"Lie down. Let's get this done with. And squeeze the dog toys, not your ass cheeks."

She got back onto the bed. "Can you talk to me while you work?"

"What do you want me to talk about?"

"Anything." She buried her face in her pillow.

He turned on the juice and found himself looking at her ass in a whole new light. "The ancient Egyptians were into tattoos," he said, wondering how that ass would look if she'd prop a pillow under it. "In fact, some of the best preserved mummies have elaborate tattoo work on their bodies."

When he touched the needle to her skin, he discovered that the dog toys she'd chosen made irritating squeaking sounds.

"The Egyptians were also the first people to practice circumcision. Other primitive tribes were into different types of piercing and scarification, but nothing quite as brutal as actually cutting off part of a guy's dick."

Now the sounds of his buzzing iron and her squeaking dog toys were joined by the wailing of her dachshunds.

"But only the Egyptian mucky-mucks—the nobility, the pharaohs, the high priests—were allowed to be tattooed and circumcised. A privilege of rank. The riffraff and slaves, the soldiers—even if they lived in the palace—no way."

She interrupted the cacophony of high-pitched squeaks she was making with the dog toys to lift her head and say, "Are you making this up?"

He ignored the question. "One of the first things the Jews did when Moses got them out of there was start circumcising all the males. Three thousand years of pain for little boys, all for a big fuck-you to the pharaoh."

She lifted her head again. "Can you hand me that other pillow?" she said. "That's the problem with large breasts. You can't lie on your stomach too long or they hurt. I have to prop myself up higher." The pillow was right beside her on the bed.

"I'm sterile," he said. "Just grab it. I'll wait." He wondered momentarily if she was actually going to stick it under her hips to prop her ass up.

"Why don't you turn on the stereo?" she said. "I've got one of your favorite CDs in there. I forgot about it. Right there on my dresser."

"I'm sterile," he said. "I can't touch anything. How's your ass doing?"

"It's not as bad as I thought it would be."

She got off the bed and turned on the CD player, then lay back down. He recognized the music immediately. *Three of a Perfect Pair*. It was, in fact, one of his favorite albums.

"How'd you know I like King Crimson?" he asked.

"Stacy told me."

"How'd she know that?"

"I don't know. That was the CD she bought this afternoon. She told me to play it tonight when you were here, because you really liked it."

"She never even met me before this afternoon. How the fuck would she know that? That's like from twenty-five years ago."

"I told you she was weird. She's always doing stuff like that."

It took him about an hour to finish inking the outline.

"Let me slap some goo on it," he said.

"Don't you dare slap it."

"Just a figure of speech," he said, gently applying salve over the surface. "I'm going to cover it with saran wrap. You can leave it on there tonight, but starting tomorrow, as much as possible, get it exposed to the air. It's got to heal. Walk around your apartment bare-assed whenever possible. No baths or soaking in water for at least two weeks. Take quick showers. You can wash it with soap and water to keep it clean. It's going to itch like hell. Don't scratch it. I'll give you some goo to put on it. It'll scab over in a week or so. Don't get the scabs wet. Let them dry out and fall off on their own. Call me when you're ready to get some color pounded in."

She stood up.

"Still want to fuck?" he said, peeling his gloves off.

She smiled weakly. "You were right," she said, and once more without waiting for him to make a move, she moved in and kissed him. "Tell me you don't have a girlfriend," she said.

"I don't … "

"I thought I might be moving to Vegas," she said. "Depending on how this trip works out. Now I might have to reconsider."

"Well, I'm not opposed to going to Vegas to finish your work if need be. I could use a trip to Vegas. Haven't been there in a couple years. I'm not going to leave you with just an outline in any case."

"I won't be moving until the tattoo's finished. What do I owe you for today?"

"One-fifty."

She went to her dresser and got the money from her purse. "My ass is pretty damn sore. Are you still turned on?"

He wasn't, but he said, "That's what happens to guys when girls kiss them."

She kissed him on the mouth again, this time more passionately, and he put his arms around her and kissed her back, telling himself he was just trying to be polite, as his dick sprang to life once more. Suddenly, she slid down onto her knees in front of him and started to unbuckle the belt on his jeans.

"Let me relieve you," she said.

He felt panic. This couldn't possibly end well. He reached down and pulled her forcefully up to a standing position. "No," was all he said.

She looked confused. She'd expected him to surrender. She kissed him on the mouth again.

He wanted her so badly and at the same time, he just wanted to get out of there.

"You are so perfect," she said. "Perfect … "

TWENTY-ONE

"**I'M NOT TRYING** to be rude, Bart. I'm just trying to get some questions answered."

"What day is it, Dorsett?"

"It's Wednesday. See how simple that was? You asked, I answered. That's all I'm asking you to do."

"What day did you come?"

"What?"

"What day? When you first came here? To my room?"

"Wednesday. Today. The hospital called this morning and said you were regaining consciousness. I already told you this. I've been here about an hour, which is all the time the nurse said I could have with you."

"No way."

"And you've been uncooperative since I got here. They're going to throw me out pretty soon."

"My life's passing too fast … "

"Well, I wish to hell you'd fill me in on a bit of it. We know more than you think we know. You're not helping your case much."

Bart threw him a bone: "You know about the Smith and Wessons?"

"Guns? You have a cache of firearms somewhere? You want to talk about that?"

The excitement in Dorsett's voice amused him.

"Bart? Bart?"

TWENTY-TWO

HE HAD ONE tumbler to go. He had to concentrate. Whatever was happening out there had at least given him more of a chance. He had to ignore the numbness in his wrist and just hold that torsion wrench steady. If he lost the torsion wrench, he'd lose the tumblers that were already lined up and he'd have to start over.

Bingo! Just like that he popped the fourth tumbler into place and the shackle arm fell open. He yanked his arms from behind his back and as he did so, the dangling steel cuff clanked loudly against the gas tank on his bike. The cop spun to look at him, pinning him in the beam of his flashlight. Bart jumped to his feet then froze as the cop brought his pistol up and pointed it at him.

Bart raised his hands. The dizziness that had subsided returned with a vengeance. So fucking close. So goddamn fucking close. His balance was off. Escape was out of the question. He was just trying to stay upright. He focused on the trooper and let the desert spin in the background.

The look on the cop's face was priceless as he walked toward him. Bart was standing there with his hands in the air, the one open cuff dangling from the wrist that was still shackled. Naked from the waist down and barefoot, he could only guess what his own face must look like, what with the cop not twenty yards from him with his service revolver pointing dead at his head.

He could see wheels turning in the cop's head as he tried to figure it out. Bart knew he had it all backwards. The cop thought that somehow Bart had managed to slip out of one of the cuffs, then took his boots and pants off. That must have seemed like the logical progression of events that got him to this state. But what undoubtedly had the cop stumped, other than the fact that he'd never seen anyone get out of his cuffs before, was any logical explanation for why Bart had taken his pants off. Why would he undress, knowing the cop was coming back, instead of trying to escape? The cop just stood there with his mouth in an ugly twist, trying to put the pieces together, coming up with nothing.

Bart could hear Uncle Jake's voice admonishing him. "What would the Maestro do?" And that ridiculous thought caused him to do the one thing he really shouldn't have done considering the dire circumstances. He started to laugh. The utter confusion on the cop's face, the absurdity of the whole scene, him standing there barefoot with his dick dangling in the wind, his failure at proving himself in his first authentic Houdini moment when he had actually come so close to success. He didn't want to laugh. He wasn't trying to taunt the cop. It was an involuntary burst of nervous adrenaline that had been building inside him since he'd awakened in the cuffs and started plotting his escape, an unfortunate burst of neurostimulant that collided with his light-headedness.

Then he saw something click in the cop's head like he'd figured it out. His face relaxed into a stone-cold-dead expression of resolve and determination. The cop knew why his pants were off and he was weighing his options.

The cop's lips twisted into an ugly sneer. "You slimy little homo," he said.

TWENTY-THREE

THE GIANT WORM was slithering onto the bed, squirming under the sheet beside him, pressing its wet flesh against his skin.

"Mr. Black, we need to talk ... "

That wasn't the worm. Was there really a Dorsett?

"Can you hear me? Say something ... "

"You still here, Dorsett?"

"Well, I'm glad you're awake. From now on when I have to step out of the room, I'm turning on the TV to keep you from fading out. You're in some serious trouble."

"It's called death throes."

"You might wish it was, Mr. Black."

"I'm no longer Bart?"

"Let me give it to you straight, Bart. We know you and Miss Thomas were living in the Silicon Valley area about four months ago and that you both arrived in Reno about the same time."

"Is she here? In this hospital? Can I get her a message?"

"We believe you brought her to Reno, and then you brought her here to Las Vegas with you a few weeks ago."

"Pretty nifty detective work, Dormouse ... Commend your department for their diligence ... You gonna cuff me now? Or wait'll I make a run for it?"

"This is not exactly a joking situation, Bart. I do appreciate your sense of humor in the face of adversity, but it might be helpful to your case for you to be cooperative. We gave the name Miss Thomas was us-

ing in Reno to authorities in California and lo and behold, they discovered that she worked in a number of nightclubs in the Bay Area under
that name, apparently using a fake ID to get jobs she was too young for.
Does the name Angel's Showgirls ring a bell?"

"Fuck off."

"Well, the Sunnyvale police were kind enough to ask a few questions at that establishment and they discovered that you also worked
there—under the table apparently, though just for one night from
what we were told. But it was a night when she was working, so this
bullshit about having met her at a bookstore in Reno is just that—
bullshit. Maybe you'd like to tell me about the 'contest' … "

"And maybe I wouldn't … "

TWENTY-FOUR

HE GOT THE idea for the wet-panties contest as he was spritzing water onto the front of Lulu's T-shirt at the Brass Rail. If he hadn't been so hard up for money, it never would have occurred to him. It was getting more difficult to make ends meet in the Bay Area as a freelance tattoo artist. Tattoo shops were everywhere these days and if you didn't work in a shop, people didn't trust you. A lot of these joints, in Bart's opinion, did crappy work—very little original art and nothing spectacular. But they had health-department clearance and scrubbed storefronts and regular hours and ads in the yellow pages. They made the housewives and college kids who were suddenly into tattoos more comfortable than a freelancer who traveled with his works in a motorcycle saddle bag.

Bart was no scratcher. He did very fine work in antiseptic conditions. He never reused his needles and he kept his equipment clean and sterile. And despite the fact that he was a biker of the outlaw stripe, he worked hard to keep his hands clean and his nails manicured, maybe not to a brain-surgeon's standards, but for a scooter tramp, he was well above the norm.

The call from Clance had been short and sweet.

"I need you up here, man. We've got some good games and you'd be a real asset. We're building a bank and there'll be some decent money in it for you."

"What kind of money?"

"I can start you out at thirty bucks an hour," Clance said. "You've gotta do a week or so, maybe two weeks max, in training with no pay, but after that, thirty an hour. Just come up here with enough cash to survive for a couple weeks and you'll be fine. You can crash on my couch for a few days or we could clear a spot for you in my garage if you want more privacy, but there are lots of cheap places you can rent by the week. After you get enough dough together to contribute to the bank, we'll work out a percentage deal, no more hourly rate. You'll get a cut of the win like the rest of us. I'm talking big bucks, man."

"Thirty an hour to start? You're saying I'll get that whether the plays win or lose?"

"To start. After your initial training. That's the deal."

"I'm not cutting my hair, Clance. And I'm not wearing a goddamn polo shirt and khakis."

"Not necessary. I want you looking like your grimy self."

"No shit?"

"Hey, man, this is a new play. We're not card-counting anymore."

"You know there's no such thing as misdemeanor cheating in Nevada. If we get busted for cheating, it's a felony. Even first offense is a year, minimum."

"The play's legit, Bart. And it's strong. We're gonna make some real money on this one. I want you to be part of it. You were born for this play, man. What are you … four-foot-nine?"

"Fuck you."

"How tall are you?"

"What the fuck does that have to do with anything?"

"It's why you were made for this play, man. I know you're under five-six."

"I'm five-three."

"Perfect, man. Short's an asset—a huge asset. We're playin' the hole card and when you sit down, you're automatically low to the table. You won't even have to slouch."

Clance had been counting cards for about twenty years and Bart had worked with him many times. Counting strategies were widely available in dozens of books and Bart found the systems easy to memorize and employ. But he didn't have the patience for the ups and downs of the occupation and he quickly grew bored playing at the tables. Clance had worked with a lot of big counting teams, traveled all over the world, and seemed to enjoy fleecing the casinos. To Bart, it just felt like a grind and the sporadic paydays were never big enough to keep him interested in it. Thirty bucks an hour, however, with no downside, was enough to pique his interest.

Counting the hundred and fifty bucks Bart had gotten from Zoey, all he had to his name was about three hundred bucks, so the timing of Clance's call couldn't have been better. In fact, he'd been considering moving back to Berkeley for a while and sponging off his mother, a thought that made him queasy. He knew she'd let him crash in the basement of their house. She always had in the past. But she had a strict no-smoking rule that was mildly bothersome and, mostly, he just didn't like the way she looked at him like he was such an abysmal failure. Or maybe it was that he made her feel that she was an abysmal failure. Any type of conversation with her was always strained.

So this Reno gig sounded too good to pass up. Three hundred bucks might be all he'd need to get through the training period, though he wished he had more. He could live cheap but he really didn't want to crash on Clance's couch, or worse, in his garage.

The Brass Rail was a biker-friendly bar on Persian Drive in Sunnyvale that had a wet T-shirt contest every Wednesday night. Lulu was Bart's favorite dancer there. She always managed to flash him a nipple. Earlier, at the bar, one of the bartenders told him about a new joint that had just opened up. They didn't serve alcohol, so the girls could dance nude.

"Are they going to cut into your business?" Bart asked him.

"Look at this crowd. Does it look like they're hurting our business? There's no booze and they've got a ten-buck cover. All they get is the young guys who wanna look at some pussy."

"What's the name of the place?"

"Angel's Showgirls."

That's where Stacy had said she was dancing.

So Bart was standing there in front of the DJ's booth, wetting down Lulu, when it hit him. A nude joint could have a wet-panties contest. That would drive those eighteen-year-old boys nuts. He let the idea churn around in his head for a couple hours as he watched the wet T-shirt contest, thinking about how it might work and how he might actually be able to make a few bucks off it. But what kept popping into his head was that Stacy worked there. Not that she was his type or that he was even looking for his type. But she was there. Around midnight, he took a ride over to Angel's. He had trouble concentrating on how he would present his idea to the manager, because he kept thinking of Stacy. Would she be there? If she took the stage, should he sit on the rail and tip her? Jesus Christ, she'd be fucking naked.

The manager was maybe twenty-five years old, if that. He was tall, probably six-two, clean-shaven with a crew cut. He looked like a college kid, a jock. "You got a problem?" he asked Bart. He had an attitude, but then most people who ask to see the manager at a strip club probably do have a problem.

"No, man, no problem," Bart said. "I've got a proposition for you. How's business?"

"It's slow tonight. I don't need a DJ, if that's what you're looking for. And no offense, but you're too small to work as a bouncer. I've got a whole list of dudes looking for door jobs. We don't have a bar. No alcohol, you know. You might try the Kit Kat or Hip Hugger if you're looking for a DJ job."

"Nothing like that, man. I'm talking about a special-event night. I'm talking about pulling in some huge crowds, packing this place. And making more money on one night midweek than you make on Friday and Saturday combined."

The club manager just looked at him, waiting for more of an explanation, then finally said, "I'm listening."

"Do you have an office?" Bart asked. "Someplace where we can sit down for a few minutes and talk? I won't take up much of your time." Bart extended his hand. "The name's Bart," he said. "Bart Black."

The manager almost looked like he wasn't going to take his hand, then finally he extended his own hand and said, "I'm Del. Come on in. Not much going on anyway."

Bart followed him into the club. Not much going on? Dead was more like it. There were three customers in the whole place and no dancer in sight. The stage was very large for a strip club—about three feet high and maybe twenty feet square—right in the middle of the floor. Bart noticed one of the patrons handing a flask to another. The club's interpretation of the no-booze policy apparently meant BYO.

Del led Bart into his office and sat down in the big leather chair behind his desk. There was no other seat in the room, which was all but barren, so Bart just stood there.

"Have you ever been to the Brass Rail on Wednesday night for the wet T-shirt contest?" Bart asked him.

"A few times."

"I used to run a contest similar to that at a nude club in Phoenix. A wet-panties contest."

"And?"

"It was a real moneymaker."

"So, what do *you* do?" Del said "Nobody wants to see you in your wet panties. My DJ can announce the contestants, just like they do at the Rail. I don't think you have any patent on wet-panty contests."

"No, your DJ can't do it," Bart replied. "You need an MC on stage. At the Rail, they make their money selling booze. You, on the other hand, have to make your money off the girls—and I know how to sell them. So, the guys all pay their ten bucks to get in, then we charge them big bucks to see those wet panties."

"Bad idea. All you're gonna do is piss off my customers. You can't make 'em pay twice."

"That's just it, Del. We're not going to make them pay; they're going to *beg* us to pay!"

Del cocked his head and looked at him sideways. "Explain."

"First of all," Bart said. "I'm going to *auction off* the squirt guns. I'm not going to just hand the gun to some guy in the front row. If you want to wet down the girl's panties, you've got to pay for the privilege. Highest bidder gets the gun."

"How much will a guy pay for the squirt gun?"

"Fifty, maybe sixty ... What's your slowest night?"

"Monday," Del said. "Last Monday we had seven customers all

night. Only one dancer showed up. I've been thinking of closing on Mondays until business picks up."

"We'll have the first contest this Monday night," Bart said.

"I find it hard to believe any of these punk kids will pay that much," Del said. "And the dancers'll want a big cut if they've got to get wet. And I'm sure you're expecting to get paid for running the show. There's nothing in it for me."

"Del, you're not looking at the whole picture. What we're talking about here is you pulling in a big crowd on Monday night when you're normally dead. Everybody pays their ten bucks to get in and your girls sell private dances all night long, too. You take a piece of all that action. The money we get from the auctions is just icing on the cake. The dancer gets fifty percent of that. You and I get twenty-five percent each. If it's a flop, nobody shows up, and we don't make any money, you can cancel the whole thing. What have you got to lose?"

"How about we do it on Saturday night when I've got some customers in here?" Del asked.

"No, Del, trust me on this. The weekend is strictly for advertising this thing. You want your marquee out front to say 'Wet-Panties Contest Monday Night,' so everyone who drives by sees it. And all night on Friday and Saturday you have your DJ plugging the thing. Every twenty minutes he should be saying 'Don't miss the wet-panties contest this Monday night.' And make sure you tell all your weekend girls to show up on Monday night, because it's going to be a big night and they won't want to miss it. There's a hundred-buck prize for the winner."

"Where does that come from?"

"You take it outta your twenty-five percent."

"How about fifty bucks?"

"Don't be such a cheapskate! You'll get your piece from every girl, plus all of the door, plus your cut of the private dances. It's gotta be a hundred."

Del was sitting there writing notes. "You're killing me, man. I'll do a hundred, but this thing better work. What do you need besides a mic?"

"A couple of squirt guns filled with water. I'll get the guns. And a few towels, like a dozen or so. And tell all the dancers if they want to be in the contest, they have to bring a pair of white-cotton panties. Other than that, they can pick their own music and wear whatever outfit they want. They just have to understand that in a wet-panties contest, black satin doesn't cut it. White cotton is the only way to go."

† † †

On Thursday, Bart made five hundred flyers and left a stack on the counter at every bike shop in the South Bay. He was well-known as a tattoo artist and they gave him a lot of referrals. In fact, he'd pounded ink onto quite a few of the managers, clerks, and mechanics. "They don't serve alcohol at Angel's," he told them all, "so it's BYO. But keep it out of sight so the place doesn't get busted." He also posted flyers at a half-dozen South Bay tattoo parlors, as well as at a couple San Jose auto-performance shops, where he'd done ink work for hot rodders and low riders.

On Friday night Bart rode by Angel's Showgirls, just to check out the sign on the marquee.

MONDAY NIGHT—9 PM
WET PANTIES CONTEST!
YOU WET 'EM DOWN!
$100 FIRST PRIZE!

Not bad, Del.

Then he went over to the Brass Rail, the Kit Kat, and Hip Huggers, and left a flyer on every car and bike in the lots. On Saturday, he did the same thing. On Sunday, he spent the day pacing the floor of his apartment trying to figure out a spiel for auctioning off the rights to the use of a squirt gun on the crotch of an eighteen-year-old girl.

Bart purchased a couple of cheap plastic squirt guns, which he felt would be more fun than the laundry-spray bottles they used at the Brass Rail. He had no concerns about his performance—five-foot-three outlaw bikers learn pretty quickly how to be funny in rowdy situations. Nor was he concerned about how much money he might make on this fiasco, despite the fact that he could ill-afford the money he'd already spent on flyers and squirt guns. In his fantasies, all the dancers were flirting with him shamelessly backstage, while he stoically ignored them, paying attention only to Stacy, who was flirting even more blatantly than the others. He couldn't stop thinking about her. Would she be there? Would she be in the contest? What the hell would he say to her? Why was he so smitten by the girl with the decaled wrists?

† † †

When he got to the club just before nine on Monday night, there was a line at the door that stretched around the corner. The doorman was turning customers away. Dozens of choppers were parked on the street, all up and down the block. The place was packed to the rafters, standing room only. It was a madhouse. The dancer on stage was wearing only a g-string and platform stripper heels. The crowd was hooting and hollering so loudly it was almost drowning out the music. Del led Bart back to his office and shut the door behind them.

He turned to Bart with a big grin. "Looks like Sunnyvale's been dying for a wet-panties contest."

"Hey, Del, if you want to attract a crowd, all you have to do is offer a show that's a little more sophisticated, a bit more intelligent and classy, just a notch above the competition."

There was a crash of glass outside the office door. It sounded like a bottle had been thrown against the wall.

Del winced. "I have no idea what that was," he said. "We serve our drinks in paper cups. Are you ready to go?"

"I need to go over a couple points with the dancers. Can you take me to the dressing room?"

Del went to the office door and opened it. "Right there," he said, pointing at a curtained doorway across from the office. "Just walk in."

"But they don't know me. They could be … *en dishabille*."

"For chrissake, Bart, I've got to deal with a lot of shit and you've got to get this show going like ten minutes ago! Just go in. They're expecting you!"

Bart stepped out of the office and crossed the hall to the curtained doorway. A paper sign was safety-pinned to the heavy velour curtain. "DANCERS ONLY!" He peeked his head inside. Six girls in unison looked expectantly in his direction.

"Good evening, ladies," he said, and when nobody screamed, he stepped into the large brightly-lit room.

Some of the dancers were wearing robes and were either barefoot or had slippers on. One was in a plaid mini-skirt and a midriff-length white blouse that was knotted in front. Another girl, a flaming red-head, was topless, wearing a g-string and platform heels; she had one foot on a short wooden bench and was fussing with an ankle strap on her shoe. He didn't see Stacy. A couple of dancers were standing in front of a wide full-length mirror, putting on make-up. Two were sitting in folding chairs.

A long table against one wall was cluttered with magazines, soda cans, purses, cigarettes, hair spray canisters, items of clothing, jars, tubes, bottles, and one stuffed teddy bear. A few of the girls were smoking. The room had no ventilation. About fifty double-stacked lockers lined one of the walls, many with graffiti, some adorned with photos torn from magazines or snapshots of babies and little kids. There was a sink next to the big mirror and a big sign above the mirror that said, "NO SMOKING." Scrawled in red lipstick on a bottom corner of the sign were the words, "FUK U."

"The name's Bart," he said. "I'll be the MC for the contest. First question, ladies: Do you all have white-cotton panties?"

The girls who were wearing robes opened them to display little plaid pleated micro-skirts, which they lifted to show their panties.

"We all wore our schoolgirl outfits," one of the girls said. "Like, what else goes with white-cotton panties?"

He nodded. "Excellent, ladies," he said. "I can already tell you get what we're doing here tonight. Have any of you ever done the wet T-shirt contest at the Brass Rail?"

They all looked at him blankly.

"Of course not," he said. "You've got to be twenty-one to dance there, right, and you're all babies."

He went to the sink and started filling the squirt guns. It struck him then that the only reason he'd come to this place was to see Stacy. He didn't really know anything about running a wet-panties contest. That was just his excuse for getting in the door. Why was he so obsessed with her? He was uncomfortable in the dressing room. All of these dancers were out of his league. These were the girls who wouldn't give him the time of day, the girls who dated the popular guys, the tall guys, the guys with the right clothes and the right friends.

Then he noticed that Stacy was there after all, one of the girls at the mirror, putting on lipstick. She glanced at him. Those full lips, those luminous eyes. He hadn't recognized her at first in her jet-black wig. She had on a colorful silk kimono-type robe. Apparently satisfied with her lip gloss, she was now texting on her cell phone. Bart tried not to look at any of the dancers. What the fuck had he gotten himself into? His spirits flip-flopped—lifted for a moment when he saw she was there, then quickly dashed when she showed no sign of recognizing him, no little smile, or even a nod. And what the hell did he want from her anyway?

He finished filling the squirt guns. "I need a list of names," he said, all business, "in the order you'll be performing."

The topless redhead, who'd finished monkeying with her shoe straps, pulled a scrap of lined paper from where it had been tacked to the wall, beside the curtained doorway. She handed it to Bart.

He read the scribbled list to himself: *Melodie Ann, Tiffany, Daisy, Britney, Demonica, and Little Bambi.* Other than Demonica, it sounded like a kindergarten roll call.

He looked at Stacy, trying to make a connection. "Let me guess," he said to her. "You're Demonica."

"No," the girl standing next to her piped in. "I'm Demonica! She's Little Bambi."

Stacy gave him a sweet smile. "And please don't forget to say *Little Bambi,*" she said.

"Right," he said. "I'll remember that. Little Bambi." He folded the list and stuck it into the breast pocket of his denim jacket. "For the first number, we're going to get all six of you on stage at the same time. Just come out one at a time when you hear your name. I'll call them in order. Move around the stage, tease the boys, but don't take anything off yet. Get off the stage fast when the music stops. Then I'll call you out one at a time for the contest. Just play along and keep in mind, it's a roomful of perverts out there who want to see a bunch of little girls in their wet panties. We're going to make 'em pay for the privilege."

"Just make us some money," said flaming red, adjusting the Velcro closure on her plaid micro-skirt. "I need a new car seat for my little girl."

"What's your name?" he asked her.

"Melodie Ann."

He looked at the list. "You're up first," he said. "We're gonna get you a car seat, sweetie." He looked at all the dancers who were now fussing with their outfits, their hair, make-up. "You get fifty percent of the take from the auction receipts," he said, "but you get a hundred percent of your stage tips, so milk these fuckers."

"Can I ask you a question?" Melodie Ann asked, still topless, standing now in a confrontational pose with her hands on her hips.

Bart was taken aback by her defiant attitude. "Shoot," he said.

She turned toward one of the lockers and took a white blouse from a wire hanger on the door, then started to put it on, saying, without looking at him, "Do you have any idea what the fuck you're doing?"

He just stared at her as she tied the front closed, straightening it on her shoulders. Then she looked up at him and said. "Have you ever done this before?"

He shook his head. "I'm winging it," he said.

"Wingin' it," she repeated. "And you're gonna tell us how to make money out there? We know how to make money. So do whatever you feel you have to do out there on that stage, then get your ass out of our way so we can bank some cash. You think we don't already have enough palms to grease? We're tippin' out the DJ, the doorman, the bouncers, the floor managers … IMHO, Bart, you're just one more hand reachin' into my pocket."

"Amen," one of the dancers behind him said softly.

He didn't turn to see who'd said it. He hadn't been expecting this attack and he didn't know how to respond. He could see Stacy out the corner of his eye and she seemed to be trying to keep herself from laughing. "But I got a big crowd in here," he said in his defense. "I mean, look at them."

Melodie Ann smirked and shook her head. "Big mistake," she said. "This is not the Brooks Brothers crowd. This isn't even the Walmart crowd. The crowd we want is wearing Versace jackets and carrying fat Gucci wallets. These guys here tonight, these are the guys who pick us up after work. These are not the guys who peel off hundreds in the VIP room. Didn't I see your boyfriend out there, Britney?"

A small dancer with a pixie haircut sitting next to Melodie Ann looked up at her and said, "Yeah, Snake's here."

"Yeah, Snake," Melodie Ann said. "Didn't you tell me you paid his rent last month?"

Britney nodded.

"And didn't you give him that big silver bracelet he's wearing with the turquoise and onyx? What'd you pay for that, Brit?"

"Six hundred," she said.

"Snake ever buy you anything?"

Britney smiled and shrugged. "Lotsa beer," she said.

A couple of the dancers snorted laughs.

"You see, Bart," Melodie Ann went on, "These are not the money guys. These are the low-lifes we put up with when we're not workin'— and not because we like them all that much. They're just a lot less judgmental than the world out there and a lot more fun than your average college assholes. And I'm not really speakin' for myself, because I'm not into men at all. I don't hang with dudes when I'm off the clock if I can help it. I like pussy and I don't really know what girls see in dick. But that's just me."

The phone on the back wall of the dressing room rang. Demonica picked it up and said, "Speak." Then she tossed the receiver to Bart. "It's for you."

"Bart, this is Todd, the DJ. Can you hear the racket out here? We gotta get this contest going!"

"We're ready," he said. "Give me thirty seconds." He went and hung up the phone, then turned to the group. "Showtime, ladies."

Before he could say another word, Todd's voice over the PA interrupted the music. "Okay, guys, it's the moment you've been waiting for … the first contestant who's going to get his panties wet for you … Bart Black!"

Thanks, Todd. Great intro. And thanks for the thirty seconds.

Bart grabbed the mic and started toward the door. Stacy intercepted him with a playful sock in the arm. He turned to look at her, hoping she didn't see the panic in his face.

"Chill," she said with a soft smile. "She gets like that. Welcome to my world."

A loud commotion out in the theater sounded like a fight was starting. A crash of glass. A couple of loud "Fuck yous!"

"Welcome to mine," Bart said, taking a deep breath to calm himself before he hit the stage running to a cacophony of boos, hisses, and catcalls.

"Good evening, ladies and gentlemen!" he said in his best game-show-host voice, pacing the stage nervously, waiting for a modicum of quiet that never came. He looked out over lots of recognizable faces, bikers he knew from the road. Flasks were being passed around. Marijuana was in the air. "This evening, in conjunction with the National Endowment for the Arts, the J. Paul Getty Heritage Foundation, and the California Board of Cultural Enrichment, we are proud to present upon our humble stage the long-awaited Angel's Showgirls Wet-Panties Contest."

Drunken biker in the front row: "Fuck you! Bring out the girls!"

"Hey, shit-for-brains, this is a cultural event."

"You're not funny! You're boring!"

"And your mother blows dogs! We're going to start by bringing all six of tonight's contestants out onto the stage, all members of our youth Bible-study group. They'll be vying for the hundred-dollar first prize that goes to the winner." He pointed at Todd in the DJ booth and just like that, Chuck Berry's *Sweet Little Sixteen* started blasting from the speakers.

Excellent choice, Todd.

"Melodie Ann," Bart spoke into the mic and she came skipping out onto the stage with a jump-rope.

"Tiffany!"

A curvy black girl with long legs started hop-scotching around the stage, trying to keep out of Melodie Ann's way, while making her little skirt fly up as much as possible.

"Delightful Daisy!"

Out she came, going straight for the center pole and shinnying up toward the ceiling. Dollar bills were flying onto the stage, though the girls were ignoring the money.

"The adorable Britney! Be careful guys, she has a black belt in tae kwon do!"

She came out dancing with the teddy bear, swirling around in pirouettes, making that micro-mini fly.

"Our fifth contestant tonight will be the ravishing Demonica!"

Entering the stage with a riding crop and an attitude, Demonica went straight for stage front to tease the crowd.

"Our final contestant tonight will be the callipygian Little Bambi, recently awarded the Nobel Prize in philosophy for her groundbreaking work on Friedrich Nietzsche's nihilistic autobiography, *Ecce Homo*. Asked why she goes on living, she says, 'Beauty is its own excuse for being.'"

Bart hurried off the stage where he could watch the girls from behind the curtain. He wondered if Stacy noticed her elaborate intro and he felt his face flush from the feeling that he was trying too hard to impress her.

She was wearing big round glasses and had a red bow in her hair. He couldn't take his eyes off her. Chuck Berry crooned, "Sweet little sixteen, she's got the grownup blues, tight dresses and lipstick, she's sportin' high-heel shoes!"

When the song ended, the dancers scurried around the stage,

picking up dollar bills before running off. There must have been fifty or sixty bucks out there and the girls hadn't taken anything off yet. Bart took that as a good sign.

He went to the front of the stage. "Gentleman," he said. "We're going to bring our first contestant out here now, but before you get to wet her down, she has to lose a few items of clothing. She looks awfully cute in that little plaid skirt, but frankly, for a wet-panties contest, the girl's overdressed. Maestro, let's have a little undressing music for Melodie Ann!"

Todd cranked it up as Bart exited the stage. He stopped Melodie Ann as she was about the make her entrance. She was carrying her jump rope. The crowd went nuts as soon as she appeared.

"Just lose the skirt and top," he said. "Leave your panties on and don't show your pussy. When the song ends, just stay out there. I'll take over."

"Okay, boss," she said, sarcastically. "Whatever you say."

He went into the dressing room with the other five girls. They were all talking and laughing. The mood in the room was high. The dancers seemed relaxed. He was nervous as hell. He repeated to all of them the dance instructions he'd just given to Melodie Ann, then leaned back against the wall and concentrated on not looking at Stacy. Out on the floor, the crowd was going wild. Melodie Ann had them wrapped around her finger.

When the music stopped, he hurried back out, grabbing a squirt gun and towel. Melodie Ann was posing, in just her panties and heels, with one finger in her mouth.

"Now, gentlemen," he said, as he joined her at the front of the stage. "We come to the all-important audience-participation portion of our program. We're appealing here for a volunteer to help little Melodie Ann get her panties wet. Sit the fuck down, bozos! We'll do this with a semblance of decorum. I'm specifically looking for a man of culture and taste who feels he's eminently qualified for this delicate position, a man who can do it with dignity, and most importantly, a man willing to part with *five lousy bucks* for the privilege of making little Melodie Ann wet and happy."

A half-dozen guys stood up and started toward the stage.

"Hold your horses, gentlemen! Put your wallets back in your pockets! This ain't no yard sale, this is an auction … Do me a favor, sweetheart. Can you kneel down on the towel here? That's right. She looks good in that position, doesn't she, gents?"

A voice from the back of the room: "Six bucks!"

"Not so fast, asshole! The auction hasn't begun yet. Melodie Ann, can you put your hands together like you're praying? That's right, like an innocent little girl at her first holy communion, a little angel. We've already got a bid of six bucks. Who wants the gun? Do I hear ten? Anybody? Ten bucks? The bid is six. I've got six, going once, going twice—"

"Six-fifty!"

"Six-fifty? What? Are you rifling through the seat cushions? Melodie Ann, honey, do me a favor and turn around. That's right, stay down on your knees, just turn your back so we can see that cute derriere. Pull those panties up real tight and get down on all fours like a little kitty-cat … Perfect, purrfect … Do I hear—"

"Seven!"

"Seven-fifty!"

A long silence. Bart turned his back to the crowd and noticed Stacy standing behind the curtain in the wing, watching him. He wanted to go to her and explain that the girl needs a car seat for her daughter. He's just trying to make her some money. These fucking tightasses won't even part with ten bucks? Stacy's hand went to her mouth. Was it to cover a smile, a laugh, like she'd heard his thoughts and found them amusing … ?

He looked down at Melodie Ann and she was craning her neck to look up at him. The impatient look on her face said everything: *Are you just going to leave me like this all night?*

"Eight bucks!" a voice boomed.

He turned to face the crowd, saw a guy in back waving a fistful of dollars in the air. "We have a bid of eight bucks from the dapper gentleman in the back row." Bart knew the guy. Lenny was his name. He was part owner of a motorcycle garage in Oakland. Bart wondered how he'd heard about the contest. His flyer distribution never went that far north. "Do I hear nine? Anybody? We've got a bid of eight bucks. Eight even … Eight going once, twice, thrice. This gun is sold! Come on up here, sir. Just come to the front of the stage."

Lenny was a big guy, bald on top, pushing sixty but strong and healthy, with massive biceps covered in faded, decades-old, blue and black ink. He was wearing a black leather vest over an Oakland A's-logo T-shirt. He maneuvered his way through the crowd and when he got to the stage he handed Bart two fives. "I need change," he said.

Bart gave him the squirt gun and said off-mic, "I'll catch you later on the two bucks. Now be nice to the lady, Lenny."

Bart walked toward the back of the stage. All of the girls had come out to the wings to witness Melodie Ann's ordeal. She, meanwhile, was not staying still for the wet-down. She quickly went from her ass-in-the-air position to flat on her back with her legs spread, and she was grinding her pelvis as she tugged and pulled at her panties while Lenny sprayed her. An unexpected hush had come over the room. As Lenny performed the task he'd paid for, he had a beatific look of mouth-open awe on his face, oblivious to the crowd watching him.

Bart walked back up to the front. Melodie Ann was dripping wet, pretty much from the neck down. Lenny didn't even notice Bart's return.

Todd cut the music.

Bart took the squirt gun from Lenny. "You may return to your seat now, sir."

Lenny looked hypnotized.

"Let's have some music, Maestro!" he said, and Todd got another beat cranking for Melodie Ann's finale. He picked up the towel and turned to exit the stage when Melodie Ann grabbed his arm.

"Eight bucks?" she said. "And I get four of it? Whoop-de-fuckin'-do."

The girls in the dressing room pretty much ignored Bart as he re-filled the squirt gun. He heard one girl say how embarrassed she'd be if no one put in a bid for her gun. "What if nobody bids a single dollar, so

he says how about fifty cents?" That got laughs from some of the dancers. They were talking about him like he wasn't there. He couldn't even
look in Stacy's direction.

As it turned out, the bids went up with each successive girl, as
the crowd got more and more into it. Tiffany's gun went for ten even.
Daisy's went for twelve. And Britney with her teddy bear scored thirteen. Demonica came out in a blindfold and with her hands tied and
that act really had the crowd going nuts. Her squirt gun went for fifteen dollars.

But Stacy took the cake. She came out skipping with a big red
lollipop in her hand. No shoes, just little ankle socks with lace trim.
As Bart had done for all the other dancers, after introducing her strip
number, he left the stage. From the folds of the curtain, he could hear
the crowd getting riled up.

When the song ended and he went back to the stage with the
squirt gun, Stacy was already on her back with her legs spread. The
lollipop was in her mouth, just the little white stick poking out from
between her lips. Bart tossed her the towel. As she lifted her hips to
position it under her ass, he noticed moist streaks of pink on the crotch
of her panties, as well as on her stomach and breasts and inner thighs.
That lollipop had been around.

Twenty-two bucks. Once again, Lenny put in the winning bid.
He gave Bart a twenty and said, "You owe me two, bro. We're even."
He got his money's worth. Little Bambi squirmed and cooed and
writhed and moaned during the wet-down. Bart let Lenny have a full
minute with the gun. He had to bring an extra towel to dry the stage
front. Stacy was dripping wet pretty much all over, including her face.
Lenny's aggressive spray technique had washed away most of the candy streaks.

Bart retired to the wings for the dance number and again, Stacy
whipped the crowd into a frenzy herd. He watched her from the wings
briefly, astonished at the power she wielded over the audience. She
seemed to be picking out individual victims to pose and strut for, making eye contact with one after another, teasing them by starting to pull
her panties down, then changing her mind and turning her back with

feigned indifference to their collective arousal. The whole room was going apeshit for her attention.

Watching Stacy's performance from the wings, Bart saw that she held all the power, doling out her favors—a whimsical look, a sultry glance, a hint of a smile at the pleading hordes. She ignored the money flying onto the stage from all sides.

Stacy turned her back on the crowd and looked directly at Bart, like she knew he was watching her. Her self-satisfied smile seemed to say, "See how it's done?" And as soon as she turned her attention back to the audience, Bart moved deeper into the backstage area where he could no longer see her and she wouldn't see him if she turned around again. He closed his eyes and just listened to the crowd, anxious for this surreal ordeal to be over so he could get the hell out of there.

When the song ended, he returned to the stage, surprised to find Stacy standing stage front with her panties still on. All of the other girls had been naked by the end of the final song and by the time he got out there, they were crawling around the stage picking up their tips.

The crowd was going nuts, banging their fists on the tables, howling, stomping their feet, whistling, and chanting, "Take them off! Take them off!" But she just stood there and when she saw Bart beside her, she gave him a big smile with that lollipop stick in her mouth. Her teeth were pink.

"I'm getting the distinct impression that your fan club wants your panties off," he said to her.

She looked at him through half-closed eyelids and said, "Auction them off."

It took a moment for that to register. "Auction off your panties?" he said.

She looked down at them. "Why not?"

He looked at her panties. The crotch was smeared in sticky red lollipop goop. He turned on the mic.

"Gentlemen," he said, "Although this fine establishment does not have a license to serve comestibles, tonight we are going to flaunt the law by offering to the highest bidder a taste treat sweeter than mom's apple pie."

Stacy pulled her wet panties up so tight they slid into all available crevices, then she slowly pulled them down to mid-thigh level and left them there.

"Gentlemen," Bart said. "What am I bid for Little Bambi's slightly used drawers?"

The first bid was for ten dollars, then the shouting became so furious, all he could do was wait until it reached the thirty-dollar mark. At that point, it became a bidding war between Lenny and a well-dressed guy in his fifties who'd been sitting quietly at a corner table, looking out of place in his business suit and tie. They were raising each other in five-dollar increments.

"Thirty-five!"

"Forty!"

"Forty-five!"

"Fifty!"

"Make it sixty!" Lenny yelled.

"Seventy-five!" the gentleman shot back. So, Mr. Versace finally showed up.

Lenny gave up. He could see where this was going, and he just wouldn't pay a hundred bucks for a pair of sugar-coated panties.

In the end, Little Bambi also won the hundred-dollar first prize, based on audience response. The total amount Bart had collected in the squirt-gun auctions came to eighty bucks even. Forty of it was split among the dancers. None of them said a word to him or even looked at him as he doled it out. Not that he was expecting pleasantries. He remembered the fantasies he'd had about this night, how they would all be flirting with him shamelessly. What a laugh.

As the dancers were leaving the dressing room to start working the crowd for private dances, he stopped Melodie Ann and gave her a twenty dollar bill, his cut of the auction receipts. "A personal donation toward that car seat," he said.

She took the twenty, obviously surprised by his gesture, mumbled a thanks, and quickly left.

Bart found himself alone in the dressing room with Stacy, who was sitting back in her robe, smoking a cigarette, and texting.

Del walked in.

"You know you're not supposed to smoke in here," Del said. "Smoke outside."

Stacy dropped her cigarette to the cement floor and stepped on it.

"We took in eighty bucks in auction receipts," Bart said to Del. "Your take is twenty minus the hundred-dollar first prize that goes to Stacy. So, I gave Stacy the twenty, and you owe her eighty more."

"Big moneymaker, Bart. I can see this show'll make me rich."

"But look at the crowd, Del." Bart's pleading face was accompanied by the sound of glass crashing against a wall.

"Who are these animals you brought into my club, Bart? Great show, but don't come back next week. You're fired."

"Fired?"

"It's like I told you," he said. "I don't need you for this job. The whole show is the girls. Nobody gives a shit about you. I can get a hundred guys to do this for beans. Besides, you're not funny. You talk too much. And the money's in selling the panties, not the squirt guns. Next week we'll advertise it as a wet panties auction. Todd can be the MC, and I only pay him minimum wage."

"Todd?" Bart said. "That knuckle-dragging mouth-breather?"

"Don't get your ass in a sling, Bart. You had some fun tonight and you made twenty bucks."

"Fuck you, Del! I don't need this fucking job! I'm leaving town tomorrow anyway. I won't even be here next week!"

Del shook his head and as he walked out of the dressing room, Bart said softly, but loud enough for Del to hear, "Arrogant wannabe-yuppie maggot."

That got a smile out of Stacy. She was sitting in her kimono and texting, still. Without warning, she stood up and dropped the robe. She was naked—just for a moment—then she started putting on some skimpy spandex number.

Bart averted his eyes and started shuffling around, gathering up his belongings. He turned his head and caught a glimpse of buttocks being squeezed into stretchy electric-blue neon.

"I wouldn't plan on seeing that eighty bucks Del owes you any time soon," he said softly, starting toward the door.

"You really leaving town?" she asked.

"Me? Yeah. I'm going to Reno." He turned to face her. She was as dressed as she was going to be.

"What about Zoey's tattoo?"

"When she wants me to start filling it in, I'll come back for the work."

"I'm coming with you," Stacy said matter-of-factly.

"To Reno? I'd like to help you out, but I don't even have a place to live there. Clance's got some kind of gambling gig lined up for me. I've got to find a cheap room and I don't even know if the job's going to work out."

"I've got money," she said. "I'll help with expenses."

"What do you have going for you in Reno?"

"Nothing. I just want out of here."

"How much money do you have?"

"Is that an issue?"

"Stacy, I'll be straight with you. My total life savings is not much more than what I've got in my pocket. It's not going to last a long time if I'm paying your way, too. It's not just a question of gas money: It's not like I'm driving an SUV but my funds are very limited after I get there. I'll probably have to crash on Clance's floor. This isn't a vacation."

"I've got six thousand dollars," she said.

"Where'd you get that kind of money?"

She just looked at him like it was a dumb question.

"I'm traveling light, Stacy. I'm taking the clothes on my back, my tattoo works, and not much more. I've got two saddle bags on my bike. Can you fit all your stuff in one of 'em?"

"I'll make do." She took a pack of cigarettes from a leather purse on the table and stuck one in her mouth.

Bart pulled out his Bic and leaned forward to light it for her. "You wouldn't happen to have an extra one of those, would you?" he asked.

She tossed him the pack.

He shook one out, tossed the pack back to her, tore the filter off the cigarette, stuck the other end in his mouth, and lit the scraggly strands of tobacco hanging out of the torn end. They flared momentarily into a flame, then settled to a glowing ember as he puffed on it. "I don't want your money," he said. "I don't take money from women. Personal policy. But how do you know I'm not going to rape you? You don't know me."

"That wouldn't be possible."

He cocked his head and lifted an eyebrow. Was that a put-down?

"It wouldn't be rape," she said softly, looking him in the eye.

He snorted a laugh. Brave bitch.

"How old are you, Stacy?"

"Nineteen."

"I'm old enough to be your father. I could be an axe murderer for all you know."

She looked intently at him, as if trying to grasp the reason for his dissention. "I can tell you're a nice guy," she said. "I need a friend. And you're a poet. I like poetry."

"You like poetry?" he said, baffled.

"Everything that comes out of your mouth is poetry," she said. "When you were introducing me, you called me 'the callipygian Little Bambi.' I'll bet I'm the only other person in this place who knows what callipygian means."

"There's nothing poetic about a five-dollar word for a fine ass."

"But then you said, 'Beauty is its own excuse for being.' That's Emerson."

"Are you loaded right now, Stacy?"

"No. Not at the moment."

"Well, Ralph Waldo notwithstanding, I think you should know I don't give a flying fuck for poetry, art, or any other hypocritical horseshit. Every damn body was born to die, and that includes me, you, and every other idiot on this planet. So while I'm waiting for the inevitable, I'm going to get loaded, get laid, and make some fucking noise. There isn't a human being I give a shit about even one iota of what I feel for my bike."

"Do you believe in miracles?" she questioned. She pulled out her cell phone and started checking messages.

"What?"

"Do you believe in destiny?"

"I believe in disbelief."

"I'm coming with you," she said and started texting.

"You know what, Stacy? I'm seriously considering your proposition. You know why? I want to fuck you. I'm forty-three years old. I'm five-foot-three in my stocking feet. I don't wear deodorant. Look at you. Nineteen years old. You ought to go to Hollywood. You're fucking gorgeous."

"You're not that short," she said without looking up at him, still texting.

"You see these boots? You see those two-inch heels? There's another one-inch riser on the inside. I'm wearing elevator shoes! What are you, five-nine? If I take my boots off, your tits would be in my mouth."

"I'm only five-seven and I don't care how tall you are. I'm coming with you and you know it. It's not even a question, so why are we discussing it?" She flipped her phone closed, finally, and looked at him.

"You don't care if I just take you and abuse you?"

"Go ahead and do whatever you want," she said. "If it gets too bad, I'll leave. I don't take crap from anybody for long. I'm willing to risk taking some crap from you, because you make me laugh. I'd like to be with someone who has a functioning brain for a while. I'm not going to work here anymore. I might stay one more week, just so I can be in the wet-panties auction next Monday with Todd as the MC. That would be thrilling."

He pictured her on stage with Todd selling her panties. "Where's your stuff?" Bart asked her.

"San Francisco."

"Can you be ready to leave in the morning?"

"Yes."

"How are you getting home tonight?"

"Demonica. I'm staying at her place in the Marina district. She has a car."

"Write down the address for me and if I don't come to my senses by tomorrow, I'll pick you up around noon. Be ready. We'll split the trip expenses fifty-fifty. I've got to get out of here now. I've got some shit to take care of before the trip."

"I'll text it to you," she said, her phone already in hand.

"My number's—"

"I've got your number. I got it from Zoey."

She already had his cell number entered on her phone? He stood there watching her text for a second, then left the dressing room, wondering what the hell he was getting himself into. She didn't *ask* him if he would take her with him; she *told* him he was taking her.

As he was making his exit through the front door, half a dozen cops were making an entrance. Out on the street, a couple of cop cars were double-parked in front of the place with their flashers on, as well as a fire captain's vehicle. A motorcycle cop was sitting on his bike in the street. Bart recognized him. His name was Gary. He'd stopped him a number of times for not wearing a helmet, though he never gave him a ticket. Gary was okay, as cops go.

"What's going on here?" Bart asked him.

"Hey, Bart, how you doing?"

"What's with the police presence?"

"We're closing down the place."

"I thought it was legal to show pussy in this town. This isn't the only nude joint in Sunnyvale."

"The Fire Marshal's closing it," Gary said. "They did a head count and they've got something like double the legal occupancy."

Thinking of Stacy inside, Bart said, "You're not busting any dancers, are you?"

"Just the manager. If it was only a few heads, he'd just get a warning. But it's a pretty gross violation, so I imagine they'll suspend the license until there's a hearing, and there'll be a fine. Got your helmet tonight, Bart?"

"Of course I do, but do me a favor, Gary. My bike's parked half a block back. When you hear that Harley engine come to life, just don't turn around and look in my direction. Before you know it, I'll be gone like the wind."

At that moment, Angel's patrons started pouring out the front door. "I'll catch you later, Gary," Bart yelled, hurrying down the street to beat the traffic.

TWENTY-FIVE

"MY NAME'S NOT Gary."

"Huh?"

"Are you still with me, Bart?"

"What day is it?"

"I just told you not one minute ago. It's Wednesday."

"One minute?"

"You're trying my patience."

"Everything's moving ... It's too fast ... ?"

"Well, can you take a minute to tell me what you were doing in Reno?"

"Jesus, Dorsett ... Don't you have a life somewhere?"

"As I was saying before you nodded out on me, what it looks like now, Bart, is that you somehow gained the confidence of this fifteen-year-old girl—a very smart girl, exceptionally bright, but fifteen years old, just the same. You got her a bogus California ID that says she's eighteen—that's a federal offense—and put her to work in a nudie club. Real classy. I'm assuming there were drugs involved—this girl's no trailer trash and she's way too smart to get into all this shit otherwise. I note that you've had drug convictions in the past. It's all starting to add up."

"Misdemeanors ... Years ago."

"Oh, I'm sure the judge will take that into consideration. But let's talk frankly, Bart. I don't think you deserve any peace. You abducted that child. At least admit that much. You were living with her for four months. Traveling with her. It's pretty much a given that you were having sex with a minor. At least admit to me that you were fucking her."

TWENTY-SIX

BUT HE HADN'T been fucking her.

His inability to function sexually with a woman was due to psychological interference, resulting from who-knows-which of the pathetic sexual tragedies of his life or, as he mentally lumped them together, his half-night stands. He'd been to a doctor who'd told him there was no physiological problem with the plumbing, but he knew that anyway. He knew a lot about the plumbing. When your dick doesn't work, you tend to look into these things. He could give a lecture on the subject.

An erection results from cyclic guanosine monophosphate activating the intracellular protein kinases, which relax the vascular smooth muscle tissues in the penis. That's the main requirement—a nice relaxed dick. This allows the free flow of blood from the corpora cavernosa, leading to vasodilation, which is to say, a boner.

Typically, when physiological complications cause erectile dysfunction, it's due to an overabundance of phosphodiesterase type 5. That's the villain. Phosphodiesterase causes a degradative action on the cyclic guanosine monophosphate, which is a major bummer. The vascular smooth muscles can't relax enough to allow the blood to flow, leaving a limp bloodless dick. This is a problem for Viagra or Cialis, which contain phosphodiesterase type 5 inhibitors, allowing the guanosine monophosphate to activate the intracellular protein kinases. Good stuff if that's your problem.

But that wasn't Bart's problem. He knew that, because he masturbated daily, sometimes multiple times daily. Girls turned him on. He walked around with a hard-on a goodly portion of his waking hours. He had no overabundance of phosphodiesterase type 5.

Besides, he liked jacking off and he'd discovered that the more he resigned himself to it, the more he liked it. Pleasure with no downside—no health risks, no emotional damage, no cost. If there was ever a movement to promote masturbation as a lifestyle, he could be the poster boy. He could get an erection on a moment's notice and entertain it for hours on end if he had the time and inclination, and there was nothing he enjoyed more than ejaculating. Some shrinks might even categorize him as a chronic masturbator, though he would dispute that label. He considered himself sexually healthy in every sense. He was just a guy who was afraid of girls.

Viagra usually works as well in cases of psychological impotence as it does for physiological impotence. *Usually*. Even sexually healthy men who take erectile dysfunction pills report increased stamina in the bedroom. When that type 5 phosphodiesterase gets stepped on, the blood surges. In some cases, it may be the placebo effect, when there really isn't any physical problem. But Bart's limp dick wasn't amenable to boner pills, placebos or otherwise. He'd tried them all.

Technically, his psychological problem was not gynephobia, which is an irrational fear that women mean you harm. His problem was more of venstraphobia, an irrational fear of beautiful women. Some shrinks would likely argue this point, since Persephone—the last woman he'd tried to fuck and failed—wouldn't have been considered beautiful by the average person. But she was beautiful to Bart at the time he'd tried to fuck her, and he felt sure that venstraphobia, like beauty, was in the mind of the beholder. And no matter how much he read and thought about and mentally raged against the very concept of venstraphobia-induced impotence, he accepted it as his life's companion. One thing he knew about impotence was that it didn't quell desires, or stifle hopes, or suppress fantasies. He loved it when women flirted with him and he couldn't help but flirt back. He was often smitten by cupid's arrow, spent a good part of his life entertaining crushes on waitresses, strippers, and other guys' girls. Impotence, psychological or otherwise, doesn't lessen the need for physical affection and it sure as hell never stopped him from falling hard for someone.

Three incidents of sexual failure stood out in his mind as being, if not instrumental in causing his impotence, then at least instrumental in his decision to forgo any future attempts at sexual congress. These were the experiences he couldn't forget, that he'd mentally relived hundreds, thousands, of times. These were the incidents he would describe to a shrink, if he believed in shrinks, which he didn't.

His first miserable attempt at sex was during his adolescent druggie period when he was fifteen. He was stoned on pot, a bit tipsy on cheap wine, and high on various pills. He had no recollection of what the pills were, if he even knew what they were when he took them. He tried to fuck a street girl who was probably as loaded as he was. He would have put her age at somewhere in her mid-twenties. She went by the name of Ronnie and he'd known her for a few months. He was in a self-destructive phase—pretty much taking any consciousness-altering substance that came his way. The Berkeley street punks sometimes took advantage of him, though he wasn't an unwilling victim. They'd dare him to take combinations of pills for the comic relief of watching how he reacted when he got loaded. They were all older than him, mostly in their late teens and twenties. Somehow, they convinced Ronnie to fuck him for their entertainment. Or maybe they paid her. He didn't know.

So, there he was, wasted, off-balance, flat on his back in fact, not really capable of actively participating in life. It was around noon on a warm October day and they were in a narrow walkway between two buildings on Telegraph Avenue, a favorite semi-secluded spot for street people to get stoned or do drug deals in broad daylight.

He had a crush on Ronnie. She was always nice to him, always willing to pass him the joint or the bottle, so that probably had something to do with it.

He hardly knew what was happening when she took down his jeans. He looked up just as she was starting to give him head. It was like a dream, a dream come true. He'd fantasized about Ronnie many times, but never thought seriously about approaching her; he would never have had the guts, virgin that he was. Just looking at her going down on him like that, it was like he was watching an angel. He got hard as a rock very quickly. At one point she looked up laughing and said, "Man, he's got a big cock for such a little guy!"

That was when he realized they had an audience. The whole gang was there—Buzz and Wes and Derrick and Jean and some other kids he'd seen before, but didn't know, even a couple of the skuzzball alkies who sometimes bought liquor for them—standing around with their hands in their pockets and big smiles on their faces at this impromptu performance of which he was the center of attention.

While he was staring at the crowd, Ronnie got on top of him, hiked up her skirt, and mounted him in a sitting position. Still flat on his back, he was looking around at all the grinning punks enjoying the show.

"Bang him good, Ronnie!" one of the voices called out.

His dick went soft. He tried reaching up to pull Ronnie down onto him. He wanted to hide beneath her. But he had no strength and just as quickly as she'd mounted him, she climbed off.

"His woody's gone," she said, and the grinning crowd laughed.

He picked up his head and looked down at himself, lying on his back with his jeans and underpants around his ankles, a bunch of street punks, even the few he counted as friends, standing around him laughing. They laughed harder as he attempted to pull his jeans up and get to his feet. Dizzy, he fell over. He got onto his hands and knees, ass in the air, and started puking his guts out. He stayed in that position until the crowd dispersed. Show over.

After that, he avoided Ronnie and that whole group, detouring down a different street whenever he saw them. In the years that followed, he had a number of sexual encounters, all forgettable, none of which culminated in an orgasm for either him or the female involved. Because he was so short, not particularly sociable, and cultivating a rather grungy biker image, he didn't have an inordinate number of opportunities for sex. But the few that presented themselves all followed the same pattern. Hot foreplay. Dick gets hard. Dick goes in. Dick shrinks. No orgasm. Game over.

And the mythical psychiatrist he didn't believe in would also want to know about that time, ten years later, in a legal brothel on the out-skirts of Carson City. He was twenty-five. He was scuffling in Reno and Tahoe as a low-stakes card counter, often sharing cheap motel rooms with Clance, as they'd both become interested in the possibility of gambling for a living, a dream Clance pursued more persistently and successfully than Bart.

A couple of drunken truckers at the Boomtown Casino in Verdi were talking about a whorehouse located off Highway 50. Bart de-cided to go down there and check it out. Despite his history of failures at culminating a sex act, he didn't yet think of himself as incapable of doing it. He hadn't had enough encounters that allowed him to ascribe any statistical relevance to his failures. There was always one thing or another to blame. No big deal. He was young.

Honey's Ranch turned out to be a group of trailers. The front room was a bar and there were small private cubicles for sex. The first time he went there, all he did was have a beer. A number of the girls approached him and asked him if he'd like to go to their rooms, but he declined. Of the half-dozen girls in the bar area, only one appealed to him, and she never approached him. She was dark-complected with big eyes and straight black hair and had a kind of a gypsy look to her. But he was so afraid of rejection, he couldn't bring himself to make the first move.

He returned to Honey's a week or so later, determined to get up the nerve to have sex with a girl, any girl, just to prove to himself that he could. He'd showered and shaved and cleaned his nails and had a cou-ple shots of Jack Daniels. This was a big deal to him and he was nervous.

He was happy to see the gypsy girl was still there. He didn't have the nerve to choose her when the girls did their initial line-up. Again, he went straight to the bar and ordered a beer. No sooner had his beer arrived, however, than the gypsy girl sat down beside him.

"Hi, my name's Jennifer," she said. "What's yours?"

She was wearing an oversized deep purple sweatshirt that hung almost to her knees. Close up, she was really pretty. Her teeth were crooked in front. Somehow, that made her even prettier, in a gypsy way.

"Bart."

"Do you want to go to my room and talk?" she said. "If you want to just sit out here and chat for a while, that's fine, but we're not allowed to talk business out here."

He took a sip of his beer.

"You can bring your drink," she said.

He took another swig.

She leaned in close to him and whispered, "I saw you checking me out last week. How come you left so soon?"

He just looked at her, trying to think of something to say.

"It's not a commitment if you come to my room," she said. "We can just talk and if you don't want to do anything, that's fine. There's no charge for talking. We can come back out here, you can have another drink, maybe think about partying with one of the other girls ... If one of the other girls in here appeals to you, I can have her come over right now if you want."

"No," he said, finally finding his voice. "Let's go to your room."

She stood up. "You've never done this before, have you?"

He stood up hesitantly. "Not really."

"Grab your drink." She took his hand. "C'mon, we'll have fun."

She led him down a narrow hallway to her cubicle. Her bed was just a mattress on the floor covered by a thick purple quilt and a half-dozen colorful pillows. The room smelled like sandalwood incense. In front of a small mirrored vanity was a straight-back chair with a dark leather seat. No other furniture. No room for much else. The space had a bohemian quality that fit her personality. Multi-colored scarves draped the walls and the shade on the overhead light fixture was painted with pictures of birds and flowers.

She sat down cross-legged on the bed and he sat down beside her.

"Jennifer," he said.

She looked at him, expecting him to say more, but he just looked down with nothing else to say. He'd just wanted to say her name.

"Since it's your first time, I'll give you a deal," she said. "Forty bucks."

"What do I get for ... ?" he didn't finish the question.

"You get to fuck me," she said. "Or a blowjob if you prefer. If you want half and half—meaning I'll suck your cock till it's good and hard, then you fuck me—that's sixty. That's a special price just for you."

Just from hearing her say those words, his dick was getting hard. But what he wanted more than anything was to lick her pussy. "What if I want … ?"

"If you want anal, sorry, I don't do that. A couple girls here do anal, but I'm not one of them. And they won't be cheap."

"No," he said. "Not that."

"I don't do kinky stuff," she said. "No B and D, no pissing or shitting or anything like that. Come on Saturday when all the girls are here, if you want to get kinky. There might be a girl here who can take care of you."

"Jesus, I wasn't thinking of any of that stuff."

She smiled. "You're fun," she said. "You're like a guessing game. Let me see … Do you want me to do a striptease for you? I can put some music on." She did a sexy little wiggle for him, then bit down on her lower lip expectantly.

"Well … " Actually, that sounded pretty good to him.

She turned and whispered in his ear, "Do you want to eat me?" Then she backed up and looked at him with that same expectant bite on her lower lip.

He nodded.

She gave him a big smile. "Well, Bart, I don't usually let guys do that. But I like you and I've got a thing for bikers. What kind of motorcycle do you have?"

"A Harley. How'd you know I had a bike?"

"I knew it! I love Harleys! You have to give me a ride sometime. I heard you coming down the road from half a mile away. It's quiet out here. All the girls ran to the window when we heard you pull up to the gate. Mostly we get truckers on weeknights like this. Now, you have to be gentle, okay? No teeth."

"Understood."

"So, how about a special deal for seventy-five bucks?" she said. "You go down on me, then I'll go down on you, then you can fuck me.

Most guys, I'd charge a hundred just for the half and half. You get to lick my pussy just 'cause you're a sweetheart and I like you."

"It's a deal," he said.

"You have to pay me in advance," she said, standing up suddenly.

He stood up and pulled out his wallet.

She sat down on her vanity chair. "Drop your pants," she said. "I have to check you out first. Make sure you don't have any sores or scabs or anything."

He unfastened his belt buckle, unbuttoned, unzipped, and dropped his jeans.

She pulled down his boxers and started examining him. "Next month we have to start using condoms for everything," she said. "The state passed a new law. It's that AIDS thing. I'm supposed to ask you if you want to use a condom. I have some if you want one."

"Do I have to?"

"Not till next month," she said. "The girls don't like the law. There's no gay guys coming in here. Most guys don't want to use rubbers." She finished examining him, then said, "I have to take the money to the front desk. Just take your clothes off and get in the bed. I'll be right back."

He handed her the seventy-five bucks, then undressed quickly and sat down on her mattress so she wouldn't see how short he was in his stocking feet.

She came back into the cubicle and closed the door behind her. She pulled her sweatshirt over her head and just like that she was down to her panties. "Do you want the light on or off?"

"Off."

She switched off the overhead light with a pull chain and the room became very dark. A small dim night light next to the vanity provided the only illumination.

"Most guys say 'on,'" she said. "But I knew you were going to say 'off.' I like it off myself. Sometimes. It's more intimate." She quickly slid out of her panties and sat down beside him. "Do you want to lick me first?" she asked. "Or do you want me to go down on you first?"

"Can we go kind of slowly?" he asked. He could feel his heart beating. He wanted to just lay back on the bed with her and start making out, kissing, hugging, holding each other.

"We can go a little slow," she said, "but we only have half an hour. They'll knock on my door in thirty minutes and that means time's up. If you want more time, you have to pay more. But we can have lots of fun in thirty minutes. Lie back on the pillows. Let me get you hard."

He lay down and she got on top of him, straddling him with her legs. She bent over and started kissing his chest, working her way down to his stomach. "You've really got muscles," she said. "I'm used to being with these old fat guys."

He was in heaven, with an angel sent from some god he didn't even believe in. He closed his eyes when he felt her take him into her mouth and just floated in a timeless space of trust and honesty and perfect peace. His dick hardened quickly and stayed that way for the longest time as she worked it, but as soon as the thought crossed his mind that maybe he should ask her if he could come like that, he tensed and felt his erection diminishing. He tried to stop thinking about it and managed to keep his dick semi-hard. When she came back up she kissed him lightly on the cheek. "Your turn," she said, licking lightly at his earlobe. "Do me," she whispered, breathing hot air on his neck.

He tried to kiss her on the mouth, but she turned away and said, "Just go down on me." Then she rolled off of him so that he could get on top.

She let him kiss her neck and her breasts. He sucked on each of her nipples, then slowly moved down her stomach like she had done to him. The smell of her was everything he wanted in life. When he got down to her pussy, she took his head in her hands and said, "Not too hard ... very gently." He started licking her. The taste was beyond his fantasies. Immediately, his dick regained full hardness. "That's right. Up a little higher. Right there. Just like that. Just like that. Just like that ... "

Within a few minutes, though it could have been seconds or hours, she sat up and took him by the shoulders, pulling him up to her. "Now come up here and fuck me."

He did as he was told, still lost in that dream world, as she guided his dick into her. She cooed in his ear, "That's right, that's right, that's right … "

He was thinking he should ask her if she really would take a ride on his bike with him. They could go get something to eat. Maybe she'd like to take a trip, go all the way to California, Big Sur, sit on the beach, light up a doobie …

But he felt his dick going soft again and he tried to will it hard, but it wouldn't cooperate. What was happening? He wanted to fuck her more than anything in the world. He tried pumping his hips faster, harder, but his dick just continued shrinking, softening. It was useless. He collapsed on top of her for a few seconds, then rolled off beside her. He was drenched in sweat.

"Are you okay?" she said softly.

He didn't answer. He couldn't.

"Did you come?" she said.

He felt her take his dick in her hand.

"Hey, that's okay," she said, turning toward him. "That's okay," she said again. "We still have a little time. You don't have to get dressed right away."

She pulled his body up against her and held him. He felt a lump in his throat and wanted to cry, but he controlled it. He was a jumble of emotions. On one hand, he was overwhelmed by the immense importance of this act he'd just attempted to perform, this passionate and intimate communication that meant so much to him, while on the other hand, he was ashamed of his inability to consummate the act and the ultimate meaninglessness of it all because it was with a seventy-five dollar whore he'd never see again. Those sweet tender moments of foreplay meant so much to him and so little to her. He dreaded the thought of even turning on the light so they could get dressed. She started saying, "Hey, hey, it's okay, hey … " trying to comfort him, as if she cared. But it bothered him that she knew he was on the verge of tears. He just wanted to be gone.

Later, he rationalized his failure as the result of an inability to fuck a girl who didn't really want to fuck him. Where's the fun in fucking someone who's only in it for the money? But when he remembered how sweet she'd been to him and how gently she'd treated him, the thought that something was wrong with him, that he had some kind of mental block against fucking, started to nag at him. Still, as he refused to concede that he was incapable of fucking, in the years that followed, there were more forgettable half-night stands.

His third shrink-worthy attempt was another ten years later with a woman who called herself "Persephone." He met her at, of all places, a poetry reading. At the age of thirty-five, he was living back in Berkeley again.

He'd never been to a poetry reading. He had no intention of ever going to a poetry reading. But it was a Tuesday night around nine p.m. and he was sitting at the bar in a crowded Irish pub on the outskirts of south Berkeley when a scruffy bearded dude got up on the small platform stage, turned on the mic, and introduced himself as "Kendall." Then he announced that the poetry reading would be starting in a few minutes. "Any poets who haven't signed the list yet," he said, "come on up here and get signed up."

Most of the "poets" seemed to be remnants of the hippie era, some with political axes to grind, others looking for a socially acceptable soapbox from which to spout tetragrams, and a few pseudo-intellectuals who had discovered that obtuseness enhanced by the liberal use of Roget's Thesaurus led to polite applause. Not a few were just nerds trying to get laid. Most read from scraps of paper, though a few read from diary-like journals. One Asian woman read from a large ring binder, and one very disheveled black man spent most of his ten-minute stage time shuffling through the contents of a stuffed leather briefcase. He finally read two poems, each of which consisted of about ten unrelated words that made no sense at all. The crowd was nodding out.

About an hour into the reading, as Bart was finishing off his stout and about to leave, a woman who was introduced as Persephone took the stage. He guessed her to be about his age. It was hard to judge, because of her severe acne. Large bumps on her forehead, neck, and both cheeks looked like deep infections. All of her visible skin was scarred and blotched with irregular red patches. She wore sunglasses and black clothes with lots of silver and turquoise jewelry. Her hair was long and straight and flaming red, obviously dyed, which only accentuated her skin problems. She didn't have anything to read from. She just stood there with her arms at her sides, either reciting from memory or improvising, Bart wasn't sure which.

Her voice was deep and her words dark and foreboding. Powerlessness in the face of evil. Pain and suffering. Sickness and death. But somehow she turned her phrases with ironic humor that got laughs out of the otherwise still crowd. She repeated the catch-phrase, "Do you know Hades?" numerous times with an emotion in her voice that contrasted sharply with the styles of the other poets, who either read in monotones or used bombastic oratory techniques to make their obvious political points. She was the only poet who actually captured the crowd, and the applause when she left the stage was more than polite. He had no idea what her poem meant—if anything—but it was funny, in the ha-ha sense. He had laughed aloud a number of times himself. That in itself made her unique.

For the next week, he couldn't get her out of his mind. He knew the story of Persephone, as he'd read a book on the Greek deities when he was a kid, another tome from his father's library. Persephone was a beautiful young girl who was raped in her garden and kidnapped by Hades, the god of the underworld. Persephone then became the Queen of the Underworld, though the Greeks also called her the Queen of the Dead, and felt that it was dangerous to speak her name out loud.

Over the weekend, between tattoo jobs, Bart penned a rhyming poem titled "Yeah, I know Hades," determined to read it the following Tuesday night at the pub if Persephone was there. He just wanted to see if he could make her laugh. He wasn't physically attracted to her and he had no fantasies about her. He just liked the way her mind worked and he admired her guts for standing up in front of a crowd of drunks and exhibiting a little-appreciated intelligence and creativity. He wanted her to know that someone had heard her—even if it was just the grungy biker tramp who didn't know poetry from poached eggs. He felt a kinship with her as a social rebel and iconoclast.

She wasn't there the following Tuesday night when he arrived, so he ordered a Guinness and had a seat at the bar. When he saw her enter the pub about fifteen minutes later, he went and signed the list to read. She signed the list to read herself shortly thereafter. The half-dozen or so poets who read before him were a rehash of the prior week. By the time Bart Black was announced, his adrenaline was pumping. He took the stage and spent the first thirty seconds or so just pacing and strutting until the crowd hushed. He knew he was a novelty act in his biker duds. He launched into his piece, which he had memorized.

"Well, sure, I know that Hades fag; I met him as a child. His breath could make a buzzard gag, his body odor's vile. They say he drinks the venom of the serpents that he eats, then chews on lizards' innards that he relishes as sweets. He wails to Zeus and Hermes just to curse his destiny, then heads back home to home sweet hell to screw Persephone."

That was the whole poem. Twelve short lines and he was gone from that stage just as fast as he could get back to the bar. He got the same polite applause as everyone else, but he was proud of himself. Persephone sat looking down at her table, not once looking in his direction. Another poet was droning on and Bart was wondering if she'd even heard him. Then, almost as if the words he'd spoken minutes before had suddenly entered her consciousness, she stood up and walked directly toward him and stood there in front of him. Finally, she said, "That was a horrible poem."

He smiled at her. "Compared to the six guys who read before me?"

That got a little smile out of her. "On that basis," she said, "it was brilliant. It rhymed."

That's when that thing happened with the eyes. That chemistry thing. It didn't make sense to him. He wasn't physically attracted to her at all. But he liked her in that kind of way that he could only think of as some kind of chemical attraction.

"Have a seat," he said, motioning to the barstool beside him.

"I have a bottle of wine," she said. "Come to my table if you want to talk." She turned and walked away.

In the back of his mind he was telling himself to be careful. Don't lead her on. Don't give the impression that you're trying to put the make on her. You're not attracted to her.

But he felt an exhilarating rush of bravado as he made his way through the crowd to her table. He could feel the eyes of the room on him, everyone watching this drama unfold, while some dipshit on the stage was droning on about the pain of having a mean mother. Now, here he was, the novelty biker-scum act getting together with the ugly chick, the diseased girl that no one talked to. He sat down beside her and set his glass on the table.

"Why did you want to meet me?" she asked before he'd even settled in. Her wine bottle was already half empty.

"Precisely because no one else in here wants anything to do with you," he said. "Anyone who's that much of a pariah is okay in my book."

She sat staring down at her glass, every once in a while casting a sidelong glance at him.

"Don't look at me like that," she said.

"Like what?"

"Just don't look at me," she said. "I'm not much to look at."

"Should I turn my chair to the wall?"

"I don't like to be looked at."

"I see … So that's why you come down here every Tuesday night and get on the stage under a spotlight."

"Believe me," she said, looking at him directly for the first time since he'd sat down, "if I could read my poems from here, in the dark, without getting on the stage, I'd do it."

"Why write poems at all?"

"Should I just cut my wrists?" she asked matter-of-factly.

"Are those the only two options open to you? Do you wake up in the morning and lie there thinking, should I pick up a pen today or just get the razor? Pen … razor … pen … razor … ?"

She smiled at him. "That's pretty much it," she said. "That's my morning in a nutshell."

"Are these morons worth it?"

She refilled her wine glass and took a deep drink from it. "So, you think tomorrow morning I should just pick up the razor and be done with it?"

"There are other alternatives in life besides poetry and death."

"Not in my life."

"Why are you trying to impress these phonies? Do you want them to admire you? Do you want them to accept you? They won't even talk to you."

"So why are *you* trying to impress them?"

He laughed. "No, uh uh. Let me tell you something. That was the first time I've ever gotten on a stage at a poetry reading and it's certainly the last. I wasn't trying to impress anyone but you. Nobody here gives a flying fuck about anybody else. Do what I did twenty years ago. Get yourself a motorcycle, girl. Fuck these assholes. Hit the road. Feel the wind."

She pursed her lips. "Seriously," she said, "I'm not the Hell's Angels type."

"Well, we've got that in common, Persephone. I'm not the Hell's Angels type either. I'm sure the Angels are a fine upstanding bunch of lads, but frankly, I don't care piss for clubs or colors. Everybody in this world has to join a fucking group. We live in a world of sheep. I say fuck 'em all."

Just then Kendall announced that the next poet was Persephone. As soon as Bart heard her name, he turned toward the stage and yelled, "Hey, Kendall!"

The MC's eyes widened in surprise and he stood there staring at Bart with his mouth slightly open. The room went silent.

"Can you bring that mic down this way?" Bart said. "Persephone's reading her poem from here."

Kendall looked confused for a moment, looked down at the cord and started gathering it up. "I don't know if the cord will stretch that far."

"Don't make a scene," Persephone said softly, starting to rise from her seat.

Bart put his hand over her hand on the table to stop her.

Kendall just stood there staring at their table.

"Give it the old college try, Kendall," Bart said. "It's a concept piece. It was written to be read from an anonymous voice in a dark corner."

Kendall walked over to the amplifier in the back corner of the stage and dragged it to the front. Then he started weaving his way through the tables, feeding out cord as he went. He brought the mic down and handed it to Persephone. The only voices in the room were whispers.

Persephone put the mic to her mouth and bowed her head. "Pen," she said, then waited about five seconds before saying, "Razor?" Then she said it again, almost identically, just a bit softer, "Pen ... Razor?"

Then, after a long pause, when just about everyone, including Bart, wondered if that was the whole poem, she said in an emotionless matter-of-fact voice, "That's pretty much it ... my morning ... in a nutshell."

There was a good ten seconds of silence before the polite applause. Kendall came to the table and retrieved the mic. Persephone had a satisfied smile on her face.

"Well, you're not going to win a Pulitzer for that one," Bart said.

She looked at him and raised her glass of wine. "It's a work in progress."

Bart went to the poetry readings at the pub just about every week after that and he always sat with Persephone. She always drank an entire bottle of wine in the time it took him to polish off a pint of Guinness. Some nights they hardly spoke; other nights they'd talk incessantly about just about anything. He learned a lot about her. Her skin problem, for example, was a result of her having fucked up her kidneys when she attempted suicide at the age of seventeen by ingesting a bottle of her mother's sleeping pills. They revived her in the hospital after pumping her stomach, but she'd already done severe damage to her kidneys, liver, and immune system. She had a master's degree in psychology from a small college in Michigan. She was thirty-six years old. She was currently reading about Eastern religions and she was practicing yoga. She was a vegetarian and ate only organic foods. She was also an alcoholic and she chain-smoked menthol cigarettes. She was mercilessly sarcastic in her opinions of just about everything.

Bart told her things about himself he'd never told anyone. Things about his parents, his fucking up in school. She was easy to talk to and completely non-judgmental.

But any time he tried to get her to talk about what exactly she did when she wasn't at the pub, she just changed the subject or simply said, "Don't go there." She would never tell him why she had attempted suicide as a teenage girl. If he ever pushed for an answer on some topic she was sensitive about, he quickly regretted it. Something seemed to click in her head and she became paranoid, close to delusional. Suddenly, she would complain that other poets in the room hated her or, worse, were reporting on her to "the authorities."

Many times he asked her if he could give her a ride home on his bike, but she always declined. Then, early one Tuesday night, he said, "C'mon, let's get out of here. This place sucks."

"Where is there to go?"

"Anywhere but here," he said. "I'll take you for a ride. We'll go nowhere, just hit the highway. I'll have you back here in time to read if you want. You're down at the bottom of the list. Let's get some fresh air."

"I've never been on a motorcycle," she said. "What if it tips over?"

"Tips over? You mean if we're rolling down the highway at like ninety and suddenly the bike tips over? Gee, I guess we might skin our little shins." He stood up. "I'm outta here, Persephone. You coming?"

"What do I do with the bottle?" Her wine bottle was still three-quarters full.

He picked up the cork from the table and jammed it into the bottle. "I'll tell the bartender to hold it for you."

To his astonishment, she picked up her purse and rose from the table. "I'm going to trust you this once."

"Bad idea," he shot back. "You should never trust a human."

His bike was parked on the street right outside the pub entrance.

"It's an evil-looking thing, isn't it?" he said as they stood on the sidewalk looking at it. He handed her a helmet.

"I think it's beautiful," she said, trying to tuck her hair into the helmet. Some people just look downright comical in a helmet and she was one of them. "Do I have to wear this?"

"You do according to California Vehicle Code, Division Twelve, Chapter Five, Article Seven, Section Twenty-Seven-Eight-O-Three," he said. "I've already been cited for more violations than I can afford since they enacted this legislation in nineteen-ninety-two. It's unconstitutional and I'm going to fight the bastards in court. But tonight, we'll be law-abiding citizens."

He got on the bike and took the kickstand off.

She walked around to the front of the bike like she was sizing it up anew. Where moments before she had said it was beautiful, she now said, "It's kind of dirty … Do you ever wash it?"

He got the engine revved up then let it slow to an idle. "It's just the way I like it," he said. "Dynamite fast and medium clean." He looked at her as if to say, "What are you waiting for?"

She came over to the side of the bike. "How do I do this?"

There's no ladylike way to get on a motorcycle. "You hike up your skirt, step on that peg, and climb on. It won't tip over. I promise."

She was wearing a short black skirt with opaque black tights and knee-high black leather boots. It was a brisk September night. The moon was full. Riding with her on his bike was more of a pleasure than he'd anticipated; the warmth of her body pressed up against him, her arms wrapped around him, her thighs squeezing tight around his waist. He was more starved for affection than he knew.

After that night, everything was different. It was like she had let him initiate her into some secret holy order. When he looked at her, he didn't see the acne scars on her face. He just saw her eyes. He knew she was crazy, but what did that matter? He started having fantasies about making love to her. Every week he asked her to take another ride with him, but she always said no. Finally, he just came out and asked her to sleep with him.

"I can't," she said. "Not tonight."

He ignored the "I can't" and only heard the "not tonight."

"How about tomorrow night?"

"Tomorrow in the daytime."

He was stunned. "What time?"

"Noon," she said. "I'll come to your place. Write down your address."

"I'll come and pick you up. Where do you live?"

She thought for a moment, then said, "Pick me up here."

"The pub's not open at noon," he said.

"I'll wait out front."

He was living in a studio apartment in Emeryville, in the warehouse district. Technically, his place was a two-car garage that had been converted into a studio by the addition of a small bathroom with a sink, toilet, and shower stall, no tub. There was no kitchen, just a sink in the back corner, an ancient two-burner gas stove, and a small refrigerator that made a racket whenever the motor was running. He had an electric space heater that blew a fuse if he attempted to heat the room while the stereo was on. It violated a half-dozen building codes for residential quarters. But he paid the landlord in cash and utilities were included. It wasn't exactly the kind of place you'd want to bring a date. He had a beat-up old couch that was losing its stuffing, a mattress on a creaky box spring on the floor, lots of motorcycle mags lying around, bike parts, skin mags, no TV. He did his best to straighten up the place and even took the sheets to the laundromat that morning.

But he almost didn't go through with it. He viewed his prior two major sexual adventures as among the major catastrophes of his life. Now, here he was at the age of thirty-five about to give naked vulnerability another shot.

He also felt there was a good chance that Persephone would just blow him off. Was she really going to be standing outside the pub at noon? He decided that if she actually had the guts to show up, then it was game on. If she wasn't there, then that was it. Fuck the poetry readings. He had to get on with his life. He wanted to find humor in the concept of being rejected by the ugliest girl in town, but it churned his guts even to consider it.

She was there, leaning back against the building with her hand over her mouth. She saw him coming from a block away but it was half a minute or so before she came over to the bike.

"Get on." He handed her a helmet.

"I really didn't think you'd come. I'm so ugly. Why are you pursuing me?" She looked like she was about to start crying.

"Jesus Christ, Persephone, you're fucking gorgeous! Granted, you look ridiculous in that helmet."

She just stood there, looking hurt.

"You're not ugly," he said in a softer tone. "And you're the only goddamn friend I have in this world. Get on the bike, okay?"

She took out a handkerchief and blew her nose. "You're crazy," she said. Then she put her hand on his shoulder and climbed onto the bike.

† † †

She sat down on his couch.

"Do you want a glass of wine?" he said.

"No. It's cold in here."

He flipped the switch on his electric heater. So much for mood music. He sat down beside her.

"I don't know if I can go through with this," she said.

"My feelings precisely."

They turned simultaneously and looked at each other. Their eyes met and within seconds they were kissing, passionately making out, their hands all over each other.

They moved quickly to the bed. Neither of them said anything, but there they were, rolling around on that creaky mattress with their clothes slowly coming off a piece at a time. He wanted to go down on her, but she wouldn't let him. Every time he started to move down from her breasts to her belly, she would pull him up. Finally, she said, "Come inside me now."

"I have condoms."

"I had my tubes tied. Just fuck me."

His dick was hard as granite and as she guided it into her, he felt sure he'd finally be able to have sex with a girl, but within seconds he could feel it happening. The incredible shrinking dick. He tried thinking of the porno images that worked best for him when he masturbated. Why was this happening? Why couldn't he maintain a fucking hard-on?

Then she said, "I'm going to leave my husband."

He pushed himself up onto his elbows to look at her, trying to take in her remark. His cock was still in her, but was quickly becoming flaccid. "I don't believe I knew you were married."

"I didn't tell you," she said. "You have to help me. I can't do it by myself. He's a good husband and father but he's not right for me."

"Father?"

"I have children," she said. "Three children."

His dick was dead. He couldn't even pretend to himself that this fuck was going to happen. He rolled off of her onto his side. "Jesus, Persephone, why didn't you tell me this before?"

"He doesn't make love to me anymore," she said. "He doesn't even touch me. Ever. He's a good man, but he doesn't really love me. He just stays with me out of a sense of duty."

On the one hand, Bart felt relieved of having to explain his impotence to her. The whole issue had been overshadowed by this new development. On the other hand …

"Three kids," he said, still trying to take this in. "How old are they?"

"Eight, six, and five. All boys."

"And what happens to your kids when you leave your husband?"

She didn't answer.

Bart rolled onto his back and just stared at the ceiling.

After a minute she said, "You have to help me."

"What can I do?" he said. He had a sick feeling. She was dealing with shit he didn't even want to think about.

"We have to get a place," she said. "This place is too small. We need a house."

"What?" He'd just been starting to think in terms of "girlfriend" for the first time in his life, like maybe he'd finally have a date once in a while, get laid now and then, but this was lunacy.

"Do you have a job?" he asked her.

"No," she said. "I … I can't work a job. I'm too … emotionally unbalanced."

It figured.

"What does your husband do?"

"He's a policeman."

"Are you shitting me?" This was getting worse by the minute. "Is he a Berkeley cop?" Bart wondered if he knew him.

"No," she said. "Oakland. He's in vice."

Game over. "Jesus Christ … Do you know what I do for a living?"

"No."

He sat up on the bed. "I've got a lot of jobs, Persephone. You see the stuff on that bench over there? That's my tattoo equipment. I'm a tattoo artist. Freelance. I don't work in a shop. I get word of mouth customers, mostly other bikers, and I work right here. I also do motor-cycle repair. Freelance. I fix bikes. Right out there in my front yard. I'm good at it. Also, about once a month or so, I go up to Reno and play some blackjack. I'm a card counter. That's a tougher gig, because if the cards don't go my way, well, I just have to make sure I have enough gas money to get home. Sometimes, I even sell a little ganja, just enough to pay my rent when my other jobs aren't bringing anything in. I like to have enough money to keep beans on my stove.

"Now, you might wonder why I don't just get a full-time job work-ing in a fancy tattoo parlor, or in a motorcycle repair shop, or even selling mocha grande cappuccinos in a fucking Starbucks. You know why I don't do that? I'll tell you why." He stood up and pulled on his jeans. "I don't work a regular job, Persephone, because, like you, *I'm too fucking emotionally unbalanced!*"

It went downhill from there. She kept saying, "I need you." The whole time they were dressing, she was crying.

He kept answering, as gently as he could manage in his panic, "Just get dressed, sweetheart."

The whole way back to the pub, she was sobbing into his neck, quietly moaning, "Please, Bart, please!"

When they got to the pub, she got off the bike but wouldn't let go of his arm. Her face looked a mess. He just sat there numb with the engine running, waiting for her to release him.

Finally, she said, "I could leave my kids."

That hit him like a brick in the solar plexus. "No," he said as calmly as he could. "You can't do that. Don't even think that way."

She let go of his arm.

"I'm sorry," he said. "Life's a kick in the head."

And with that, he got the hell out of there. He hit the highway and rode all the way to San Jose, just to let the wind have its way with him.

He felt like he'd abandoned her. He did abandon her. But a cop and three kids? That was more baggage than he could handle. That night, stoned on weed, he tried briefly to convince himself that his dick had died because she'd dropped a bombshell on him. But he knew that wasn't the way it had happened. First the dick went, then she dropped the bomb. If she hadn't, he would have been trying to hump her with a limp dick. Either way, the afternoon romp was destined to have a sordid ending. Why hadn't he seen that coming?

So, at the age of thirty-five, he decided that he'd had it with women. He didn't know why he couldn't perform as a man in their presence, but he was done trying to make it work. He didn't need women anyway. Jacking off suited him just fine. And in the eight years since he'd abandoned Persephone at the side of the road, he hadn't tried to bed a woman since.

Flattered as he was by Stacy's attentions, he had no aspirations of attempting to have sex with her. She was a trophy girlfriend in the truest sense. People who saw them together assumed she was his girl. Even she seemed to assume it. But to him, she was just a decoration. It couldn't go any further than that; he wasn't about to reveal his impotence to a nineteen-year-old kid, regardless of how much he liked her. He would just keep telling her she was too young and eventually she'd meet some other guy. Hormones and chemistry would take it from there.

TWENTY-SEVEN

"WE FOUND YOUR websites, Bart."

"Websites?"

"Or should I say Stacy's websites?"

"Is it still Wednesday?"

"It's ten minutes later than the last time you asked."

"Isn't your hour up yet?"

"I want to know what you know about these sites. How big is this thing? Is this a "movement" or just you and a bunch of your biker buddies trying to cause trouble? Using that poor girl as a scapegoat for whatever illicit activities you're involved in. Who's behind this thing? Where's the money coming from?"

"Too many questions, Dorsett."

"And no answers. This whole thing is going to be wide open in the next few days. The feds are interested. The FBI. DEA. Homeland Security. Zoey Berrington is already behind bars."

"But she wasn't there ... "

"Stacy was living with her. We got a warrant to search her residence and what should we find but a phony ID mill. I'm giving you a chance, Bart. Tell me what you know and save yourself a lot of trouble. The feds won't treat you as kindly as I am."

"Fuck off ... Tell 'em to waterboard me."

TWENTY-EIGHT

THE COP'S VOICE surprised him. He looked so tough, so brawny, but his voice was weak and tinny. "I learned something tonight," he said. "I never knew a faggot could ride a Harley. You must be damn proud of that big dick of yours. Damn proud. Couldn't wait to whip it out for me, you sick fuckin' bastard." The cop walked a few steps closer to him, waving his gun haphazardly. "I been offered all kinds of bribes. Goes with the territory. Fifties, hundreds … I've had whores offer to suck me off right there on the highway just to get out of a speedin' ticket. Goes with the territory. But you're the first sonofabitch to offer me a dick." He took a few more steps closer. "You think I'm queer? You think I can't resist? Kneel down you homo bastard. Get on yer fuckin' knees! I'm gonna waste your ass and leave your carcass out here for the coyotes. Say your prayers, faggot."

Bart knelt down, keeping his hands in the air. Now that lump on his head was starting to pulse. He felt sick. The cop took a few more steps toward him, stopping when he was about ten feet away.

"You want to suck my dick?" he said. "I'll bet you do it better'n them cunts down the road. You wouldn't know about that, would you?"

The cop took a couple steps closer, unzipping his fly as he walked, still pointing the gun at him.

That's when they both heard the car engine rev up. The cop spun around just as his patrol car lurched forward, barreling into his legs and knocking him backwards. Bart jumped aside or the cop would have plowed into him on his way down. Instead, the back of the cop's head smashed into one of the knuckles on the front valve cover of Bart's bike. His bike was a "knucklehead" in Harley argot, due to the big heads on the rocker-box shaft bolts that resemble knuckles on a clenched fist. Harley stopped making knuckleheads in the late forties, but aesthetically, Bart had always thought the knuckleheads were the finest-looking V-twins Harley ever built. Now he had another reason to like them. The cop was out cold.

Stacy was at the wheel of the cop's car. She looked panicky.

"Cool it," he said. "He's conked. Back up the car and let's get the fuck out of here."

She backed up slowly, cranking the steering wheel, so that the headlights were no longer pointing dead at him. It was just starting to sink in that he had passed his Houdini moment with flying colors, using Houdini's top secret last-resort method—the accomplice.

TWENTY-NINE

"BART, ARE YOU still with me? You awake?"

"Jesus, Dogdirt … What day is it?"

"We have more to go over. Now pay attention. This is serious. "

"Will your shift never end? Must be fuckin' midnight."

"No, because I'd be home in bed, not sitting here trying to squeeze blood out of a damn rock. But my hour's up and I expect to be booted out of here any time now so they can change your diaper and I can go to lunch. Now listen. We learned a lot about you in the four days you were napping. You're in way over your head, Bart. Getting Stacy a fake California driver's license so she could work in strip clubs was only your first federal offense. Then you transport her out of state to Reno—another federal offense—and three months later when her cover gets blown in Reno, it's on to Las Vegas. And although we can't find any employment records for you going back ten years—in either California or Nevada—you're in possession of thirty-nine thousand dollars *in cash*, which leads us to believe you were involving this young lady in more than just nude dancing."

"Tryin' to wiggle my toe … Big toe on my right foot … Can you tell me if it's moving? I think it is … "

"Do you fully understand the implications of that second federal offense, Bart? When you brought her from California to Nevada, you crossed a state line. As we have every reason to believe you brought her here for immoral purposes, it appears you've violated the Mann Act."

"Never crossed a state line with her."
Big, big, big lie …

THIRTY

SHORTLY AFTER CROSSING the California/Nevada state line, in room 26 of the Starlight Motel on the outskirts of Reno, Bart started to get a handle on just how crazy Stacy was. After lugging their stuff up to the room, he plopped down onto one of the beds and Stacy sat down on the wooden straight-backed chair in front of the small desk.

"I've got to call Clance," he said. "He'll probably want me over at his place right away. Do you want to come?"

"Why'd you get two beds?" she asked. "I thought you said you wanted to sleep with me."

"I didn't say I wanted to sleep with you. I said I wanted to fuck you. But that doesn't mean I'm going to fuck you."

"Yes you are," she said. "You're a man. When it comes to sex, men adhere to hedonistic utilitarianism."

"You wanna run that by me again?"

"Henry Sidgwick," she said. "He was a nineteenth century English philosopher. He wrote *The Methods of Ethics*. Eighteen-seventy-four."

"You sure it wasn't the B-Fifty-Twos? *I Know What Boys Like*, nineteen-eighty-four?"

"That wasn't the B-Fifty-Twos," she said. "That was the Waitresses. They probably read Sidgwick."

"Philosophy major?" he said.

"No, chemistry. But I've read a lot of philosophy on my own."

The quilted bedspread he was lying on had cigarette burns along one side. He touched one of the indented black holes; it felt like hard plastic.

"How old did you say you were?" he asked.

"Nineteen."

"You don't look nineteen. You're a smart girl. What the hell were you doing working in a strip joint?"

"I needed the money."

"For school? I always thought that was a joke. Every stripper says she's putting herself through college, when most of them are just putting themselves through a kilo of coke."

"I needed the money to get out of the Bay Area," she said.

"Where were you going to school?"

"Stanford."

"That's not cheap."

"I'm on a full scholarship."

"Are you going back?"

"Not right away. Can I touch your beard?"

"What?"

"It looks so soft." She reached her hand up slowly, giving him ample time to move or protest, but he didn't.

When her hand was inches from his face, he closed his eyes, then felt a light brush of her fingertips.

"Ooh," she said. "I wish I could grow a beard."

He opened his eyes and felt his face break into a smile. Who was this girl and why the hell was she with him? "What are you running from?" he said.

She thought for a moment then said, "Stupid people."

"Then you're going to love Reno, the armpit of the Southwest. It's known for the incredible intelligence of the derelicts and hustlers who compose the majority of the population here."

"Comprise," she corrected him. "And I wasn't running to Reno; I was running to you."

How long could this go on? "I don't know what kind of fantasies you've built up, Stacy, but it ain't me, babe. If you hang out with me for any length of time, I'm sure I'll disappoint you on as massive a level as anyone else ever has." He got up from the mattress and noticed that the worn carpet had blackened cigarette burns that looked similar to those on the bedspread.

"I've got to call Clance," he said, flipping his cell phone open.

"Look, Bart," she said. "I'm not going to beat around the bush. There's a reason I'm here and a reason you're here, but you don't know it yet."

He closed his phone before making the call and propped a pillow against the headboard. He sat back down. "That sounds like beating around the bush to me. Are you trying to tell me something? Because I know why I'm here. I'm here for thirty bucks an hour. Why are *you* here?"

"What if I told you I was God?"

Was this the weirdness Zoey had warned him about? "Then I'd say that dude who paid seventy-five bucks for your panties got himself a bargain." He thought immediately of Persephone. Jesus, he could pick 'em. "I'm hungry," he said. "I say we hit the buffet at Circus Circus before we head over to Clance's. Unless, of course, you'd like to rustle up some loaves and fishes."

"I don't do miracles," she said.

"Damn, I must be psychic! I knew you were going to say that!"

"I know you don't believe me, but do me a favor and don't tell other people."

"You mean I can't tell Clance I'm dating the Savior?"

"We're not dating. And I don't like that name."

"How about 'Yahweh'?"

"You can call me that if I can call you 'Midge'."

A chill ran through him. "Are you going to tell me where you got that from?"

The atmosphere had quickly become brittle.

"Just call me Stacy."

"You know, Stacy, I thought I liked you. Now I'm not so sure." He felt like she'd hit him below the belt. What else did she know about him? "Are you going to tell me where you got that?"

She just looked at him.

"Why'd you call me that?"

"You were hurting my feelings, Bart. You weren't taking me seriously."

He smirked. "Okay, I'll take you seriously," he said. "What's it like being God?"

"You just want to make fun of me."

"Hey, they mocked Jesus, too. So tell me what it's like."

"It's lonely."

"Are you on acid right now?"

She screwed up her face. "No," she said.

"I had that trip once. I was sixteen. Took some acid with Clance. Scared the fuckin' shit out of me. Thought I was God. Everything I saw was my own creation. Nothing was real. It was like a movie and I knew what was going to happen next and it just kept happening. But I couldn't do miracles—not because I was trying and failing—I was too scared shitless to try."

"I can do miracles," she said.

"No, you can't. Lots of people have had that trip. The tragedies are the nut cases who jump out of windows to prove it. Don't go playing in traffic, girl. Why don't you try and make that ashtray float? You do that and I'll fall down on my knees and worship your ass."

"I'm not here to entertain you with magic tricks. I'm here for a reason and you have to help me. I need an apostle, Bart."

"An apostle? Does it pay more than thirty fuckin' bucks an hour? Tell me where you learned my nickname. And cut the God bullshit."

"I'm hungry," she said. "Let's go eat. We'll talk later."

"Well, until I see that ashtray doing loop-de-loops, I don't wanna hear any more God crap. And you *are* going to tell me where you heard my nickname or you can get your own fuckin' room and get the fuck outta my life. I don't need some punk-ass brat gettin' in my face with Midge, Midge, Midge, Midge, Midge. I ever hear that word come out of your yap again, you'll need a fuckin' miracle to get your teeth back in your mouth. Is that understood, Savior?"

"I'm sorry," she said softly, "I didn't mean—"

"Can it!" he cut her off. "You're on thin fuckin' ice."

She put her hand on his arm very lightly. "I know you'd never hurt me," she said.

He fixed his eyes on hers and knew she did know that. But he said, "You don't know shit, Stacy. God, my ass. Get your fuckin' coat on."

He left Clance a text message from the Circus Circus buffet. Clance texted back that he'd call him in the a.m.

As he and Stacy were eating, he kept thinking of Brenda, a Berkeley street girl the local punks all said was schizophrenic. She was crazy, that was certain, and the word on the street was that Brenda believed she was God. Often talking to herself, rarely acknowledging anyone else, even if they tried to talk to her. One day she came into the comic book store when Bart was there just hanging with Clance. She sat down on the floor and took a pair of scissors out of a large cloth bag she was carrying and started cutting small squares of material from the loose cotton dress she was wearing.

"Brenda, you can't stay here," Clance said.

Without looking up, she poked the scissors into her dress, just above the hem, and twisted them to increase the size of the hole. "I made you say that," she responded.

"You gotta leave the store, Brenda."

"You're just saying what I want you to say," she said, cutting a neat square in her dress that was filled with cutout squares.

This was just a few months after Bart had taken his I-am-God acid trip and it struck him that Brenda was on the same trip, but without the help of acid. He took a step toward her and said, "C'mon, Brenda, I'll walk you outside."

She looked up at him with alarm and pointed her scissors at him, jabbing them in his direction, essentially telling him to keep his distance.

Brenda had been around the avenue for years and he'd never heard about her being dangerous to anyone. But he took the threat seriously. If she really thought he was some figment of her imagination, she might stab him. Clance said, "Leave her be," and she ended up sitting there for twenty minutes or so, then got up and walked back outside.

Now Bart was wondering if Stacy was schizo. She wasn't exactly Brenda. She didn't walk around babbling to herself. She apparently was able to hold a job, at least in a strip club. But if she really thought she was God, she could be dangerous.

After gorging themselves at the buffet and with the night free, he decided to give Stacy a cook's tour of the Reno casinos. When they walked into the Eldorado, she slipped her hand inside his arm and they walked like that from casino to casino. He felt proud to have her on his arm. Damn, she looked good. When they stopped to look at a game, she would put her arm around him and lean on him lightly, just enough to let him know she wanted to be closer to him than an acquaintance, closer than a friend. He loved the smell of her hair, the warmth of her body. He stopped caring if she was crazy. She was his girl. It was pushing midnight when they got back to the motel room, and there were those beds. Suddenly, he wished he was alone.

"Which bed do you want?" he said.

She looked at him like the question wasn't registering, then she went and sat down on the bed closest to the bathroom. "This one," she said. She took off her jacket and tossed it on the desk.

He took off his own jacket, then sat down on the other bed and yanked his boots off.

Stacy got the straight-back chair and set it in front of him, then sat down facing him. "Help me get my boots off," she said.

She almost tipped over backwards when he pried the first boot off. He couldn't tell if she'd really almost fallen or if she was trying to entertain him, maybe soften the mood a bit. He appreciated her effort. When he got the second boot off, less dramatically, she stretched out both of her legs and put her feet up on the mattress of his bed, between his legs.

"Can I have a foot massage?" she said in a little girl voice. "Please, Bart? My boots are new and they're still stiff. My feeet huuurrt … "

"Aw, gimme your footsie-wootsie," he said, mocking her tone of voice. He picked up one of her feet and started rubbing it through the thin yellow cotton sock.

"I think I'm getting a blister," she said. "Can you take my socks off? I hope my feet don't smell too bad."

He peeled off her socks. He could definitely smell her feet, but it registered as anything but bad. He felt his dick stir. Great. Just what he needed. He pressed his thumb into the soft part of her sole.

"Oh, yes," she said, closing her eyes. "Don't stop. Just keep doing that."

"I feel like the reddleman," he said.

She opened her eyes and looked at him. "Thomas Hardy's reddleman?"

Damn, she was quick. "Do you know of any other reddleman?" he asked.

"No, but why do you feel like that?"

"Think about it."

She closed her eyes again and laid back, stretching her arms up over her head, arching her back. Was she trying to tease him? "I like riddles," she said, stretching from side to side. "Don't tell me ... I'll figure it out ... "

When he was fourteen he read *Return of the Native*—not for school; it was a book his father had. The reddleman was the friendless, lonely, town freak. There was a scene where Eustacia Vye—the knockout babe that all the men lusted after—granted the reddleman a few moments of holding her hand. And though Hardy's prose was far from graphic, he fully conveyed—at least to a fourteen-year-old boy—that this hand holding was the supreme sexual experience of the reddleman's life.

"Can you do the other foot now?" Stacy said. "Do it just like that one. I'll do your feet when you're done with mine."

"I don't need a foot massage," he said, taking her other foot. "My boots fit just fine."

His dick was hard as a rock. He wanted to adjust it upwards in his jeans, but there was no inconspicuous way to accomplish it. It wasn't that her feet turned him on so much as just touching her and seeing the pleasure in her face. Having seen her naked at the club, it wasn't difficult for him to mentally undress her. She had her eyes closed and her head tipped back and he was drinking her in.

Suddenly, she pulled her feet away from him and sat up.

"Give me a foot," she said.

He didn't want a foot massage. He wanted to hit the shower and jack-off.

She reached down and lifted one of his feet to her lap. He didn't fight her.

"Your feet are so big," she said, peeling off his crew sock.

"I got them from my father. Part of my inheritance."

"I'll bet you know about reflexology," she said.

"That word is not in my vocabulary."

"It's the same as acupressure," she said. "But Westernized. Every part of your foot corresponds to a different part of your body. If you have stomach problems, you relieve the tension in the sole of your foot here, and this area here at the side relates to your arms and shoulders, and right here at the base of your big toe, this is for your throat and neck. Do you have tension anywhere?"

He almost said, "My dick," but stopped himself in time, cracking a weak smile.

"I know what you were going to say," she said matter-of-factly, then picked up his other foot and peeled the sock off. Now both of his feet were in her lap. He lay back on the bed and closed his eyes. She worked on his feet for a while, then, out of nowhere, said, "Would you like a blow job?"

Yeah, right. He pulled his feet from her lap and set them on the floor as he sat up straight. "Time for bed," he said. "Clance is calling in the morning."

"The reddleman was like the town fool, wasn't he?" she said.

"Did you actually read the book?" he asked.

She thought for a moment, then said, "No, not really. But I read critiques of it."

"Stacy, you're very smart, but you're also a big fat phony."

"But he was the town fool, wasn't he?" she said.

"That's close enough."

She stood up and without warning pulled her T-shirt up over her head and tossed it over the back of the chair. "I'm going to take a shower and go to bed," she announced.

She wasn't wearing a bra and her nipples bounced as she walked to the bathroom in her jeans. Her breasts were not much more than slight swells on her chest with the kind of knobby nipples girls get in puberty when they first start to develop. Later, when she came out of the shower, he had his back to her and was pretending to be asleep. But with her in the bed beside his bed, sleep didn't come easily.

† † †

In the morning—it was close to noon—they were sitting in their respective beds smoking a wake-up cigarette, when she said, "We have to talk, Bart. I want you to understand this God thing."

"I already understand. You're God, but you don't do miracles, and for some reason you had to work in a strip club. Can I ask you a personal question? Have you always been God, or is this a recent development in your life?"

"I've known it for as long as I can remember, but I tried not to think about it for a long time. Do you know how lonely it is to be a solitary consciousness in a total void? So I created all of this. I made a world so complex, it confuses even me. I've succeeded in my goal. Almost."

"So, you created me?"

"Yes. Not just you. All of this."

"Because you were lonely."

"That's the best I can describe it in terms you'd understand."

"Have you ever taken acid?'

"Bart, I created it."

"Ha! I mean it, baby, you've gotta take this show on the road. One hit of acid and I'm right there with you. But it's just a trip. You do know that, right? You can't keep walking around thinking that way."

"Bart, I'm not like Brenda."

"What?"

"I'm not like Brenda. You don't see me cutting holes in my dress, do you?"

Fuck. Jesus fuck. Fuck a fuckin duck. "What do you know about Brenda?" he said. She must have talked to Clance. He was the only other one there. Jesus fuck.

"She's not important right now. Right now, I'm scared."

"Of what?"

"I'm scared of what we have to do, Bart. The moment I walked into Zoey's living room, I knew you were the one."

"What one?"

"My apostle."

"Are you ready to make that ashtray float for me?"

"I already told you I don't do miracles."

"And why is that, exactly?"

"Get me another cigarette and I'll tell you."

He got up from the bed and picked up her purse from the desk and looked inside it, rummaging around. There was a lot of stuff in it, but he didn't see cigarettes. He wanted to dump the contents onto the desk, but he didn't feel he had the right. He decided not to mention to her the small card he found that said CustomDecals4U.com. It was covered with tiny ECCE HOMOs. So much for her "birthmarks." He was tempted to pull the decals out and wave them in her face, but he didn't want to drive her away. She was crazy, but he wanted her to stay. He decided to ignore the decals.

He found her Salems in a zippered pocket of her purse, the only item in that pocket. He made a mental note to buy a pack of unfiltered Luckies. He shook out a couple cigarettes from the pack, stuck one in his mouth, lit it, then passed it to her after taking a puff. Then he tore the filter off the other one, tossed the filter into the waste basket, stuck the other end between his lips and lit it for himself.

"I'm waiting," he said.

"Look," she said, "Jesus tried the miracle thing and it was a disaster."

"What disaster? It's two thousand years later and he's still got a bigger fan club than Oprah."

"Yes, but the miracles scared people. Everybody thinks they want to see miracles, but miracles send the wrong message."

"And that message would be … ?"

"That God's powerful and majestic and worthy of praise and, quite frankly, scary as shit. But that's not the message I'm trying to convey."

"And your message is … ?"

"I'm sorry."

"You're sorry?"

"I want to tell people I'm sorry. And if I could do anything about their pain, I would. But this is the best I can do. And also … there's no heaven, no hell, it's just me and this world I've created, and that's it."

"That's your message?"

"It is what it is."

"You're mentally ill. You have to know that."

"Make love to me."

"Show me a miracle first."

"Then you'll make love to me?"

"Just show me a fuckin' miracle."

"Okay, one miracle." She picked up the deck of cards from Bart's stuff on the bedside table. "Pick a card," she said, fanning the deck.

"You're showing me a card trick?"

"Pick a card."

He picked a card and looked at it. Three of spades. "Jesus never would have stooped to this."

"Jesus never would have offered you a blowjob either. Now put the card back in the deck, shuffle the cards, and put the deck down on the bed."

He picked up the deck and flung it onto the floor with enough force to cause cards to skid and tumble and fly every which way over the grimy worn carpet. "That's my trick," he said. "Fifty-two-card pick-up."

She sighed. "Please," she said. "Just hold me."

He stood there for a moment, resisting, then he sat down on her bed stiffly and put his arms around her.

She drew him down onto the mattress and nuzzled her face into his neck. "I just want you to like me," she said.

She was naked under her T-shirt. He felt a surge of blood to his dick and it jumped against her body. It happened so fast it startled him. All he was wearing was a T-shirt and boxer shorts. He started to pull back from her, but she rolled to face him and put her hands on the small of his back, pulling him tight against her.

His dick was stiffening, creeping up against her belly.

She loosened her hug and started to reach for it.

He twisted away from her and caught her hand in his.

"Just get dressed," he said.

He got off the bed and picked his jeans up off the chair and started to pull them on. His dick was still hard as a crowbar inside his boxer shorts and it wasn't going to tuck into his jeans very easily. He jammed it in sideways and zipped up.

That got a laugh out of her. "You can't walk around like that!" she said.

"Just get your clothes on," he said in a calm voice, the way one would talk to a mental patient. "We're late. Clance said noon."

He sat down on the edge of his bed and started pulling his boots on.

She came over and plopped down next to him and put an arm around his shoulder buddy-buddy-like. "Don't go all weird on me, okay?" she said. "We're going to have sex, but we can take it slow. I'll wait until you're ready."

"Don't hold your breath. I haven't had sex with a woman in eight years." Hey, why not tell the truth?

"I know that."

"I'm impotent, okay? Don't take it personally. It has nothing to do with you."

"It's obviously not physiological."

"Look, I don't have time for these games right now. I have to get over to Clance's. I'm here for a job. Get your clothes on."

She stood up and grabbed the panties she'd worn the previous day from the foot of her bed and pulled them on. "We have to go shopping after your meeting," she said. "I have to buy some clothes."

He wasn't angry with her at this point, though he was pissed at himself for getting involved with another psychiatric case when he was here to make some money. But, Jesus, it felt good to hold her. He had no idea where this thing was going. The reddleman never got past the hand-holding stage. Eustacia Vye was not supposed to be running around his room in thong panties.

THIRTY-ONE

"BART, I'M LOSING my patience. I'm trying to help you out here, but you're not giving me anything. When this thing comes to trial, they're going to throw the book at you."

"Got nothing on me."

"We know a lot more than you think, Bart."

"Know where Stacy is?"

"Why don't you give me some names and I might be more willing to see what I can find out about her?"

"Fuck off."

"You think you're being honorable protecting the people behind this thing? You know they're all going to turn on you when they're given half a chance. I'm giving you first shot. Just between you and me. No one has to know about this. I'm just looking for a lead. The tape recorder's off. You have full deniability. If you cooperate, I can work a deal for you. Just some names."

"No one else involved … Just me."

"I don't believe that, Bart. Not for one second. We've found two-hundred forty-one websites connected to this event you staged."

"No shit? Really? Two-hundred forty-one?"

"I'm trying to get a handle on the mob that caused the disturbance, specifically, the fanatics dressed in black who were not part of the Gay Pride organization or the Slutwalk crowd. We got the guy with the gun. He was dressed in black and had a number of devil tattoos on his arms just like yours. All accounts point to you being the ring leader of this mob."

"Look, Dorsett ... Try to understand ... You have no leverage ... Not sure you're even real ... I never talk to my hallucinations."

"Believe me, Bart, you're not hallucinating now."

"Don't mean that as a put-down ... Just don't know what's real ... Pretty soon I'll be snoozing ... You'll be sittin' in your car ... Scarfing down Krispy Kremes ... That's destiny."

"Bart, I can help you."

"Horseshit."

"If I can get you information on Stacy's whereabouts, will you talk?"

"Want more than that ... "

"How about information on her condition and maybe get a message to her? Would that do it?"

"Yes."

"You'll talk?"

"Yes."

"I'll see what I can do. Now don't go to sleep. I'll be right back."

THIRTY-TWO

HE PULLED ON his jeans, keeping an eye on the cop in case he started to move. He didn't know if Stacy had actually saved his life, because he didn't know if the cop was really planning to shoot him or just trying to scare the shit out of him. But that sealed it for him with Stacy. She might have gotten him into this mess, but she damn well did what she had to do to get him out of it. He would die for this girl if it ever came to that.

By the time she got out of the car and came over to him, his jeans were on and he was sitting in the dirt pulling his boots on.

She was crying. "He was going to kill you!"

Bart stood up. "I just hope he doesn't wake up while I'm trying to get his head off my bike."

"Why did he make you take your pants off?" she said, wiping away tears with her forearm.

He heard a small laugh come out of him. "It's a long story," he said. "I'll tell you what happened when we get to Vegas."

She went up to him and put her arms around him. He held her for a moment.

"I thought I was a goner, Stacy. I owe you one. A big one."

He let go of her and walked over to where the cop was sprawled with his head on the valve cover. That's when he noticed the cop's eyes were wide open and seeing nothing. It took his breath away.

He heard Stacy come up behind. She let out a cry.

"I was just trying to stop him," she said. Her body started shaking.

She knelt down in the dust beside the dead man and cradled his head in her arms. "I'm sorry, I'm sorry," she said, moaning softly. "I didn't mean to—"

Bart watched her, trying to take in what had happened. The sky was starting to lighten to gray in the east. He thought about the blood on his bike, the blood that was now on Stacy's arms and her hands, her jeans.

"We've got to get the fuck out of here," he said.

In grabbing the cop's arm to pull him away from the bike, Bart noticed that the gun was still firmly in his hand. He decided to leave it there, but moved it aside while pulling the body, so that the barrel wasn't pointing at him. The cop's head dropped to the dirt like a rock and the sound made Bart sway on his feet. A lot of blood had come out of the back of the cop's head and was still draining. He'd caught the knuckle perfectly and cracked his skull. Bart wondered where the nearest service station was where he could rinse the blood off his engine.

"Why did he have to attack you?" Stacy asked, tears streaming down her face. "Why did this have to happen?"

"No time for that now. He's dead and we have to get out of here."

"What if he has someone waiting for him? Someone who loves him?"

"You have to let it go, okay? There's nothing we can do. They'll be out here looking for him any time now. It's our word versus a dead cop." He looked around, trying to think. "Dust your hands off in the dirt, then go wipe your fingerprints off the steering wheel and door handle and anything else you may have touched on the car. They'll have a CSI team out here scouring this place for clues. Cut the engine, but leave the lights on for now. I've got to find my picking tools and anything else I dropped. And I've got to get this other cuff off my wrist. Jesus."

He was able to find every tool he'd dropped in the dirt, thanks to those belt-stud handles. His head was throbbing. He got the other cuff off his wrist in less than a minute while Stacy looked around the area for any other signs that they'd been there. When she came back she wasn't crying anymore.

"I don't see any footprints," she said dully. "I don't even see tire tracks from the car or bike. It's really hard-packed dirt out here."

"Believe me, there's tracks, there's footprints, god knows what else, but we can't do anything about that." Bart hooked the cop's handcuffs back onto his belt, then wiped them off with the tail of his shirt. "Go cut the headlights now," he said. "And shut the door so the interior light goes out. And don't get anymore prints on anything."

He got his bike uprighted. By now, he was sure the cop had never radioed for assistance. Way too much time had passed. He had to get them rolling and most of all off the fucking Extraterrestrial Highway. He kicked the engine to life as soon as Stacy got back to him.

"Do you want this?" she said. She was holding a small square of paper with some numbers on it.

"What is it?"

"It was on the clipboard on his dash," she said. "It's the only page he had anything written on."

Then he recognized what it was—his bike's plate number.

"I definitely want that," he said, taking it from her and putting it in his mouth, chewing it vigorously. "Get on."

"There's something else I have to show you," she said. She put both hands into her jacket pockets, then pulled them out.

It looked like she had balls of gray fuzz in each fist.

"What is it?" he said, swallowing the paper wad.

"They're kittens."

"Kittens? Are they alive?"

"Of course they're alive," she said. "Do you think I'd carry dead kittens around?"

"Where'd you get them? They're hardly bigger than mice."

"I don't know if they'll live," she said. "But they're going to have to live without their mother because that bastard just shot her out there."

"Just leave 'em. They can't be more than a week old, if that. Their eyes aren't even open. They can't survive without their mother's milk."

"We'll get them some milk when we get to Vegas. We have to take care of them, Bart."

"Whatever. Just stuff the kitty-cats back in your pockets and get on the bike. Why would he shoot a cat?"

"Because he was very fucked-up," she said.

"Well, he's no longer fucked up. He's just dead."

She climbed on. He felt her arms go around his chest, her thighs hugging his hips. "Now hold on tight, because I'm heading back to the highway with my lights off. It's going to be a bumpy ride." He glanced back at her. "Where's your helmet?"

She made a face. "Somewhere out there," she said.

"The last thing we need is to get pulled over for you not having a helmet on," he said. "And I'm sure your prints are on it, as well as mine. How far out there?"

"Way out there. At least a half-mile, maybe more."

"Then we'll have to risk leaving it. We've got to get the fuck out of here. Let's book."

And with that, they fled the scene of the crime.

PART TWO:

On the Lam

THIRTY-THREE

WHEN THEY ARRIVED in Vegas, they got a room at a cheap motel on the outskirts of town near the Motor Speedway. Bart paid in cash and never showed his ID. He couldn't sleep and he sensed that Stacy was awake, but they didn't talk. A cop was lying dead in the desert and the hard knot on the top of his skull was the size of a pigeon egg. He had no aspirin. The front desk had no aspirin. And although he knew a 24-hour convenience store was within minutes of their motel, he was afraid to leave the safety of their room.

He sat up in the bed, propped against his pillow, chain-smoking, thinking about Stacy's helmet out there, somewhere. He wondered how far from the scene she'd left it. Half a mile? If it was far enough away, there was a chance they wouldn't find it. Shit. He knew they'd find it.

The combination heater/air-conditioner that ran along the floor beneath the bedroom window made a rattling sound every time the fan started and a loud clunking sound every time it turned itself off.

At one point, after Stacy's breathing evened out and he thought she'd probably fallen asleep, he turned on his bedside lamp and saw that the kittens she had bundled up in a blanket beside her had stopped squirming and purring. He picked up a kitten. It was dead. The body was limp and lifeless. He tried shaking it gently, tapping the chest. The head just rolled back, mouth open, dead. He carefully picked up the other kitten from the makeshift nest. Also dead.

He wrapped both kittens in a T-shirt and placed the bundle near the door, hoping Stacy wouldn't be too upset when she awoke. He considered taking their bodies down to the dumpster and disposing of them forthwith, but decided against it. Better to let her deal with them however she saw fit. He imagined she'd insist on a burial with some kind of ceremony. She'd place flowers atop their graves.

Later, when he heard Stacy stir, he made two cups of coffee with the cheap drip coffee maker next to the bathroom sink.

When he returned to the bedroom with the coffee, she was sitting up in the bed, holding her face in her hands.

He put her cup of coffee on the nightstand beside her.

"The kittens?" she said between her fingers, still not looking up.

"Gone," he said. "I wrapped them in a T-shirt. They're by the door."

She nodded, but her face was still in her hands.

He went around the bed and sat down on the other side. He sipped his coffee, but he was already wired, his head buzzing.

"We have to get new IDs," he said. "Both of us."

"Okay."

"Your 'Wanted' poster's on a milk carton. You've been living with me for the past four months. If they're looking for you, they're looking for me. People at that bookstore knew you were living with me. A lot of people knew that. I'll call Clance later and see if there's any heat coming down on you from that picture. And you should call Zoey about the IDs. We'll go shopping later and get some different clothes. We both have to change our looks."

The air conditioner fan kicked on with a noisy rattle and Bart threw one of his boots at it. It immediately quieted down.

"I knew you'd fix it," she said.

"And how did you know that? I didn't know I would fix it. I was just pissed off at the racket the damn thing was making." He heard his voice getting loud. "You have some kind of fantasy that I'm going to take care of you. But I can't even take care of myself. If I knew how to fix crazy, I would've fixed myself a long time ago."

"I'm not looking for a therapist, Bart."

"So why are you with me?"

"I already told you. I need an apostle."

"Oh, just fucking terrific, the God crap again. Well, how about this, Stacy? I mean, I'm just curious … If you're God, why don't you just make everything better? Why don't you bring that cop back to life and make everyone forget what happened?"

"I can't make it any better. You change one piece and it all goes completely haywire someplace else. This is the best I can do."

"So, it's not that God's indifferent … just incompetent?"

"I understand why you're angry."

"You don't understand shit about me."

"I do understand and I didn't mean for it to be so hard, but now the world is on its own, just going where it goes."

"So you're the one that arranged for the death of that cop, not to mention my pygmy DNA, and now you're apologizing?"

"You're not a pygmy; you're just short. But, yes, I'm responsible for both death and pygmies."

"So you admit you're responsible for all the misery in the world? All the people with deformities and diseases and horrible injuries and amputations. You're responsible for all this? You're the reason I've got a dick that doesn't work? And you're telling me you're sorry?"

"Your dick works fine, Bart, and yes, I'm sorry for your pain and everyone's pain and I'm sorry for that cop last night. Do you think people will forgive me?"

"People?"

"Will *you* forgive me?"

"Stacy, if I believed for one second that you were ultimately responsible for all the shit in my life … I don't know what I'd do, but I don't think forgiveness would be at the top of my list."

"But what about the good stuff? There's lots of good in the world."

"For an awful lot of people, not enough."

"So, you don't think people will forgive me?"

"You'll get the same reception Jesus got."

"I hated being Jesus."

"So, now you were Jesus in a past life?"

"There's no real past. Time's an illusion I created. Jesus was the

Third Person of the Blessed Trinity. I'm the Fourth Person of the Blessed Quad."

"Baby, you're killing me. Don't start telling me stories about what life was like when you were Jesus! Not right now, okay?"

"They didn't even write about the best stuff. They couldn't comprehend the best stuff. People just see and hear what they want to see and hear."

"Will you ever get off this God kick?"

"How can I?"

"Oh, fuck it. Let's go for a ride."

"Where?"

"Into the wind. We gotta blow this craziness away. No helmets. I'm telling you, baby, the wind is God. The wind forgives your sins, rights your wrongs. Just let yourself feel it."

† † †

They had been in Vegas for four days. They spent most of their time in the motel room, sporadically watching TV and reading. The room was small and dark, with fake wood paneling on three walls and a scuffed brown carpet. Bart didn't think it would be safe to be seen until they both had new IDs and a different look. Stacy spent a lot of time on her laptop and almost as much time texting on her cell phone. Bart made fast-food runs, on foot, as necessary. They avoided restaurants. They made a few trips to buy clothes, hair dye, and a couple dozen used books on a variety of subjects so they wouldn't go stir crazy. Still, those walls were closing in on him.

It was getting near eleven p.m. and he and Stacy were lying on their backs on the bed in their room, wearing T-shirts, socks, and underwear, staring at the ceiling and sharing a cigarette. Bart was planning on going to the MGM Grand in a few hours to try out his yuppie disguise and look for hole-card opportunities when the grave-shift dealers came on. Clance was planning to be in town within the next few weeks with their crew and Bart wanted to have some flashers lined up and ready to go.

The television was on, though they weren't watching it. The eleven o'clock news opened with a story that got them to prop themselves up on their elbows to watch:

"Another Area Fifty-One mystery! The Nevada Highway Patrol has reported that one of its officers, thirty-eight-year-old Trooper John Wade Newhouse, was slain in the line of duty last week. Missing for three days, his body was discovered yesterday morning in the desert about three miles from Highway Three-Seventy-Five near the restricted territory of Area Fifty-One. That particular stretch of highway is known as the Extraterrestrial Highway, due to the hundreds of reported UFO sightings in that region since the nineteen-fifties. Officer Newhouse's patrol car was close to his body.

"The Fox News team is going live right now to the Nevada Highway Patrol's southern command office in Las Vegas. Our own Miles Sherwood is on the scene with NHP spokesman Lieutenant Marvin Welter."

"Lieutenant, what can you tell us about Officer Newhouse's death?"

"We are investigating it as a homicide. Officer Newhouse died from blunt-force trauma to the head approximately seventy-two hours prior to our finding him. The autopsy also showed fractures in both legs. We do not know why he was near Area Fifty-One. Until we complete our investigation, we have no further comment."

"Back to you, Bob."

"We take you now to the little town of Rachel, Nevada, where our own Stephanie Ng is on the scene with Jacqueline Mattison, a spokesperson for an organization that calls itself 'They Are Real,' a group that has been investigating UFO activity in the region for more than thirty years."

"Thank you, Bob. Ms. Mattison, what can you tell

us about the mysterious death of this state trooper near Area Fifty-One?"

"We believe the NHP is purposely withholding facts in this case, Stephanie. In our opinion, this was clearly another alien abduction, and the first such abduction we know of that has resulted in a death. We are very concerned about this. We've had a rash of reports of UFO activity in Area Fifty-One in the past six months, and we've been waiting for something like this to happen."

"After the Highway Patrol found the body, how did you learn about it, Ms. Mattison, since the NHP blocked access to it?"

"The Highway Patrol did not find the body. We discovered Officer Newhouse's vehicle out there yesterday during one of our regular telescopic sweeps of the area and we contacted the NHP and informed them that there appeared to be a body lying close by the vehicle. They would not allow us into the area. But we spoke with a number of the NHP officers who went to the scene to investigate and their statements to us this morning are highly suspicious and indicative of another government cover-up."

"Back to you, Bob."

"We're returning now to Miles Sherwood who is still with Lieutenant Welter in Las Vegas."

"Thank you, Bob.

"Lieutenant, we've learned that Officer Newhouse had been relieved of active duty twice in the past year for psychiatric reasons. Do you think that has any bearing on this case?"

"If our staff physician cleared him, obviously we felt he was mentally fit for duty. Officer Newhouse had simply been undergoing stress due to personal problems. He was a fine trooper with an excellent record."

"Back to you, Bob."

Bart and Stacy turned their heads in unison to look at each other.

"Maybe the cops know more than they're saying," Bart said. "They do that kind of stuff."

His cell phone rang. It was plugged into the wall, recharging on the floor in the corner of the room. It was the first time it had rung since they'd left Reno, and he was afraid to answer it. He knew it could be Clance. The caller ID was blocked. Clance's caller ID was always blocked. He answered.

"Oh, hey, Zoey," he said, thinking finally, *my new ID*. "When are you coming back to Vegas?"

"Let me talk to her!" Stacy said. She grabbed for the phone.

Bart slapped her hand away and said, "Wait!"

They both heard the anger in his voice.

She slumped down onto the bed. He'd never struck her like that before.

THIRTY-FOUR

"DORSETT? YOU STILL with me?"

"I'm right here, Bart."

"What'd the doc say?"

"They're getting some information on Stacy. I don't have anything yet."

"Have a question for you, Dorsett."

"You're turning the tables on me?"

"Good cop, bad cop … What do you usually play?"

"Come again?"

"Good cop or bad cop?"

"Bad cop."

"I thought so … You're okay, Dorsett … It can't still be Wednesday … can it?"

"It most certainly can and is."

"You been here all day?"

"I've been here almost two hours, but it seems like all day. Are you going to answer some questions for me now?"

"Not yet … First, Stacy."

"There's a baseball game on. The Angels versus the Mariners. Do you want to listen to it?"

"No."

"Tell me about Satanism. Is it something you really believe in or just something you do for shock value?"

"Tell me about bein' a cop … Somethin' you believe in? Or just somethin' you do because ... you want people to think you're a dick?"

"I'm trying to be friendly here, Bart. Anybody ever tell you you have a nasty attitude?"

THIRTY-FIVE

HE'D BEEN WEARING the outlaw-biker uniform for so long, he thought it was an intrinsic part of his nature, like his age or nationality. He'd simply thought of himself biologically as a biker life form.

No longer.

Bart Black was transforming himself into a yuppie nerd. He'd purchased a stack of polo shirts and a few pairs of khaki slacks. He'd ditched his boots and now wore rubber-soled brown loafers. Stacy had cut his hair. He'd shaved his beard and regretted not leaving the mustache, so immediately began regrowing the hair above his lip. His cheeks and neck were unnaturally white where his beard had been. He tried to avoid looking in the mirror. He didn't like the person he saw.

Meanwhile, Stacy was going Goth. She'd dyed her hair jet black and got it chopped into Bettie-Page-style bangs. For some reason beyond Bart's comprehension, she started sticking a large red feather in her hair, which he told her made her look like a punk Indian. She, of course, corrected him.

"Punk Native American."

She took to painting her nails black and she favored heavy black eye-liner with a fire-engine-red rouge to shade her eyelids, possibly to match the feather. She did a thirty-minute shop at Hot Topic and came out with bags full of black skirts, jeans, and tops, most decorated with silver or chrome studs and chains.

After ten days in the motel, it was finally the day of Zoey's return to Las Vegas. As they were picking out the outfits they'd put on for their new fake ID, Stacy said, "I've been thinking of talking to Clance. Do you think he'd understand where I'm coming from?"

"Probably," Bart said, cutting the tag off of a polo shirt with nail clippers. "Clance is smart. He ran away from home every other week when he was a kid. I didn't know him then. He told me his father used to beat the crap out of him just for kicks."

"No, I don't mean that. I mean about being God and telling people I'm sorry."

He took a deep breath. "Look, I never talked religion with him, but I think it's fair to say he won't give a rat's ass for your theories. He worships Harleys. Heaven is the wind in your armpits."

"So you don't give a rat's ass for what you call my theories?"

"I think I've stated my opinion clearly. Did you ever talk to Zoey about it?"

"She just humored me. But I have other followers," she said.

"You have followers?" he said with a laugh. "Who are they?"

"On my blogs, lots of them. You'd be surprised. Also, some of the dancers I worked with in San Francisco and Sunnyvale."

"You told these followers you were God?"

"Sure. And I told them I was sorry. Lots of them understood. That's why I think Clance might understand, and maybe some of the other guys on the team. They're disaffiliated. They're outsiders."

"I doubt there's a single dancer you talked to who really believes you're God. As for Clance and the team, baby, these are not religious people. They're not going to join some dopey cult. Gamblers worship logic, the odds. They worship math. Clance will advise me very strongly to disassociate myself from you a.s.a.p., if for no other reason than the r.o.r."

"What's r.o.r.?"

"Risk of ruin. It's a gambler's term. It means your likelihood of tapping out. Placing your case bet and losing. Clance would not see a high probability of success in my having anything to do with you at this point."

"I like Clance. Why would he think that?"

"Because you're a negative expectation bet. If I stay with you, I'm going down. The only reason I'm sticking with you is that I know life itself is a negative expectation bet. Trying to beat death is like trying to use a system to beat craps. If you stay in the game, you'll go broke."

"But you can beat craps if you cheat," she said. "Use loaded dice."

"Gimme a break, Stacy. Can you load the dice of life?" He made no attempt to hide the sarcasm in his voice.

"Sure," she said with a gleam of confidence in her eyes. "And if you bet the pass line when I'm shooting, you can't lose. You gotta have faith in me, Bart."

He sat down on the edge of his bed. The springs squeaked. Again he wondered if she had any awareness of the depth of their dilemma. "Look, Stacy. I know you're way ahead of most sixteen-year-olds in brains. You're way ahead of most everyone in brains. And you're probably quite a bit beyond anyone your age in life experience. But you're still sixteen and you're so smart, you should be in school figuring out what you want to do with your life. You can do anything you want."

"I know what I want," she said. "I want to tell people I'm sorry, and then I want a family."

"Kids? You want kids? Do I look like father material?"

"I didn't say I wanted kids. I said I wanted a family."

"I don't know what to do, Stacy. I don't want to abandon you, because you're too crazy to survive on your own. But I'm too old for you and you are fucking jailbait. Oh, yes, and we murdered a cop and left a fuckton of clues and I'm trying to change my name and what I look like. This is the worst dilemma of my life and it's all because of you. What the hell happened to you anyway? Why did you run away from home? What the fuck kind of parents did you have?"

She ignored his questions and opened her laptop and started typing.

† † †

Zoey was waiting for them in the lobby at Turnberry 3, one of the upscale high-rises on Paradise Road. After hugging Stacy and giving Bart a cold look, she led them through the foyer to the elevators, marveling at how different they both looked since she'd last seen them. They were in full regalia—the yuppie nerd, Charles Boles, and his Gothic-punk girlfriend, Maggie.

Zoey was wearing an ornate Christian Audigier T-shirt and jeans. Her twenty-second-floor flat was ultra-modern, with high ceilings, mirrored wall sconces, long, low-slung, sectional sofas, and black end-tables that matched the media console that dominated the far wall. An abstract sculpture against the wall next to the hallway appeared to have been constructed of plumber's pipes.

"Is this a one-bedroom?" Bart asked before they'd even sat down.

"Two," she said. "Actually three, but one of the bedrooms is being used as a storage room by my friend Marcos. He owns this place. I'm just subletting. He's in Italy right now and I'm hoping he stays there a long time. I like it here, despite the crappy view."

Bart walked over to the picture window where Stacy was gazing out at the unfortunate view of the Fontainebleau hotel's unfinished parking-lot structure.

"Drinks?" Zoey asked. "I've got O.J., Red Bull, ginseng tea, Drambuie … "

"Do you have a room for Stacy?" Bart asked, turning from the window. Might as well get straight to the point.

"Sure."

"Hey!" Stacy protested. "I don't need a place to stay! We're going to get our own place, Bart!"

He looked at her. "You're sixteen," he said flatly. "I can't live with you."

"Bart! No!" She came up close to him. "You can't just dump me like this!"

"I'm not dumping you, baby. Really. I'm just finding you a place to live where you'll be safe."

"Well, fuck you!"

Zoey put her arm around Stacy. "It's okay, Stace. You'll be better off with me for now. Bart's right."

Stacy twisted away from her. "You planned this," she said. "You didn't even tell me. You could at least have talked to me about it." Her eyes darted back and forth between Bart and Zoey.

"Cool your jets," Bart said as calmly as he could. "We're talking about it now."

"Really, Stace," Zoey said.

"You guys think you're running this show," Stacy said. "But you're not running my life. I don't have to put up with this." She calmly walked to the door and looked at Bart. "I'm taking a cab back to the motel. I'll get a room of my own. I'm taking my money, Bart. It's been nice knowing you."

"Stop and think, Stace," Zoey said. "It really is safer for you to stay here. You'll have your own room. Look how comfortable this place is. I'll make you a new ID and you can get something else going here. This'll be a good setup for you."

Stacy let Zoey speak, but she never took her eyes off Bart. "I thought you had feelings for me," she said. "You're supposed to be my protector. You're going to abandon me as soon as things get tough?"

"I'm not abandoning you. You'll be safer here, safer than you could possibly be with me."

"I thought you knew me. You don't know me at all."

Bart looked at Zoey. "Can I have a few minutes here?" he said.

Zoey put her hands up as if to say, "Say no more," and quickly exited the room.

"You scare me," Bart said. "This God trip you're on. I'm not going to play along with it. You're mentally ill. I'm worried about you. You don't seem to understand how much trouble we could be in."

She looked down at the floor. He put his hand on her shoulder and she looked up at him again. "I love you," he said. "Okay? I'm saying it. Does that count for anything?"

He watched her face soften. Her breathing slowed. She relaxed her shoulders, then said, "Okay, I'll stay here."

"You'll be safe here, baby. You can't be safe with me. This is the best I can do right now."

"Zoey!" Stacy called loudly.

Zoey came running back into the room.

"Is it really okay if I stay here?"

"It's fine, Stace. I'll be glad to have you. C'mon, I'll get you some towels and stuff. We can get your clothes from the motel tomorrow."

Bart went back to the living room and flopped down onto the sofa. He stretched his legs out in front of him, laid his head back, and closed his eyes. He sat there a long time. He could hear Zoey and Stacy talking in another room, further away, then he heard the shower running.

It was just starting to hit him that the Stacy episode of his life would soon be over.

Zoey came into the living room.

"I still need a new ID," he said.

"I know. Do you want to do it now? I'll make you a Michigan driver's license."

"How about a Nevada license?"

"Not a good idea. The IDs look good, but they're not perfect. You don't want to try and pass off a Nevada license in Nevada. And California's too close. Same problem. I can do Michigan or Ohio, Indiana … What name do you want on it?"

"Charles Boles."

She led him into a room cluttered with boxes stacked on chairs, a bicycle leaning up against a bookcase, a mattress standing against one wall, where she had a camera set up in front of a white screen.

"Sit on that stool and look at the red dot," she said. "And how about a smile; you look half-dead."

She flashed a photo and told him she'd have the ID in a day or two. "You're now a resident of Saginaw, Michigan," she said.

When they got back to the living room, he could still hear the shower running. He walked to the door.

"I can finish your tattoo while I'm here," he said. "I brought my gear."

"Forget it. I already have an appointment at Hart and Huntington."

"What the hell is Hart and Huntington?"

"It's a tattoo parlor at the Hard Rock. They said they could fill in the colors in thirty minutes."

"Maybe for a hack job."

"They do nice work. Go look at their stuff."

"They can't color it the way I'd color it. Do you want a work of art on your ass or a fucking cartoon?"

"Probably not a good idea for you to be coming around, don't you think?"

He nodded and put his hand on the doorknob. He heard the water stop running. "She said you were going to get her a job in a Pahrump whorehouse. Is that true?"

"It's true I told her that. I thought it would scare her into going back home, going back to school, doing something with her life. She'd never be able to get a sheriff's card to work in a brothel."

"I thought your IDs looked perfect."

"How they look is one thing, but when they run the background check on her, it won't hold up."

He let that sink in for a moment, then he nodded toward the pipe sculpture. "You ought to call building maintenance to report a plumbing problem. That shit's supposed to be on the other side of the wall."

He opened the door and stepped through it. Walking out was like wrenching his feet out of quicksand.

They both listened for a moment. The blow dryer started.

Zoey said, "You know, girls can marry at sixteen in this state with parental approval."

"Like that's about to happen … You lived with her. She's not only sixteen, she's living in fantasyland. She's not ready to get married to anyone. I care about her because she has guts and she doesn't give a shit what most people think of her. I admire her and I don't have admiration for very many humans on this planet. But that's not a reason to marry someone. Did she tell you she was God?"

"I think she got that out of some book she read on Vedantic Hinduism. She's read a lot about religion. It's kind of a central belief of some Hindu mystics."

The blow dryer stopped.

He shook his head and started walking away, then said over his shoulder, "I'll call you to work out a place where you can pass me the ID."

"See ya," said Zoey, as the door closed behind him.

He had one thought in mind: He had to get on his bike and hit the road, let the wind have its way with him.

† † †

The next day, Bart stayed away from the motel during the time when Zoey and Stacy were supposed to stop by for Stacy's things. When he got back to the motel, he was surprised to see they'd removed every trace of her stay. Her dirty coffee cup from the previous morning had disappeared from the nightstand. Her long black hairs had been cleaned from the tub and sink. He went immediately to look for a holey sock she'd tossed into the back of the closet a week earlier, but even that had been picked up. It looked like they'd taken some Windex and rags and gone over all of the fixtures in the room. The only thing left was the smell of her skin on the sheets.

He turned on the TV and turned it off again. He walked to the window and looked out at the broken asphalt parking lot where his bike was parked between two pickups, as hidden from the street as possible.

Then he called Clance. "I've got eight dealers lined up," Bart said. "When are you coming down?"

"Day after tomorrow. Me and Debbie have a couple things to wrap up here ... The cops are looking for you and Stacy now."

"Did they question you?"

"Not yet. Somebody in the building told me a couple cops knocked on my door yesterday when we were out, but I don't know that I can avoid them for two more days. Debbie went over to the bookstore last week and casually asked about Stacy. The manager told her she's a runaway and the cops were looking for her and her skuzzy motorcycle-bum boyfriend. I assume that's you. Debbie just acted dumb, like she didn't know you and she didn't really know Stacy that well. But she found out it was the bookstore clerk who called the cops. I suspect the cops questioned people at your apartment, since the bookstore had Stacy's address."

"Well, the apartment was in my name, so they know who I am."

"I told you ya shoulda cut her loose, man."

"I did."

"Really?"

"She's back living with Zoey now."

"No shit?"

"How many of our crew are coming to Vegas?"

"Six of us. Me and Debbie, Jimmie, Johnny, Sam, and Lisa. Four of the other guys are coming out later. Plus, I got us an investor. Wally's gonna put some serious money behind us. Mid-six figures. How come you only have eight dealers? You've been there two weeks."

"Hey, I've got a lot more than eight. Maybe a hundred and eight. Most of them we can't play. It's a fucking hole-card battlefield out here. At least three other teams and lots of rogue players are fighting over the same dealers, trying to lock up tables, picking off each others' signals. I've got eight dealers I don't think any of them know about yet and that's a miracle. One team of Asian kids is just running wild. It's a pretty nasty atmosphere. Barry's here with his boys."

"I knew it! Have they seen you yet?"

"I changed my look pretty radically. The beard's history. I'm sure they haven't recognized me. But they're right in the middle of it. They almost got into a fight with the Asians a few nights ago."

"In the casino? Which one?"

"Luxor. Out in the parking lot. Nothing happened … just an argument. Lots of fuck-yous. I've got to warn you, man, you're coming into a war zone. Tell the guys to wear body armor."

"Yeah, right. I'll see you in two days."

"Have a good one."

The room's silence got to him again. He picked up the newspaper he'd bought on the way home. He hadn't even noticed the front page story that filled the bottom half of the page:

Slain NHP Officer Implicated in Drug Ring

According to information released yesterday by the
Nevada Highway Patrol, Trooper John Wade Newhouse,
whose body was found bludgeoned to death next to his
patrol car less than two miles from Area 51, appears to
have been involved in an illegal drug deal gone awry.

The case was cracked when a guard at the High
Desert State Prison near Indian Springs was arrested for
selling illicit drugs to inmates and named Officer Newhouse as one of his suppliers. A subsequent search of Officer Newhouse's residence turned up small quantities of
illicit drugs, including heroin, marijuana, cocaine, and
methamphetamine, and a large amount of cash.

According to an NHP source: "Officer Newhouse
apparently got involved in a drug deal with a motorcycle
gang. A helmet and motorcycle tracks were found at the
scene."

They found the helmet, he thought. They were probably looking for
him already. And if they weren't looking for him, they were going to
be harassing the bike clubs. They'd find someone to blame this on. It
was a cop, even if he was a bad cop. Somebody's head was going to roll.

In his mind's eye he saw his bike with the blood smeared on the
engine and Stacy with the blood on her hands, crying. He tossed the
paper onto the bed and headed off to scout more dealers.

† † †

Bart parked his bike on the lower level of the public garage behind
the MGM Grand. He took the escalator up to the MGM's cavernous
hotel lobby, crossing briskly into the gaming area. The MGM has multiple blackjack pits, spread widely throughout the huge casino. Most of
the open blackjack games were being dealt from six decks, immediately

identifiable by the dealing shoe on the right side of the table and the tall discard tray on the left. He scouted a few of the shoe games, but saw nothing that interested him.

He paused briefly at each of the open hand-held games, just long enough to ascertain whether or not the dealer might be a flasher. He found a couple possibilities, worth checking when he could get the right seat to play. He went into a men's room, scribbled some notes on the dealers, and revisited the tables in time to catch one of the seats he needed being vacated. The dealer turned out to be a fifty-percenter. Unfortunately, the square occupying the seat of the most promising dealer looked like he'd settled in for a marathon session. Bart hung out a bit longer, but made a quick exit when he saw a pit boss taking note of him. He headed back to the parking garage.

As he started down the aisle where he'd left his bike, he saw that a cop car was blocking the aisle right in front of it. Two Metro cops and two MGM Grand security guards were surrounding the bike, talking calmly.

He had to think fast. If he suddenly turned around and went the opposite direction, it would look suspicious. *Keep walking*, he said to himself. *Don't look at them. Normal pace.*

He passed right in front of them, then took the escalator at the end of the aisle to the second level of the garage. He felt sick. The cops had his bike! His treasured knucklehead chopper. His *life*.

He took a quick look back, tasting the exhaust fumes in the air. He saw one of the cops rushing down the aisle on the lower level toward the escalator.

"Jesus fuck!" he said through clenched teeth, dodging around cars to get to the stairwell that led to an exit to the street. Crunched for time, he ducked behind a van parked near the stairwell, and through the van's windows saw the cop was arriving at the top of the escalator. He looked around and a second cop joined him. They talked for a minute then one of the cops started walking toward the shop area.

He's going to look for me in the casino, Bart thought, barely breathing.

The other cop was still standing there, now talking into his walkie-talkie. Then he headed toward the up escalator that would bring him to the next level of the garage.

As soon as the cop disappeared, Bart stood up and hurried to the fire exit that led to the outside stairwell. He looked out and saw no cop cars on the street. The traffic on Tropicana was heavy, as usual. Across the street to the west, there was a line of cabs in front of Hooters casino. He stepped outside into the night air, took a deep breath and hit the street running.

When he was safely in the back seat of a cab and rolling east on Trop, he closed his eyes and said good-bye to his bike. His new look was already in danger. He'd have to get a warning to Stacy. But before he could call Zoey, he'd have to pick up a new phone, one of those throwaway jobs.

Why did the cops follow him? His disguise was so perfect. Every aspect of it was so unbiker, so the opposite of him. But he knew the answer. Of course, it was his height. It was the one aspect of his appearance he could do nothing about, his lifelong plague.

He spent little time in his room, just enough to pack his gear, wipe down the room, and catch another cab to another motel down the road. He'd have to keep moving. And now, he didn't even have the wind to console him. He'd lost his name, his identity, and now his bike. He didn't even know who he was anymore.

THIRTY-SIX

"I SAW YOUR mug shot today."

"Dorsett?"

"It was on a casino-surveillance flyer from Reno. You and some big Chinese dude. It said you were suspected of using a blackjack computer."

"That's bullshit ... Never used a computer ... Sore losers ... Damn ... Knew I pushed it too far ... Why the hell you looking at surveillance photos?"

"Just part of the investigation. Information comes forward."

"Have a confession to make, Dorsett."

"I'm all ears. Can I turn the tape on?"

Bart heard the sound of the tape recorder being clicked on.

"When I was seven years old ... tortured some worms."

He heard the tape recorder being clicked off.

"You're in luck," Dorsett said. "The statute of limitations has run out."

"Serious, Dorsett ... Set up a torture camp ... In my backyard ... After a hard rain ... Tortured 'em ... Impaled 'em on twigs ... Crushed 'em with stones ... Cruel ... Heartless ... Disgusts me now ... Never told anyone before ... Had nightmares about worms ... For years."

"Why'd you do it?"

"Don't know ... Pretty fucked up ... Lotta stress ... Some kinda power trip ... Stopped having those dreams long time ago ... But now they're back ... Just one Saturday morning in my miserable childhood

… Worms been plaguing me ever since … Is the nurse still here?"

"She's here. She's always here."

"Why are you here, Dorsett? You stopped asking questions."

"Are you feeling ready to talk?"

"I'm waitin' for you … What about Stacy?"

"First, tell me what you were doing near Area Fifty-One on the night of July twenty-eighth."

Bart said nothing. He knew this was coming. He knew it!

"We've been on to you since day one, Bart. You know we found a helmet out there with Miss Thomas' prints all over it. We're pretty sure some of the partial prints on it are yours. Do you recall losing a helmet out there?"

Again, he made no response.

"And there's a service station attendant out on Highway Ninety-Three just north of Coyote Springs who remembers seeing a biker that night that he described as 'a pint-size bad guy' who stopped to use the water to wash his engine. No gas. Just spent a few minutes spraying water all over his engine. He remembered you because of the girl who went inside for a carton of milk. Described her as 'a knockout blonde bimbo.' Said it looked like she had dried blood on her jeans. He felt sure he could identify you if he saw you again. Do you always wash your engine at three a.m.? What was on your engine that you were so anxious to clean off?"

"Wasn't me," Bart said.

"Don't play games with me, Bart. Oh, yes, and there were some unusual tire tracks out there in the desert, you know those fat chopper tires some bikers like to put on their rear wheels? Our tire expert says they're from Avon's Venom series. You wouldn't happen to have a rear tire like that on your bike, would you? And where is your bike, by the way?"

"Fuck you."

"I just want you to clear up the mystery because we are stumped. We have to assume it was some kind of drug deal, because how else could you have lured that trooper out into the desert with no backup?

But what the hell happened? And who the hell was running around barefoot out there?"

"No comment."

"That's what I figured. That's why I stopped asking you questions. But did you really think you got away with it? How fuckin' crazy are you? You all but sign your name to it, then you drive an hour south to lead a parade. 'Til we got your bike, we thought you were in Mexico. I don't think you'll be remembered as a mastermind."

"Get screwed, Dogshit."

"Is that true about the worms, though? That's pretty sick."

"Just go away … "

THIRTY-SEVEN

"YOU CAN'T CALL me Bart anymore. The name's Boles, Charles Boles."

Bart and Clance were talking in Clance's hotel room, along with Debbie, Jimmy, Sam and Lisa.

"Nice disguise," Clance said. "Can I call you Chuck?"

"Make it Charlie. No, Chas. Chas sounds nerdier."

"You better be careful ridin' your bike, Chas. They're probably watching for your plate all over the state."

Bart was weighing the risk of telling Clance that his bike was already history. Would Clance think he was too dangerous for the team to play with? "Toss me a beer," Bart said.

Clance took a beer from the cooler at his feet and lobbed it underhand to Bart. "The cops came to talk to me day before yesterday," he said. "Asking about you and Stacy. I told them you left town weeks ago. Said I thought you went back to California. Asked me if you were living with her. Said as far as I knew she was just some girl you went out with once or twice. Said they wanted you for questioning. I don't think they had enough on you to get a warrant."

"Maybe we should go to Mississippi," Bart said. "How are the games in Biloxi?"

"Don't sweat it, man. Just get your bike tag changed. They'll be looking for a California plate."

He had to be straight with Clance. "Too late. They already impounded my bike."

"Are you shittin' me?"

"I wish."

"How're you gettin' around, man?"

"I'm not."

"Well, you definitely look different. I'm not sure I'd've recognized you if I passed you on the street. You gotta get a used car or something, Chas. Shit. Just what we need is your mug flashing on surveillance screens."

"You think they'd recognize me if I was sitting down?"

Clance considered it for a moment, but pretty quickly said, "No. We'll do fine. I've been itchin' to hit this town since Wally came on board with some serious cash. They just don't take big action well in Reno and you can forget about Mississippi. Not enough hand-helds. We're gonna make a mint here and if you're up for it, I'm up for it."

Bart was definitely up for it, but he wondered if Clance would be if he knew about the dead cop. Clance would probably advise him to get on the next bus to bumfuck and don't call when you get there. What the hell good could he do for Stacy here anyway? He hadn't even seen her since he'd pawned her off on Zoey. But he kept thinking that if he could just get a big enough score, he could whisk her away to some hidden paradise, where they could … what? She was sixteen fucking years old. He was an old man with a broke dick and no foreseeable future.

"Hey! Chas! Chas!"

Bart opened his eyes to find the whole team staring at him.

"You okay, man?" Clance asked. "You're spacin' out on me."

"Fuckin' headache," Bart said. "Sorry … I got the dealer lined up for a play tomorrow night," he changed the subject. "You're gonna love this, Clance. I found another index flasher. I can get her hole card about forty, maybe fifty percent, but I can top-card her almost every time. Sam, did you and Lisa get those signals down?"

Sam was a big guy in his forties with a full beard and a quick smile. "We're ready," he said.

"Speak for yourself," Lisa piped in. "I need some practice." She and Sam had been together since college. She was pretty and voluptuous, "built for distraction," was how Clance described her.

"Okay, we both need to brush up," Sam said. "But we're raring to go. Let's start practicing the signals right now."

"We're going to do it different this time," Bart said. "We're going to take over the table, steering to the max. Lisa, you're going to be sitting between Sam and Jimmy, playing table minimum. It's going to be your job to eat cards, or not, as necessary to make Jimmy's hand. You'll be making lots of idiotic plays. I'll be at third base, trying to bust the dealer. You gotta pay attention to me. I'll be signaling all of you how to play your hands."

"Now we're talkin'," Clance said. "The practice session is underway!"

† † †

With Wally's $300K cash infusion, and the substantial edge they had on this play, they should have been betting much more. But Clance wanted to play it safe on this first attempt with this new strategy. They were at a quarter-minimum table, spread out in their seats to keep the squares off the game, with Sam and Jimmy pretty much flat-betting a thousand per hand. Lisa was betting a single quarter and Bart was betting one black chip.

They were crushing the game, but Bart didn't like the feel of it. It was taking him too long to figure out the best play. The problem was he had to wait for the damn dealer to give up the index so he could signal the players on their decisions. The dealer was a small Asian woman with kewpie-doll make-up. She always flashed the top card, but wasted too much time futzing around in her check tray, keeping it neat and organized. With all of the players waiting for him to signal their plays, it just wasn't flowing like a regular blackjack game.

Sam had bought in for $10K, but now had multiple stacks of yellows in front of him. Jimmy was doing almost as well. Lisa was the perfect screwball girlfriend. She was making plays even Johnny the Jap had never attempted. Standing on soft fourteen. Hitting 16 against a 6. Hitting 17 against anything. Sam kept reprimanding her, but she'd just tell him to play his own damn cards and let her play hers like she wanted. She had the floor men and bosses in stitches.

Still, it didn't feel right.

An hour into the play, with Sam and Jimmy up about $65K between them, another suit entered the pit and he seemed to be burning the table seriously. Then Bart felt that the guy who had been watching the table from behind him for the past ten minutes wasn't just a square spectator. He'd been there too long and he knew something was going down. Sam signaled Bart that he had the same suspicion. Too much heat. But calling off the play was Bart's decision to make, and he hated abandoning such a lucrative opportunity.

That's when Stacy showed up. She was in her full Goth get-up, red feather and all. She just stood there behind Sam, watching the table. When she caught Bart's eye, she moved over to the next table and started pretending to watch that game, just a tourist, wandering through the pit, looking at the action. He knew none of his teammates at the table had recognized her in her Goth disguise. But Bart felt violated. What the hell was she doing?

He gave the signal to call off the play and pushed his small stack of chips toward the dealer to get colored up. He stood up and tossed the dealer a nickel chip before exiting stage right.

He brushed past Stacy without pausing or looking in her direction and said, in a voice only she could hear in the din of the casino, "Are you fucking nuts?" Then he kept walking briskly toward the exit, praying that she'd follow him and not wanting to admit to himself that was what he wanted.

The next surprise: Just before he got to the exit doors, he passed Clance in the aisle, not the person he was hoping to see just then. Now, if Stacy was following him, Clance would see her and he would definitely recognize her. Clance had been over to Zoey's place a couple times since hitting town. Jesus fuck. Clance was going to think he'd set something up to meet Stacy. How else would she just happen to be there?

Bart hit the Strip, the hot air hitting him like a blast from an oven after the cool air-conditioned environment of the casino. It was near midnight, but the Strip didn't cool at night in the summer. Bart kept walking, still not looking back to see if Stacy was following him. But he knew she was. He knew it.

The Strip was crowded. He continued to walk at an accelerated pace toward Planet Hollywood, refusing to slow down to make it easy for her to follow. He wasn't trying to lose her. He just wanted to know that she was trying hard to catch him. That it wasn't an accidental crossing of paths.

The crowd on the sidewalk bunched up at a corner, waiting for the signal to change. He had to stop.

He turned around for the first time since he'd gotten up from his seat in the casino.

She was right in his face.

"Hey, stranger," she said.

"You're living dangerously," he said.

"I'm hungry."

"Let's go have breakfast," he said.

"Breakfast? It's night time."

"It's Vegas, baby. I feel like bacon and eggs. Let's go to a coffee shop. We'll talk."

"Where?"

"Downtown," he said. "I gotta get out of this neighborhood. We'll catch a cab."

"Golden Gate?"

"Wherever you want."

"Buy me a piece of pie?"

"Anything you want, baby."

† † †

After a few seconds of attempting to shake pepper onto his plate, Bart unscrewed the top of the shaker and blackened his potatoes and eggs. He picked up his fork and stabbed a home fry, swabbed it in his egg yolk, pointed at Stacy with the forked potato and said, "Maybe we can cut a deal here. Meet up half way, in a way. Know what I mean?"

Stacy sipped a spoonful of her chicken noodle soup and said nothing.

"Personally, I couldn't care less if you think you're God, or Napoleon, or whatever the fuck. I see no technical difference between you thinking you're the Fourth Person of the Blessed Quad and every other fool on this planet thinking there's an old man up in the sky. I'm willing to concede that it makes you no crazier than anyone else. But the thing is that *they've* all come to a mutual agreement that there's an old man up in the sky, while *you're* the only one who thinks you're the old man up in the sky. So, what I'm proposing is you keep your opinions to yourself, not because they're right and you're wrong, but because there're millions of them and only one of you."

"I told you I have followers, Bart."

"What, three strippers in Sunnyvale?"

"I have followers on my blogs."

"Doesn't matter. The Internet's a freak show. Everybody has followers. Do you have a Facebook page or what?"

"Yes, but I also have my own blog: GodsGuilty-dot-com. And I'm getting clicks every day from my feeder blogs."

"Feeder blogs?"

"I have to tell people I'm sorry, Bart. So I set up blogs for all the different religions in the world so I could apologize."

"For all the religions in the world? How many feeder blogs is that?"

"Don't ask."

"You collecting offerings on these sites, or what?"

"No."

"Then you're missing the boat, babe. That's my two cents. If you want anyone to believe you're God, you've got to demand top dollar."

A brown plastic coffee pot was hovering over Bart's mug. He looked up and nodded to the waitress, who refilled his cup, then disappeared.

Stacy was sitting there with her eyes closed; then she opened them and sipped another spoonful of soup.

He spooned sugar into his coffee. "I told you that first night in Reno I'd disappoint you. I warned you. I knew I couldn't live up to whatever fantasies you had about me. So why did you come after me in the casino? You could have turned the other way when you saw me."

"I wasn't there accidentally," she said. "I knew you were scouting that joint and I knew you'd find that dealer. I've been watching that game for a week, waiting for you to show up."

"Why?"

"Do you have to ask? How about I missed you?"

"It wasn't more of that apostle shit?"

"That too," she said.

"Then we're back to square one," he said.

"You!" she said. "You worshipped Satan. Why is it so hard for you to believe I could be God?"

"I was a kid, Stacy. A few years before that I believed in Santa Claus and the Tooth Fairy."

She opened her mouth as if to speak, but stopped. She stood up and walked around to his side of the table. "Push your chair back," she said.

"I'm not done eating," he said. "Sit down."

She put a hand on his shoulder, hiked up her skirt, swung a leg up over the table, squeezed her butt between him and the edge of the table and sat down on his lap facing him, straddling him, her body pressed up against his tight as could be, her face just inches in front of his.

"How does that feel?" she said.

He spoke in a gruff whisper. "Stacy, I do not embarrass easily."

"I'm not trying to embarrass you," she said.

"But you're making a scene. Did you forget the cops are looking for us and we're trying to keep a low profile?"

"There's nobody back here right now," she said.

"Come on, you're pissing me off."

"No, I'm not," she said, leaning into him so that her parted lips were tickling his ear lobe. "I'm turning you on," she whispered. Her breath was hot in his ear. She started grinding her hips in his lap.

He felt his dick jump.

She backed her face away from his a few inches and said, "You like that?"

"You're not being fair," he said. "C'mon, baby, get off me, okay?" But his dick jumped again, this time staying pressed up against her crotch.

"That's holy," she said softly. "That's the prelude to sex: the most spiritual act a human being can perform."

She just looked at him for a minute, neither of them speaking.

He looked back at her, trying to figure out what the fuck was going on. "Jesus Christ, I want to fuck you," he said with his lips, but not even a whisper.

She got off his lap and held out her hand. "You want a miracle?" she said. "Let's get a room."

"You know I can't do what you want."

"You said you loved me."

"In a moment of weakness."

"Say it again," she said. "Right now, all I want is for you to love me. That's all I want in the whole universe. I … want … you … to love … me."

"Crazy bitch," he said in a half-whisper. "I fuckin' love you and you know it."

"Then, let's get a room," she said, still holding out her hand.

He got up and tossed a twenty onto the table, then took her hand and led her through the casino to the Golden Gate's hotel registration desk. Within a few minutes, he had a room under the name of Charles Boles from Saginaw, Michigan, and they were on the elevator to the third floor.

He slid the cardkey into the lock slot but nothing happened. He tried again; still nothing. Stacy took the cardkey from him, turned it 180 degrees, then slid it into the lock slot. The lock clicked and a little green light went on.

Bart pushed the door open, then looked at Stacy.

She stepped into the room and he followed. The door clicked closed behind them.

He slid his hand up and down the wall, searching for a light switch that wasn't there. He felt her hand on his arm.

Facing him directly, she put her arms around him, pulling him toward her. "Kiss me," she said, moving in on him.

Her lips lightly touched his, brushing against them softly. He stood perfectly still, his lips slightly parted, feeling the warmth of her breath on his mouth.

"Come with me," she said, taking his hand and leading him further into the dark room. But suddenly, they were making a turn into a dark alleyway along the side of a building.

She put her arms around him, her hands on the small of his back, pulling him toward her.

"I'm not going to make out with you in this stinking alley—"

Again, her lips touched his, lightly.

"Hold me," she whispered.

He surrendered, putting his hands on her waist, barely touching her as he felt her body moving closer, pressing against him. The alley smelled of urine and sadness and garbage and broken dreams. He closed his eyes.

He was fifteen years old. It wasn't Stacy who was kissing him. It was Ronnie, the Berkeley street girl who'd tried to fuck him in the alley when he was wasted on drugs. She pressed her lips against his and he gave in to the urgency he felt inside her. Her kiss was hard and needy, almost frantic in its attempt to tell him she was sorry, she needed the money, she needed the drugs. He felt how she felt in her dead-end life, her anger, her frustration, her sadness. They kissed passionately. He felt her body relax into his embrace and they rocked back and forth, side to side, holding each other, consoling each other …

"I want to fuck you, Ronnie," he said, "Right here, right now, I want to fuck you." He backed away to look into her eyes and found himself looking at Stacy.

"You're fucking with my head," he said.

"Kiss me."

"You're fucking with my head."

But the moment her lips touched his, he surrendered and found himself kissing Jennifer, the Carson City prostitute who'd tried to comfort him when his dick wouldn't cooperate. She told him with her kiss that it was just the wrong place, the wrong time, that if their paths had crossed at some other juncture of their lives, it would have been different, it would have been good and real, she would have taken that ride with him all the way to Big Sur ... Her kisses were wet and sexy. She pressed her breasts against his chest and accepted his tongue into her mouth and pushed hers into his, tasting everything they'd missed that sad night in that dumpy little trailer.

He slid his hand over her ass and lifted her short skirt, then slipped his hand into her panties, worked his middle finger into her wet slit. He was kissing his way down her chest and belly when he looked up to see it wasn't Jennifer he was finger-fucking, but Stacy.

She looked down at him with lust in her eyes.

"I'm sorry," he said, taking his hand away. "You're fuckin' with my head, goddamn it!"

She put her hand to his lips to quiet him, and patted the bed beside her. He looked at the bed. They were in his low-rent little Emeryville studio. "Get on the bed," she said, sitting down on the mattress. When he sat down beside her, bewildered, she reached her hand behind his head and moved in for another kiss.

He was thirty-five and it was Persephone this time and his first impulse was to pull away, to hide in shame over his abandonment of this woman.

"I'm sorry," he said, twisting away from the kiss.

But she started kissing his mouth harder, long and deep passionate kisses until he stopped fighting it, and it wasn't Persephone anymore, it was Stacy and he knew it was Stacy, kissing him how he'd always wanted to be kissed, like nothing in the world mattered except these kisses.

He felt his dick stiffening inside his trousers and he pushed her back against the bed and pressed his pelvis against her so she could feel how badly he wanted her. All those nights she'd slept in the bed next to him, the endless torture.

He looked at her face. Her eyes were wet and her mascara was running down her face. Her lipstick was smeared across her mouth.

"Stacy, I'm going crazy. You're driving me crazy."

He looked into her eyes, trying to see what was inside of her. Then he said, "You own me, you own my heart, my soul … I worship you."

She laughed. He tried to read the conflicting emotions in her face. Tears ran down her cheeks into her hairline. He kissed the corners of her eyes, tasted the salty drops, felt his dick stiffening even more. "I want to fuck you so bad," he said, and she started removing his clothes.

† † †

"Whoever would have thought Heaven would have a soundtrack by the Doors?" he said.

"That's the Fremont Street Experience," she said. "Do you want to go out and watch the light show?"

Jim Morrison's voice rumbled through the walls of their little room at the Golden Gate. *Strange days have tracked us down …*

"I never want to leave this room," he said.

They were both naked. He was lying on his back with his head and shoulders propped on two pillows. Stacy was on her side, pressed up against him, with one leg curled over his thighs. A thin sheet covered them up to their waists.

Bart took a cigarette from the nightstand and lit it, passing it to her for a drag.

"I could be arrested for this," he said. "And I don't fucking care. You know you've accomplished what no other woman in my life has ever been able to do."

"It was a piece of cake," she said.

"I guess I just needed to be with a woman who's totally deranged. I've finally found my type."

"I'm not deranged. I'm God."

THIRTY-EIGHT

"WHY ARE YOU crying? Bart? Bart? Can you hear me?"

"Goddamn it, Dorsett ... Thought you were gone."

"Why are you crying?"

"Not crying."

"I've been sitting here with you for almost an hour and this is the first time I've seen tears."

"It's called pain, Dorsett ... Wouldn't happen to have any reds, would you?"

"Reds?"

"How about a joint? Can you light up a fatty for me?"

"I wish I could, Bart."

"I'm getting stronger, Dorsett ... I can move my right leg ... but the left one's still unresponsive ... Can you touch my left leg?"

"Can't do it. I have orders not to touch you."

"You go to church, Dorsett?"

"Sometimes."

"How often?"

"When the wife drags me."

"You ever pray?"

"Only when I'm shooting dice."

"Oh ... You're a craps man ..."

"Love the game."

"It's a sucker bet, Dorsett."

THIRTY-NINE

BART KICKED AT the door and hollered, "Room service!" He was holding a tray that had a pot of coffee, cups and saucers, and two pieces of pie.

Stacy answered quickly and let him into the room. She was still in her bare feet, wearing only a T-shirt and panties.

He set the tray on the small circular table by the window, where the morning sun was filtering through the curtains.

When she seated herself at the table, he served the coconut cream pie to her, then the hot apple pie with ice cream to himself. The Golden Gate Hotel had no room service, but with a 24-hour coffee shop just around the corner from the elevators, it was no problem.

He sat down and poured the coffee.

"So, ask me a question I shouldn't know the answer to," Stacy said.

"Okay, what kind of motorcycle did I have before my Harley?"

"A Triton."

"How'd you know that?"

She smiled.

"Where is it right now?"

"In a tool shed behind your mother's house in Berkeley."

"Jesus. Is it still running?"

"Not unless you replace the battery."

"How'd the battery die?"

"It's not dead. You removed it when you put the bike in the shed to store it. The battery's in a corrugated cardboard box next to the bike. It could use a recharge, but it's not dead."

"Unfuckingreal … You went and saw my mother, right?"

"Nope."

"Really, did I talk to you about this?"

"No. But go ahead, ask me something you know you never talked to me about."

"Okay. What CD did I listen to before I went to the casino yesterday?"

"*Blues for Allah*. Grateful Dead. You kept replaying the cut titled 'Crazy Fingers.' You just bought it two days ago."

"Are you stalking me?"

"You bought it to replace the LP you loaned to Dusty twenty years ago that he never returned. How could you go twenty years without it?"

He set his fork down and sat back. "You're unreal," he said. "Who's Dusty?"

"He used to be your pot connection in Berkeley, till he moved to Monterey."

"Jesus fuck, Stacy … What's my favorite line from that song?"

"*Gone are the days we stop to decide where we should go, we just ride.*"

"Jesus fucking Christ!"

"Ask me something else."

"No. Show me your web site."

"Really?"

"Really. I want to see it."

She got her smart phone from the nightstand and by the time she got back to the table, she had her blog on the screen. She handed it to Bart and sat back down.

"I designed it myself," she said. "GodsGuilty-dot-com. Check it out."

Bart read the announcement on the front page:

This Saturday at 7 p.m. in Las Vegas
GAY PRIDE PARADE AND MARCH OF THE SLUTS!
Gather in front of the Erotic Heritage Museum for a walk up the Las Vegas Strip
Let's Stop Traffic! Wear Black!
Rally at 9 p.m. after the March
  — *Stacy, Fourth Person of the Blessed Quad*

There was a navigation block on the left side of the front page.

"That's the list of all my feeder blogs," Stacy said.

"How many are there?"

"Hundreds. I cover all of the religions where any followers might have Internet access."

"I see you have a new Ten Commandments," Bart said.

"That's my latest post, inspired by you. Read it."

Bart read aloud: "Don't worship."

He looked at Stacy.

"I don't want to be worshiped," she said. "I want to be forgiven. Read it. I want your opinion."

"Did Moses get any of them right? What about, 'Honor thy father and thy mother'?"

"That's an idiotic commandment. There are parents who torture their children, molest their children, teach them horrible things. Moses just stuck that one in there because his kids thought he was an asshole. Which he was. A righteous kid thinks for himself and rebels against his parents if they deserve it. I made it, 'Honor those worthy of honor.'"

"How about, 'Thou shalt not steal'?"

"I made it, 'Thou shalt share.' People aren't supposed to own property, Bart. And you can only steal if people own things. You're supposed to be hunter gatherers and those who manage to find food are supposed to share with those who didn't."

"How about, 'Thou shalt not commit adultery'?"

"I hate that whole bizarre marriage scene with all that possessiveness and jealousy. Life is simpler than that. Hunt. Gather. Fuck. That's all there is to it. I changed it to 'Have a lot of sex, but keep it holy.'"

"Well, you may win some followers on that one," he said.

"If I don't, humans have a real hell in front of them, and it's not that far away. Not too many years from now, people will be battling over their shit with machetes and homemade bombs."

"They're already doing that," he said. "I like your commandments."

"I knew you'd like them," she said. "It really all comes down to hunt, gather, fuck."

"How about 'Remember to keep holy the Sabbath Day'?"

"Dumb," she said. "I made it 'Remember to keep holy.' Why would you keep holy only one day a week?"

"Do you always sign your posts, 'Stacy, Fourth Person of the Blessed Quad'?"

"Yes."

"What comes up when you Google your name?"

"I never tried it."

He Googled "stacy fourth person of the blessed quad."

"Wow," he said. "You're on a lot of sites."

"My main site should be up at the top," she said. "And my feeder blogs should come after."

"You've already got an entry in Wikipedia," he said. "And look—a Facebook page dedicated to the Quadite religion. How long have you been doing your blog?"

"About a year. And it's not a religion."

"It is now. Jesus Christ, Stacy."

"At least I got people thinking."

"You've got some of the Christians upset," he said. "Look at this one. They're trying to organize a counter-demonstration. Look, this one here says you're a Satanist."

"This is America. It's free speech, that's all."

"It's not as free as you think," Bart said. "There's something else I need to know."

"Okay. What?"

"What exactly happened to you that made you run away from home at fifteen?"

"It was just time to leave. I had no connection there. I knew what I was here for and what I had to do."

"Your parents wouldn't buy your God trip?"

"I never told them about it. I came here as a human being and I'm suffering as a human being. All they knew was the human side of me."

"So no angel came down and told your mother she'd be the next Virgin Mary?"

"My mother wasn't a virgin, her name wasn't Mary, and no—no angel told anybody anything. The Jesus trip didn't go very well. I decided for the comeback to show up with no fanfare, no angels, no wise men following stars, just pop myself into the first newly fertilized human embryo and see what it's like to enter this world the way everybody else does."

"So, how's it working out for you?"

"It is what it is. It's not easy. I didn't know I was God at first. I was born as dumb as everyone else. But by the time I met you, I knew what was happening."

He decided to stop fighting it. She was who she was.

In the distance a siren wailed. Bart pictured the cops surrounding his bike in the MGM Grand parking garage, then the face of the dead cop in the desert.

"You know, we need to get a plan together," he said. "We need to get out of Vegas right away. I'm thinking maybe Mexico or Costa Rica, someplace nobody'll ask questions."

"I can't go anywhere until after the march."

"What march?"

"On Friday night," she said. "They're combining the Gay Pride Parade with the Slutwalk this year, and I'm going to march with my followers and give a sermon. I've been posting about this on my blog for the last month."

"A Slutwalk?"

"It's women saying they're human and should be treated with dignity and respect. I'm asking you to support me in this. We can leave Las Vegas right after."

"It's dangerous," he said.

"I have people coming. I promise we can leave right after."

"Look, I've got to go settle accounts with Clance. Get my cut from our last play and tell him I'm going to be disappearing for a while."

"Why don't I come with you?" she said.

"You can't come with me to talk to Clance," he said. "This is business. I'll pay for the room until Friday. You can wait for me here."

"I need to get my stuff from Zoey's."

"Do you have cab fare?"

"Yes."

"You go get your stuff. I'll go see Clance and get my stuff from my motel room. I'll meet you back here later this afternoon."

"You're not just splitting on me again, are you?"

He just looked at her.

"I'll meet you here later," she said.

FORTY

"DORSETT... GOTTA DO me a favor."

"If I can, Bart."

"Talk to the doc or whoever ... Find out about Stacy ... Want to know if she's okay ... Wherever she is ... Can I get a message to her?"

There was a long silence. Bart didn't like the sound of it.

"You hear what I said, Dorsett?"

"I heard you, Bart."

"You said you would do that for me."

"I can't. I lied to you, Bart. I'm sorry. She was never in any hospital. She died at the scene."

There was a longer silence.

"Fuck you."

"I'm sorry."

"I hope you rot in hell ... You sonofabitch ... Why would you do that?"

"I'm sorry. Really I am. I thought I could get more information out of you if you thought she was alive."

"They killed her?"

"I'm sorry, Bart. I'm really sorry."

FORTY-ONE

AFTER PICKING UP his duffel bag with all of his worldly possessions at his motel room, he took a cab to the Loose Caboose on Flamingo, the spot Clance chose for them to meet.

They sat in a booth in back and both ordered coffee.

Clance tossed him a fat envelope. "Your cut," he said. "I thought you were coming back last night, man. We've gotta talk. We've got our next play scheduled."

"Where?"

"That dealer you found at the Hilton. She'll be on the tables Friday night. Let's get her. Zoey says we can practice at her place until I get my crib set up. I want you to get the signals down with Sam and Lisa. Too bad the heat came down last night. Sam says your decision to call the play was wise."

"I can't make it on Friday night."

"What do you mean you can't make it?" Clance raised his voice. "This is why we're in Vegas, man! Are you telling me you have a scheduling conflict?"

"I have to do something with Stacy on Friday."

"Do something? Are you outta your freakin' mind? We got the numbers, the strategy worked out, the dealer, the bankroll …"

"I have to go to a march. It's on Friday. I can't change it."

"A what?"

"The Gay Pride Parade and Slutwalk. Why don't you come?"

"I repeat: The what?"

"It's a march. It's going to be like the sixties."

"Stop fuckin' with me, Bart," Clance said. "Just be at Zoey's tomorrow night at ten for practice."

"I'm serious, Clance. I can't make it Friday. How about Thursday?"

"Thursday's no good. The high-limit pit's too dead. Surveillance'll have nothing else to look at but us. How about Saturday?"

"I'm blowing town Saturday," Bart said.

"The cops?"

Bart nodded.

"Then Friday it is," Clance said.

"Can't. I've got this march."

"Are you trippin', man? You been out in the desert eatin' mushrooms? You're losin' it, Bart. Just tell me you're stoned and we'll talk later."

"This is really important to Stacy."

"Important to Stacy? What about what's important to me, man? What's important to the team? Isn't that why we're all here? You already fucked us over in Reno for your dippy teenybopper girlfriend. Didn't you tell me it was over with her? And what the fuck was she doing with you last night? You know you're not supposed to bring outsiders in on our plays. Especially her! I keep cuttin' you slack, man, but you're pushin' my limits. I thought you said you kissed her off."

"Yeah … well, she kissed me back on."

"I'm renting a blackjack table, Bart. It's bein' delivered to Zoey's tomorrow afternoon. Johnny's in town now, so we're all going to be there. We're going to rotate our players in and out of the game to get maximum time against this dealer before she's fixed or some other team spots her and wrecks it for us."

"I really can't make it on Friday, Clance. What about Debbie? She could do it."

"Debbie's eyes suck." Clance was struggling visibly for self-control. "Hey, man, I know you dig the chick, but try to focus. I told you weeks ago to cut that bitch loose. Do you have any idea how important it is for us—and I mean all of us—to keep a low profile? Do you know what it means to stay under the radar? It doesn't mean playing hippie games with teenage girls the cops are lookin' for."

Again, Bart saw that dead cop's face, the blood …

"You think you're fuckin' indispensable," Clance went on, "But you're not. Right now, you're costin' me money and you're makin' me nervous. I believe I mentioned that Wally's putting three hundred large behind us. You know why? Because he trusts me. And right now, I'm startin' to think I can't trust you. You got a choice here, Bart. If you intend to do this play with us Friday night, be at Zoey's tomorrow night at ten. Otherwise, have a nice life with Stacy."

† † †

"Was he angry?" Stacy asked, when he got back to their room at the Golden Gate.

"He's been my friend for thirty years," Bart said. "He saved my life when I was a kid. He's the only person, aside from you, who ever saved my life."

"And I'm glad he did," she said. "Seconal is awful stuff. You really might have died."

It took a moment for her words to register. Then he said, "Do you have to know every fuckin' detail of my life?"

† † †

It was Clance who got him off of drugs. Bart had spent two years building a bike in Clance's garage. Clance was of the opinion that any biker with a set of wrenches and a few odd tools should be able to take his bike apart piece by piece—the frame, engine, transmission, brakes, clutch, everything—and put it back together again, knowing the function and purpose of every hose, clamp, gear, housing, rocker, cover plate, engine component, mounting bracket, interface, sprocket, lifter, bearing, tappet, solenoid, pushrod, gasket, vent line, nut, and bolt.

Bart was getting close to the age when he'd actually be able to get a license to ride the thing when Clance laid down the law. At the time, Bart was high on reds and yellows, the street names for Seconals and

Nembutals, both barbiturates, very cheap and easy to score on the streets of Berkeley in the 1980s. He'd just walked into Clance's garage, stubbing his toe and kicking over a coffee can half-filled with dirty gasoline that they used to wash greasy engine parts.

Clance flew off the handle. "Every goddamn time I see you you're fuckin' stoned outta your gourd! I'm not gonna let you wreck this machine, Bart. If you wanna toke up some weed now and then, hey, that's your business. But you're eatin' any goddamn pill anyone puts in front of you. You passed out in here twice already, scarin' the shit outta me. You puked on the floor yesterday. How many times have I had to take tools away from you so you wouldn't lose a finger 'cuz you were too wasted on some kinda shit or other to handle a wrench?"

"Hey, man, I'm sorry," Bart said, swaying on his feet.

"Plus, look at you ... I told you two years ago to put on some fuckin' muscle. Shit, I got more muscle in my big toes than you've got in your biceps. You haven't touched my weights. You think muscle's gonna just appear on your arms? How many times have I had to help you pick up that engine? What the fuck're you gonna do out on the road if you dump your bike? Call me? Your bike's startin' to look road ready, but I'll be damned if I'll let you ride it."

Bart just stood there with his head pulled down into his shoulders. Clance had never gotten really pissed off at him before.

"Here's the deal, Bart. Fuck off. You can't come in here wasted anymore. Come back tomorrow if you're ready to work. I'm gonna register this bike in my name. I'll let you ride it when you're not stoned, assuming you can show me that you've got the strength to upright it. Feel free to use my weight bench any time. Now get the fuck outta here and don't *ever* let me see you like this again. If you go a year without getting' fucked up on shit, I'll sign the bike over to you."

With that two-minute tirade, Clance accomplished what the church, the school, and Bart's parents had all failed at. His immediate resolve to quit drugs had nothing to do with morality, nothing to do with health and well-being, nothing to do with fear of incarceration; nothing to do with what was socially acceptable. In fact, quite the opposite. He wanted that bike *because* he wanted to be socially unacceptable. He wanted to be a badass motherfucker nobody would mess with. That was the only way of life he saw that seemed to make life worth living.

No more drugs. No more getting wasted. Not if he wanted to feel that Triton thundering between his legs. Bart was amazed at how quickly Clance sobered him up. He went home that afternoon and flushed his whole stash of pills down the toilet—the diet pills he'd stolen from his mother that had some kind of speed in them. The old codeines he'd copped from his father's medicine cabinet while his father lay in bed dying. Some pills he didn't even know what they were. But mostly, he was throwing away his precious reds. Seconals. He loved reds, possibly the greatest memory erasers ever created.

He could use some reds right now.

FORTY-TWO

"BART, I'M GOING to the cafeteria for a cup of coffee. I'll be gone about five minutes. Do you want the TV on?"

"Just leave. Don't come back."

"How about the radio?"

"We've got a radio?"

"FM only."

"Find some hard rock."

A voice came from the speaker overhead: "*... our pledge drive ... just nine more subscribers to get that thousand-dollar matching grant. If you've been waiting to become a member, please do it now ...*"

"I don't know how to change the station, Bart. There's no dial on the speaker."

"Turn it off."

The radio went dead.

"I'll be back soon."

"Just do me one favor, Dorsett ... Pull the plug ... Whatever it takes ..."

"I can't do that, Bart."

PART THREE:

Captured

FORTY-THREE

BART SCANNED THE street apprehensively. The parking lot in front of the Erotic Heritage Museum was crowded with women in torn underwear and eight-inch platform heels, men in dresses and trollop make-up, streetwalkers, strippers, women with bared breasts save for Band-Aids over their nipples. Many carried signs with slogans: "NO MEANS NO!" "A DRESS IS NOT A YES!" "I'M GAY AND I'M PROUD!" "WOMEN'S HEALTH MATTERS!"

Stacy looked fired up. "Bart, these are my people!"

"What about them?" he said, pointing at a group of religious nuts, a few carrying signs that quoted Bible verses: "VENGEANCE IS MINE SAITH THE LORD!" "WHOREMONGERS AND ADULTERERS GOD WILL JUDGE!"

Half a dozen cop cars were parked on the street in front of the museum. Despite his new disguise, he was nervous around the cops. He was wearing six-inch platform pimp shoes, a long blonde wig that Stacy had picked up for him at a dancers' emporium, a pair of over-size metallic sunglasses, and he'd used Stacy's mascara to thicken and darken his mustache. Otherwise, he'd stuck to her color scheme in a black T-shirt and pegged black jeans. He was carrying a walking stick with a brass handle and hoped that, as Stacy's bodyguard, he wouldn't have to use it.

He lowered his head and caught a glimpse of his cheerless expression in one of the dark glass windows of the museum. *I'll be glad when this night is over*, he thought.

A small knot of people dressed in black congregated in one corner of the lot. The women in this group outnumbered the men by about two to one. Many of their outfits were on the skimpy side. A few wore black bikini bathing suits or lingerie ensembles. One of the men—who was at least six-foot-five and sported a full curly brown beard speckled with black and silver glitter—was wearing a miniskirt with thigh-high stockings and a black garter belt. His tube top hid his obviously fake breasts.

Bart was trying to count the number of those in all black—*their people*. Stacy had specified on her blog that all of her followers in the march should be dressed in black. Stacy had on a black halter top with a large white button that said GOD'S GUILTY pinned over one tit. She also had that bright red feather clipped into her hair. He spotted her talking excitedly with a small group of scantily-clad women he guessed to be her dancer friends.

In scanning the crowd, he did a double-take on a dude wearing plastic Mickey Mouse ears, a familiar face … Was that the guy who used to host the poetry readings at the pub in Berkeley? There was quite a bit of gray in his beard now.

"Hey, Kendall!"

Kendall looked at Bart without registering recognition. Bart noticed that one of the mouse ears said "DON'T" and the other said "WORSHIP," Stacy's first commandment.

"It's me. Bart Black. From the poetry readings."

"Oh … oh, yeah … Man, it's been like five or six years." A kind, rather wan smile appeared on his grizzled face.

"More like eight," Bart said.

"You were Persephone's friend."

"Right. What the hell are you doing here?"

"Are you kidding, man? I wouldn't miss this for the world! Gay Pride teaming up with the March of the Sluts, man, what an idea. We've got a little poetry contingent here from Berkeley. Tom's here. Bert's here. Bert's the one who found this thing. I think he was surfing porno sites, but he says he was Googling Buddhism. Andy's here. Sally's here. You remember those guys? They're wandering around here somewhere. We all did the slutwalk in San Francisco last year."

Bart didn't remember a single one of them, not by name. "Maybe if I saw them," he said. "How's Persephone?"

"Oh, man, didn't you hear?"

"Hear what?"

"Oh, man, that was a long time ago. She OD'd on pills. Way back then. I kept looking for you after that, because I thought you might know her family. Thought maybe we could get some of her poetry together, publish it in a chapbook, you know, in her memory."

"Shit. I'm sorry to hear that." He felt sick in his gut. "She had three kids," he said. He tipped his head back, just feeling the warm night air on his face. How old were they? They'd be teenagers now … For chrissake, Persephone, was it that bad? Was it that fucking bad? But he'd known in his heart that when he rode away that day, it was the end for her. She had nothing left but poetry or death and her poetry was going nowhere.

He felt a hand on his forearm and looked down to see Stacy standing in front of him. She was carrying a large black plastic bag of the type generally used for household trash or lawn clippings and had a small cardboard box tucked under one arm.

"Are you okay?" she said. "You look ill."

"I just heard some sad news about an old friend," he said. "This is Kendall. He's a poet … This is Stacy. How can I describe you, Stacy?"

Kendall's face lit up. "Stacy? *The* Stacy? Fourth Person of the Blessed Quad?" He started bowing in mock worship and she smiled at the adulation. "This is so cool," he said. "You gotta do this every year. It'll get bigger than Burning Man. We could've gotten a hundred people from Berkeley if we'd known about it sooner. I'll help you promote it next year."

She touched his upper arm and said, "I like your bling."

Bart had noticed the weird necklace Kendall was wearing, but hadn't paid it any mind. Now he looked at it more closely. It was a conglomeration of beer bottle caps and Zig-Zag cigarette paper packages strung onto some kind of wire. At the bottom, a silver crucifix hung upside-down, with the classic crucified Christ in a loin cloth, but the face of Jesus had been meticulously painted in brightly-colored clown make-up.

A kid about ten years old ran up to them. He was wearing a Halloween Batman costume.

"This is my grandson, Jello," Kendall said.

"Jello?" Bart said. "Like the dessert?"

"Actually, he was named after Jello Biafra," Kendall said. "My daughter-in-law's a big Dead Kennedys fan."

"That is so cool you brought your grandson," Stacy said. "I was afraid there wouldn't be any kids."

"Kids?" Bart said. "Stacy, this is a slut march. We don't want kids participating."

She gave him a look and touched Kendall's arm again. "Send me an email," she said to him.

Jello went running after another kid about his age in a Darth Vader outfit. Kendall went chasing after them.

"Is that blood?" Bart said, pointing to a bright red smear on the white cardboard box Stacy was holding.

Stacy looked at the blood, then turned her wrists up to see that the skin beneath her ECCE HOMO decals was starting to bleed. The decals had loosened and were sliding from the bloodied areas of her wrists. She handed the box to Bart, then took a tissue from her hip pocket and wiped them off, removing the decals.

"Your birthmarks fell off," he said.

"The decals came off," she said. "The birthmarks are still there." She turned both wrists up again to show him the small red spots that looked like common port wine stains. Tiny droplets of blood were slowly reforming over them.

"It's okay," she said. "It just happens. The fact is I've already gone too far in remembering who I am, so I won't be here much longer. This isn't working for me anymore."

"You're scaring the shit out of me," he said.

"I'm sorry," she said. "I'm really sorry."

She took the box back from Bart, then said, "Did you do a head count?"

"People in black clothes," he said. "Your disciples. I counted thirty-three. That includes you and me. Other sluts and LGBTers—not wearing black—lots more than that. Then there are the religious kooks. Some of them are wearing black, but I didn't count them."

"It's a perfect-size crowd," she said.

"I was worried you'd be disappointed."

"These are all my people," she said. "Even if they don't know it yet. It's almost eight o'clock. We're going to start moving soon."

She dropped the plastic bag she was still holding and a man in black helped her climb onto the bed of an old Ford pick-up truck. The black-clad group gathered around her. She raised her voice to be heard above the din. "Okay, guys! I want to thank you all for dressing in black. My apostle, Bart, will now distribute our sacramental vizards."

"What the hell's a vizard?" Bart said.

She pointed to the plastic bag she'd dropped on the ground.

He picked it up and looked inside. It was filled with novelty eyeglasses. He pulled out a pair and looked at them—cheap black plastic lensless frame, big rubber nose, fake plastic eyebrows and mustache. "We're all going as Groucho?" he said.

She squatted down on her haunches to get onto a level where she could talk to him privately. "First impressions are important. People think God has no sense of humor."

"I don't think Jesus was known for his repartee."

"Are you kidding? You should have seen Jesus in his prime."

"But the Bible doesn't mention a single joke he ever told."

"What about 'Blessed are the meek; for they shall inherit the earth'?"

"That was a joke?"

"C'mon, Bart, pass out the vizards."

She took the pair of Groucho glasses that Bart was holding and put them on, then stood back up and raised her hands to quiet her followers. "Throughout the march, we will all wear the sacramental vizard!"

The people in black began reaching for the glasses.

"C'mon, Bart, pass 'em out!" she called down to him.

He traded his metallic wraparounds for a pair, then started distributing them to those in black. He liked the glasses. He could now walk right in front of the cops without worry.

"As we march, stay close to the person in front of you, because we don't want to be broken up," Stacy announced to the crowd. "While we march, we'll be singing: 'Row, row, row your boat, gently down the stream. Merrily, merrily, merrily, merrily, life is but a dream.' You all know the words.

"If anyone on the street asks you what we're doing," Stacy went on, "don't answer them. Speak to no one. Just keep singing. I have some cards here you can pass out to the public." She held up the cardboard box, then opened it and placed it at her feet on the bed of the pick-up. "Grab a handful of cards before you get in line. And think about the words you're singing as we march—'gently down the stream' and 'life is but a dream.' If we just keep moving and singing, it *will* feel like a dream."

It already feels like a dream! Bart thought.

"While walking, place your hands in front of you, like this," Stacy went on, "with your fists closed as if you're holding oars, and move them like this in a continual rowing motion." She demonstrated as her followers in the crowd, now in their vizards, practiced the motion.

The Gay Pride Parade started moving out, crossing Industrial Road onto Fashion Show Drive. The Slutwalkers were mustering.

Bart picked up a handful of the business cards from the box Stacy had brought. They were disappearing fast as the vizard-wearing Grouchos came forward to help themselves. Bart looked at one of the cards. It said: GODSGUILTY.COM. That's all.

"Remember everyone," Stacy addressed the crowd. "I'll lead and you should all just fall in behind whoever's in front of you!" Leaning toward Bart, without turning to face him, she said, *sotto voce*, "Does that make sense?"

"Baby, you're not seriously asking me that, are you?"

"Sing," Stacy said, then facing the crowd once again, she started in: "Row, row, row your boat, gently down the stream …"

Bart joined in in a flat, off-key voice, much louder than hers, "Merrily, merrily, merrily, merrily, life is but a dream!" He heard others joining in, then another group started a second round, and soon the crowd had a third round going.

Stacy gave Bart a look that said, "Here goes nothin'," as she jumped down from the truck bed and started rowing her arms as she followed the slutwalkers across Industrial Road down Fashion Show Drive toward the Strip.

Bart watched as the crowd fell in behind her, rowing their arms, all singing loudly. In front of them he could hear the slutwalkers chanting "No means no!" and "Yes means yes!" The pedestrians and cops on the sidewalk looked puzzled as the boat-rowers, many of them wearing very little, passed them singing. A few of the spectators smiled. Some of the slutwalkers started walking alongside the rowing Grouchos, holding up their protest signs, but joining in the song. Bart felt as if he were watching Moses part the Red Sea, but he was the only one who could see it.

He joined the boat rowers bringing up the rear, playing sweep. He was fascinated by the reactions of the pedestrians, some of whom looked away, as if they'd seen nothing out of the ordinary. Most of those who looked had smiles on their faces. Confused smiles, but smiles.

Some of the cars passing by on the street slowed down to watch the spectacle and a few started honking their horns in support. One guy jumped out of his Lexus and started taking pictures of the Groucho caravan.

It seemed to take forever for all of the Grouchos to get from one side of Fashion Show Drive to the other. Bringing up the rear, the stragglers, including Bart, were walking against the Don't Walk sign. The honking horns created a din and more and more people started getting out of their cars to see what the hold-up was.

Bart was relieved at getting the last Groucho off the street and onto the sidewalk on the other side. Stacy was so far in front at this point, he had to walk out into the street to see her. A couple of Metro cops on bicycles were now walking their bikes in the street near him. He had his cop radar on high alert, but sensed no danger.

The pedestrian and street traffic picked up as soon as they turned onto Las Vegas Boulevard. He had no idea where this march was headed. Obviously, with the cooperative police presence, the march organizers had obtained a permit. Singing the boat-rowing song had become almost meditative, like a mantra, and what Stacy had said was true. The repetition of the words did make it feel like a dream.

As they approached Treasure Island, some of the pedestrians he passed asked questions:

"What is this?"

Row, row, row your boat, gently down the stream ...

"Is this part of the Siren show?"

"Are you guys the pirates?"

Merrily, merrily, merrily, merrily, life is but a dream ...

He just handed out cards and kept singing, rowing, with his hands wrapped around his walking stick as if it were a brass-tipped oar.

When the Gay Pride marchers got to the Mirage, they crossed the pedestrian bridge and started retracing their route, heading back toward the museum. Bart jogged ahead to catch up to Stacy for instructions. He had no idea what she had planned. But she just gave him a look and kept rowing and singing. She hardly seemed to notice him. She was in some kind of trance. He surrendered to the insanity, fell back in line again, and sang louder. She turned and smiled at him, a smile that meant more to him at that moment than anything in the world.

As the marchers turned from Las Vegas Boulevard back onto Fashion Show Drive, where there were far fewer tourists and pedestrians, the chants of the LGBTers and the slutwalkers grew less frequent. The Grouchos never stopped their song, though—all around him he heard *Row, row, row your boat, Row, row, row your boat, Merrily, merrily, merrily, Merrily, merrily, merrily ...*

As they approached the museum parking lot, he saw that the Christian groups were still waiting. He noticed a group of men in clerical garb—priests or ministers of some sort. The Christian numbers had grown. There were more picket signs. One sign read, "THE BI-BLE IS GOD'S WORD!" Another said, "BLASPHEMERS BURN IN HELL!" A third was just a large photo of Stacy's face—copied from her blog and blown-up to poster size—with a Hitler mustache scribbled above her upper lip. *These are enemies*, he thought.

As the gays and sluts and Grouchos converged on the parking lot, where a small wooden stage had been erected for the speakers, Stacy stepped out of the line to talk with Bart.

"Don't hurt anyone," she said.

He opened his mouth, but before he could say a word, she put her hand on his arm to shush him.

"These people," she said. "They're my creations. All of them. Be careful with that stick. Don't hurt anyone."

One of the Christian protesters with a bullhorn, who was standing on the hood of a car across the street from the museum, started speaking loudly about hell and damnation.

Some of the sluts and gays tried drowning him out by resuming their chants, "I'm gay and I'm proud!" and "A dress is not a yes!" Loud arguments started breaking out from crowd to crowd.

Stacy just stood there, as if waiting for the ruckus to die down.

"Come on," Bart said to her. "We gotta get outta here."

One of the gay priders was now standing on the pickup bed, shouting obscenities at the man with the bullhorn. The Christians started shouting, "God hates gays! God hates gays!" The chanters were pumping their fists and their voices were angry. The cops, vastly out-numbered, were looking around nervously. One of them was talking on his radio; others had their billy clubs already drawn.

"Let's go," Bart said to Stacy once more.

But she didn't seem to hear him. She was back in that trance. And before he could figure out what she was doing, she stepped up onto the empty speakers' stage and ripped off her halter top. She stood there bare-breasted in all her messianic, nubile, sixteen-year-old glory.

The Christians began to yell at her and boo. One woman was shouting, "Whore!" A man carrying a Bible was demanding that the police arrest her. She just closed her eyes and stood there, her face turned up toward the sky, stretching out her arms.

As the cops started approaching, a group of the slutwalkers quickly surrounded the stage where Stacy stood, locking arms to keep both the cops and Christians at bay.

That was when the first bottle flew. It smashed onto the top of the pickup roof and shards of glass rained into the crowd, one big piece hitting the wall behind Stacy and landing a foot in front of her on the stage where she stood. She looked down, startled, saw what it was, then removed the rest of her clothes and again stretched out her arms.

Bart knew he had to get her off of that stage and out of there. What the fuck was she doing? She was making herself a target.

He saw a van arrive with cops in riot gear and he made a charge for the stage. "Let me through!" he shouted. "I have to get her down from there!" But his voice was lost in the noise of the crowd that was now packed so tightly up against the stage, he couldn't get near it.

Stacy just stood there naked, with her arms stretched high and her eyes closed, still lost in her private reverie, listening to some inner music.

That's when a bottle hit her, and someone had already broken this one before throwing it. The jagged glass edge hit her in the ribcage and cut her. She was only ten feet away from him and she seemed unaware of the wound in her side. Another broken bottle hit her in the shoulder, then sliced down across one of her breasts. A thin rivulet of deep red blood ran from the cut down her cream-white stomach.

The sight of her blood finally panicked Bart enough that he managed to fight his way through the slutwalk guard. But before he could get onto the stage, a group of Christians got hold of him and stopped his advance. They were pummeling him from all sides. He felt a rib crack, then another. A blow to his head with something hard almost knocked him out. Had he known he'd been bonked with the brass handle of his own walking stick—which one of the protesters had wrested from him—he would have appreciated the irony and thought, *It figures.* He was locked in a bear hug from behind, then something hit him in the mouth, breaking teeth, cracking his jaw.

Many of the slutwalkers and gays were now involved in the brawl with the nutcases from the religious groups. Through his blurred vision, he saw Kendall running away with his grandson, little Jello. The police in riot gear were now putting on gas masks. How long till the tear gas hit?

Then a shot rang out, followed by screams of panic, followed by a volley of gunfire. Bart looked immediately for Stacy, but she was no longer on the stage. Had she been hit, or did she finally duck for cover?

A hot sting in his gut told him that at least one of those bullets had hit him in a place where a Band-Aid wouldn't do much good. But the sound of the gunshots had given him a ferocious strength, and he broke out of the bear hug he was trapped in, elbows and fists flailing furiously at his captors. He managed to open his mouth and bite down with his broken teeth on the hand that was still attempting to suffocate him, heard the fingers break, tasted blood, couldn't see through the blur of his tears, couldn't get his bearings, hardly knew which way was up, just punched and kicked like a wild man at every human within striking distance.

He broke away from his captors just in time to see Stacy's nude limp body being carried away. He tried to run to her, but he was too dizzy to even stand, coughing and wheezing in the clouds of CS gas all around him.

"Stacy!" he cried. "Baby! Baby! Baby!"

Then there was a cop's arm around his neck, and the world went black.

FORTY-FOUR

"ARE YOU STILL with me, Bart?"

Bart heard the question, but Dorsett sounded so far away.

"Bart? You still hanging in there?"

He felt like his insides were going to sleep.

"Bart?"

"Of course, I hear you."

"Bart?"

"That's my name."

Then he realized he wasn't actually speaking.

"Bart?" This time it was Stacy's voice. "Don't worry about it. I'm here."

She was radiant and beautiful and unwounded.

"I knew you'd come, baby. I was waiting for you."

She smiled and reached for his hand.

"Come with me," she said.

"Where are we going, baby?"

"Into the wind," she said.

ABOUT THE AUTHOR

ARNOLD SNYDER IS a professional gambler and ordained minister who lives in the Nevada hills west of Las Vegas. He prefers the company of his five dogs to most humans. In 2002, he was induct-  ed into the Blackjack Hall of Fame. He is the author of *The Seven Spiritual Laws of Making Big Bucks, Topless Vegas, Sadistic Sudoku, The Poker Tournament Formula, Blackbelt in Blackjack,* and numerous other books on games and gambling. He maintains a fiction blog at: write-aholic.com. You may contact him directly at: GodsGuilty@gmail.com.

ABOUT VEGAS LIT

VEGAS LIT IS the fiction imprint of Huntington Press, a specialty publisher of Las Vegas- and gambling-related books and periodicals, including the award-winning consumer newsletter, *Anthony Curtis' Las Vegas Advisor.*

Huntington Press ✦ 3665 Procyon Street
Las Vegas, Nevada 89103 ✦ LasVegasAdvisor.com
e-mail: books@huntingtonpress.com